CW00409384

Nork from Nowhere

Best wishes
Mike

Nork from Nowhere

AN ORPHAN BOY'S AMAZING
JOURNEY TO BELONGING

Mike Leaver

The Book Guild Ltd

First published in Great Britain in 2021 by
The Book Guild Ltd
9 Priory Business Park
Wistow Road, Kibworth
Leicestershire, LE8 0RX
Freephone: 0800 999 2982
www.bookguild.co.uk
Email: info@bookguild.co.uk
Twitter: @bookguild

Copyright © 2021 Mike Leaver

The right of Mike Leaver to be identified as the author of this
work has been asserted by him in accordance with the
Copyright, Design and Patents Act 1988.

All rights reserved. No part of this publication may be
reproduced, transmitted, or stored in a retrieval system, in any form or by any means,
without permission in writing from the publisher, nor be otherwise circulated in
any form of binding or cover other than that in which it is published and without
a similar condition being imposed on the subsequent purchaser.

Typeset in 12pt Minion Pro

Printed on FSC accredited paper
Printed and bound in Great Britain by 4edge Limited

ISBN 978 1913913 342

British Library Cataloguing in Publication Data.
A catalogue record for this book is available from the British Library.

TO MY STATE-BOARDING SCHOOL

For giving me the opportunity to study running away to a
very advanced level…

Successfully completing the course at the age of twelve.

ONE

The radio alarm burst into life with a dawn chorus of pop music. From beneath the bedclothes, a hand appeared, its fingers well spaced to ensure the sleep button had nowhere to hide. The hand, being well accustomed to the procedure, then retreated beneath the bedclothes, without even bothering to tell the brain what had happened.

Many blissful hours passed before Sara rolled over and bumped into something solid. Was this more important than the headache? Probably. She opened one eye to confirm her suspicions. There was a man in her bed. Why? She was certain he had not been there last night!

She gave him an exploratory prod with a finger to see if he was real, and if so, what he would do. He rolled over and fell out of the single bed with a bump.

"Nice party," he mumbled in his sleep. He then reached up and pulled the bedclothes towards him.

Sara, realising she was naked, tried to pull the covers back, until the man decided the 'tug of war' was not worth the effort, and let go, to send her crashing from the other side of the bed, the blankets falling on top of her. Warm and safe, she recollected her thoughts – wild thoughts, party thoughts – and finally vague images of things that might have happened after her first-ever taste of alcohol. As to the man on the bedroom floor, she had no idea where he had come from.

Frantically, she fought her way out of the blankets to look under the bed. The individual lying the other side gave the impression of being unconscious. Ugh, he was really old, and looked like 'Mr Potato Head' who took them for History at school. *Mother and Father would not like him*, she thought, *better not take him home.*

Then she woke up completely; this was home! The night before had been her first grown-up party while her parents were away for the weekend…well, not so much a party, more a discreet gathering for a few sensible school friends, which did nothing to explain the unfortunate circumstance of having a naked man lying on her bedroom floor. Then she heard a car crunching across the gravel of their driveway. "Oh my giddy aunt," she breathed. It was zero hour and, very possibly, her 'giddy aunt' was in the vehicle, expecting to come in for a nice cup of tea.

No longer on ceremony, Sara jumped up, and with extreme gymnastic skill, trampolined onto the bed, her next landing being aimed at the man lying on the floor. Hoping no other explanation was necessary, she wrapped a sheet around her and ran into the corridor. On reaching the stairs, she made the sort of leap that would have sent her early-years' ballet teacher into a swoon of delight. But Sara's only thought, as her flight came under the influence of gravity, was that her father would kill her if he found her like this. To survive she needed to throw the bolts on the front door before he could enter, though perhaps, subconsciously, she did have a plan B. She could crash-land at the bottom of the stairs with a shattering of bone, then to lay there, oblivious to everything that was happening until, hopefully, she regained consciousness in an ambulance, being rushed away to the safety of a hospital.

Passing the front room, she skidded to a halt, unable to comprehend what she saw. It looked like a battlefield at a nudist camp! Nobody moved, except for a man lying on the floor. Directly in front of his face was a toppled-over parrot cage. Both man and parrot seemed equally happy in a shared cloud of funny-smelling smoke.

"Well bugger me," said the man, "bugger, bugger, bugger!"

"Well bugger me," repeated Father's pride and joy, "bugger, bugger, bugger."

"Get 'em off, missus," chuckled the guy.

"Get 'em off, missus," replied the parrot, apparently quite pleased by all the new words he was learning.

Father's parting words drifted into Sara's mind. "In before 2100 hours," he had commanded, "and no boyfriends back to stay."

He was like that, her father, always commanding things using the military language he had learned while doing something important in the British Army. Though, with regards to her curfew hours, he was probably just too embarrassed to say nine o'clock in the evening, given that she was now grown up, and the word 'midnight' would have been more appropriate.

Sara realised she could not face the confrontation. As the key entered the lock, she grabbed some bad-looking pills from a table, and ran in the opposite direction. On reaching

3

the back door, she heard a scream, followed by a loud bump, presumably her mother falling to the floor in a dead faint.

Racing from the door, Sara headed towards a low, decorative hedge that edged the croquet lawn. Leaping over this, she changed direction to make a hundred-yard dash around a wire fence that surrounded the tennis court. This brought her to a gate that opened onto their back field.

According to her father, this field was a horse paddock, which made her mother very cross, since it implied her hobby of keeping llamas was of secondary importance. Sara now had a much simpler view of the field; it was a great open space, and not a place to dawdle when only wearing a sheet. Thankfully, her school attached great importance to cross-country running, a skill that now propelled her across the field at such a speed, neither the horses nor llamas had time to react to the flash of white racing across it. On reaching the far side, Sara opened a gate that gave access to a path that wandered into the ancient woodland beyond. Ten minutes later, she collapsed against a stile that fronted a lane. Her house – or more precisely, a nudist war zone – was now around half a mile to her right.

What Sara found most confusing about what she had just witnessed came down to numbers. Her house could easily accommodate fifty guests, yet her recent escape had involved jumping over people in corridors, who would not fit elsewhere. The gathering, she concluded, was obviously a major event in the 'hippy' calendar. That is what her parents would call it anyway, a highly distasteful thing that went on in the Sixties, when everybody ran about naked, experimenting with the sort of pills she now held in her hand. She felt certain her removal of the evidence had been minimal. When they cleared up the mess, they would probably find a dead body.

So how did this compare with the gathering she had planned for a few friends? Well, had it gone ahead, it would still have been quite naughty since it had been organised without telling her parents. They would have insisted on chaperones – these generally being relics of the Victorian era – who believed young ladies should learn the etiquette required to visit stately homes, where a rich husband, of royal connection, might be acquired. Her parents would also have expected a Mozart string quartet to be playing quietly in the background.

At that, Sara gave up trying to compare what she had planned to what had actually happened; in truth, she had not organised a discreet social gathering, but planted a seed from which had grown a 'hippy happening'.

She wished she had not run; it had been an impulse action, that gave no consideration to how vulnerable she might feel ten minutes later, when leaning on a stile, wearing only a sheet. It would have been much better for everyone, if her reckless descent of the stairs had resulted in plan B, meaning she could have gone straight to hospital in an ambulance.

But such a fortuitous accident had eluded her; the alternative path leading to a world of which she had no understanding. After stepping back from the stile, she unscrewed the cap from the bottle of pills, and scattered the contents into a bush…that would probably grow up really happy. Then, after throwing the container away, she had two free hands, allowing her to organise her sheet into something less prone to accidents. Pulled under one arm and knotted across the other shoulder, it could even be legal…in some countries…where her father was not a local magistrate, who believed any skirt that did not reach a lady's ankles was a crime against civilisation.

Sara knew very little about alcohol, except that in the very early stages it had made her giggly, and later indulgences might be linked to a headache. But neither of these consequences would have affected her ability to get up early this morning, then make certain any evidence of her discreet social gathering had been removed.

Yet she had been oblivious to the world around her for many hours. Could alcohol do that? She did not know, but the pills she had just thrown into the bushes…well, not necessarily those pills, but others? She had not knowingly taken anything but, as far as her memory was concerned, last night had never happened.

'Click.'

At the unexpected sound, she spun around to discover a horrible little man peering at her through a camera. His smile suggested he was wearing false teeth, purchased from a second-hand shop.

'Click, click.'

She wanted to turn away in disgust, but this would allow the man to attack her from behind. Also, she needed to destroy the film; the photograph of her walking through the woods in a sheet could not possibly be allowed to have a wider circulation. Her only option was to make him more scared of her than she was of him, or at least test whether his perversion was the sort that made him run away when challenged.

"Drop dead," she said, feeling this was the best way of recovering the film.

At first, the man had seemed surprised to see her, but now he appeared to be growing in confidence. He took a step towards her; she a step sideways, away from the stile.

"When it sees the wife," he said, "it drops dead. Now it's playtime!"

Sara could make no sense of it, and frowned, until the man unzipped his trousers to expose a grandfatherly penis.

The man smiled proudly. "I only show it to those who want to look at it," he said.

"You're the guy in the woods?" said Sara, just to establish he was a really bad person, who needed to be in prison.

He looked down at his penis. "Did you hear that?" he said. "We're famous."

"To schoolgirls?" questioned Sara indignantly.

The man failed to take it as a question. "We're famous to schoolgirls," he said, still talking to his penis. "I expect they think about you all the time."

"No," retorted Sara, "because you are the pervert who always runs away, right?"

The man shrugged his shoulders, then took a £10 note from his pocket. He folded this in half and placed it across his penis.

"Recover this with your sweet lips," he said, "and it's yours for keeps."

It occurred to Sara that she had been right to think about his thingy by using its biological name. It was sufficiently old to be of no interest to anyone, except as a biological curiosity, in the same way a dead rat preserved in formaldehyde bore no resemblance to the sort that ran about with wiggly tails, squeaking and eating cheese. Now she thought about it in these terms, the penis seemed less threatening; the fact he expected her to take the £10 note from it, ridiculous. Still, he needed to be locked up, and of equal importance, she needed that film. When the police eventually raided his house, they could not be allowed to find her sheet photograph on his bedroom wall, later to be used as evidence in a court of law... possibly presided over by her father.

Suddenly, she jumped back into reality. A rapidly approaching siren would bring a police car speeding around the bend at any moment. It must be going to her house, the next farmhouse down the lane being more than a mile, and that would be approached from the opposite direction. She jumped behind a tree and, though not completely hidden, she thought it would offer sufficient camouflage when viewed from a speeding car. Two riot vans, their mesh windscreen shields down, followed.

She gave an exasperated sigh; her father must have telephoned the police. There were some things in life that you needed to sort out without attracting too much attention, but her father's mind often got muddled.

Sara looked into the bushes to locate the pervert. She was clearly in much more trouble than him, and needed that film. When his freedom came to an end, she had no intention of being part of his 'Babes in the Wood' collection.

"We need to talk," she said at no bush in particular.

The man knew about undergrowth, and what you could see through. To a normal person, he would have been completely hidden, yet she appeared to be looking directly at him. The police had unnerved him also; something big was happening here. Slowly he emerged from his carefully arranged camouflage.

Sara realised the recent events had greatly reduced the pervert's confidence.

"They've probably found the dead body," she said.

The pervert, visibly shaken, stammered something about only showing it to living people, and knowing nothing about any dead bodies. Sara wondered if he had questioned why she might be standing in a wood, wearing only a sheet, or if he just considered it his good fortune.

"Not yours, silly," she said, "the one we sacrificed last night."

The pervert backed away. "No," he said.

"Obviously," said Sara, "the Grand Master's hardly going to come all this way without a sacrifice to do his wotnots over."

"Wotnots?" said the pervert, in a way that suggested he was beginning to question her evilness.

"Clearly we do the knots," she responded, "it's very skilled work tying somebody up with their own intestines."

On hearing this, the pervert turned on his heels and ran. Sara smiled at her powers over men.

"Witch goddess," she breathed, waving her arms like she imagined they did at 'happenings'.

In the next instant, her smile vanished; the pervert had fled with the camera, her photograph taking flight to the wider world, where presumably other perverts would huddle in groups to look at her image. Then came the ambulances, speeding down the lane with their sirens wailing like full-volume opera singers. 'Big trouble,' they seemed to be screeching, over and over again, like they did in opera.

Sara ran, nowhere in particular, it just seemed the right thing to do, to put some distance between herself and the nudist war zone that had previously been her house – a place she could not return to, not tonight, next week, or just possibly ever.

An hour or so later, Sara was sitting on a grassy bank gazing across a rather wide river. Not that it had halted her progress, because she was an exceptionally good swimmer, but the bank had provided her with a place to sit while inspecting her naked feet for any damage caused by all the chaotic running. Eventually, she realised that using them to walk home would result in a trail of blood that some dog would follow, until it came across her lifeless body, drained of all fluid. Then, remembering she no longer had a home, she burst into tears.

As the tears faded, her mind wandered back to the house where she used to live: her father going crazy at each new indiscretion he found; her mother panicking that she would be banned from the fundraising committee of the Women's Institute. Only the Drug Squad would take it in their stride. There were people to be arrested, sent to hospital, or classified as innocent victims of the corruption organised by herself.

On the positive side, Sara reckoned she would have left home next year anyway. It was what her parents expected, going away to university and stuff. She was the last of four, only 'number three' having brought disgrace on their family name by not getting into 'Oxbridge'. On hearing the news, her father had gone ballistic.

"Birmingham University!" he had raged. "I expect you intend to get there using a corporation bus. They are bright yellow, you know!"

Sara tried to imagine how her father would be reacting to the embarrassment she had just caused. Get a shotgun from his hunting cabinet, probably.

Eventually, Sara's gaze lifted to the far side of the river. According to her father, it was where the working-class people lived. When she was little, he would often tell her stories about it – all the crime, drunken behaviour, and the way the residents only went to the public bath house once a week. Sometimes, his stories had made her so frightened she needed to hide behind the settee, hands half covering her ears.

Obviously, the other side of the river was not a place she had ever been…but now? Over there, lost within a great sprawling mass of unwashed bodies, she would be completely anonymous. Certainly it was not a place her parents would ever find her. Also, to avoid starvation, she needed to find work.

Sara was still gazing across the river when her thoughts became distracted by a hallucination in the form of a boy, floating upstream, clinging to a fencing panel. She knew the seaside was sufficiently close for the incoming tide to make the river go 'backwards', but this did not explain how the hallucination was now turning into something rather more real. Her hallucination theory came to a complete end when the boy stopped moving and spluttered "Ouch." A moment later, he stood up, with the water just covering his knees. Then he stood on one leg, while lifting the other, to inspect the knee for any damage, presumably connected to his utterance of the word 'ouch'.

After returning the leg to the river bed, he looked upstream, apparently surprised to see his fencing panel racing away, without himself as a passenger. However, the loss of his transport did not seem to worry him greatly, since his only response was to lift his other leg in order to inspect his other knee.

Presently, Sara's attention was drawn to the boy's mop of

black curly hair that had obviously been cut using the pudding-bowl method. His face was so white, she thought his entire life must have been spent in darkness, perhaps locked in a cellar; not for being naughty, because his expression radiated a look of complete innocence, but because he frequently did odd things that grown-ups did not understand. Ah! Hence his fencing-panel mode of transport. Sara then lowered her gaze, causing her to take a sharp intake of breath. The boy was so thin, it seemed probable that he had not eaten for the previous week.

After inspecting his second knee, the boy looked around until he saw her sitting on the bank. She responded with a smile, not to make friends, but because…well, smiling was fundamental to her nature. Sadly, this gave the boy the confidence to paddle towards her, scrambling up the bank to stand by her side while cascading water into his own private puddle.

"Do you speak English?" he asked carefully.

His game of pretend clearly involved a wild imagination. Perhaps if she played along, he might go away happy…or at least, sooner. But what game should she be pretending? Ah, to be foreign, the fencing panel presumably being a pretend boat?

Sara knew a smattering of more obscure languages from her various holidays abroad, not sufficient to communicate, but enough to confuse the locals. She was well able to ask the way to the bathroom in ten different languages, and be given a cheese sandwich in return!

"*Ja,*" she said, "*Engle Klinger.*"

"I only speak English," said the boy, appearing to cheer up, now that she had agreed to play his game.

Sara pointed up river. "*Townal-hopper.*" She managed a weak smile; as far as children's games go, this was quite funny. "*Townal-hopper, das weg,*" she added.

The boy sat beside her. She noticed he was wearing shoes, the things she now wanted more than anything else in the whole world, and the boy used these precious items to go swimming. This made her rather cross.

"Huh," she said.

But the boy seemed unaware of her annoyance. "What... country...this?" he asked, speaking carefully, with an obvious gap between each word.

"What country do you want it to be?" she asked.

"Don't care so long as it's not..."

The boy knew he must never say that word again. If people did not know where he came from, they could never send him back. Then he looked at the lady in her strange national dress. It made her look lopsided, due to one arm being kept inside her clothes. Her hair was a great tangle of ginger curls, which made it look as if she had been dragged through a hedge backwards. He thought she looked very sad.

"You speak English very well – quickly," he said.

The lady shrugged. "I am a witch," she said, "I read your thoughts."

The boy took one bounce away from her.

"But only a good witch," she added, with a kind smile.

The boy studied the lady, and decided she would cause him no harm, so long as he remained good.

"I am also good," he said, just so there could be no misunderstanding.

Then the lady stood up and started to walk away. He got up to follow; if he was walking with a grown-up, the authorities would not question him. But after a few paces, the lady hobbled, then sat back down to rub her feet.

A year before, he would have believed she had arrived on a broomstick that had probably broken down. Now, he thought, she probably just needed shoes. Grown-ups always pretended to be organised, but sometimes he knew they were not. If they did not make mistakes, they would not have let him escape.

"You need shoes," he said.

The lady clapped her hands, but no shoes appeared. He decided she could not be a very good witch. Strangely, she then started to cry.

He had not cried since the age of six, after he had spelled the word God without using a capital 'G'. This had caused a furious monk to tell him the 'Devil had entered his soul', and needed to be driven out by using a cane. In response to the tears that followed, the monk told him the ability to cry meant he was turning into a girl.

Girls were never allowed inside the high walls that surrounded the garden so, at the age of six, he had never actually seen one. However, he knew they always had to wear a skirt, and walk around playing with dolls. The idea that he might turn into a girl had worried him for weeks, especially given his idea that girls always turned into women. Only by wearing trousers did you always become a man. He had no understanding why this should be so, but the lady on the river bank, who was still crying, proved his ideas were correct.

Not knowing how he should react to the lady's tears, he looked down to study her feet.

"If I get you some shoes," he said, "would you let me sleep with you?"

"No," yelped the lady mid-tears. "Definitely not!" she added, just so there could be no misunderstanding on the subject.

Sara then remembered the naked man on her bedroom floor, causing her to lose confidence in her own respectability. Did the pervert who had folded a £10 note across his thingy think her body language indicated she was a tart, who would do it with anybody who asked? The boy certainly thought so.

"Huh," she said, this her second attempt to show him how cross she was. Then, wishing to bring all conversation to an end, she turned away to avoid eye contact.

"You should go home now," she said, "before your parents come looking for you."

"Don't have any," said the boy, "like you don't have no shoes. So, if I get you some shoes, can you be my mother?"

"It's not a game any more," said Sara, "so please, just go away."

The boy had no particular place to go and, having associated himself with a grown-up who had not handed him over to the authorities, he felt no particular need to run anywhere at the moment. Instead, he turned his attention to the river. It had stopped moving, and he thought he understood what was going on. If they waited long enough, the water would go away, leaving sand on which the lady could walk. So long as he watched to make sure the water did not come back, they could walk inland to find some shoes. Whichever way his mind turned, it all came back to shoes. In truth, she probably needed these more than he needed a mother, but both of them would benefit from the arrangement. Then, realising the lady had stopped crying, he turned to discover she was now looking at him.

"You must have parents," she said.

The boy shook his head, then pointed to the sky.

"They went to live up there," he said, "before I arrived."

He had already told her that his parents had gone away, but her grasp of English was obviously not that good.

Sara was going to shout at him for saying such things, and being a nuisance generally. She stopped herself just in time. Children played some strange games, but not pointing to the sky.

"That's not possible," she said, "unless they live in an aeroplane."

The boy's smile made her tummy feel funny.

"Do you think so?" he asked.

Feeling out of her depth with such a strange boy, she let the subject drop for fear of saying the wrong thing. Instead, she asked where he came from, but the boy only put his hand across his mouth.

"So," she asked, "you don't want to go back from where you started?"

The boy shook his head.

"Neither do I," she said, "but sometimes we must, to whoever looks after us."

The boy removed the hand from his mouth. "Nobody looks after me," he said, "though you can if you want. But I don't want the man to look after me, he looks strange."

"There's no man," she said. "I am also alone in the world."

The boy pointed towards some bushes. "The man behind those," he said.

Sara's mind flashed back to the pervert. "I can't see any man," she said, more to reassure herself than to correct the boy's mistaken belief.

"You wouldn't," responded the boy, "I was looking at you, you were looking at me, and the man lives in the bushes."

"Looking at me?"

"Is he your friend?"

Sara looked around for the terror that lurked in the woods. She could sense it; a pervert was clearly on her tracks; he might really believe she was a witch, and these have a reputation for running about in groups, without wearing any clothes. It had been silly to think he would give up at the mere risk of being a human sacrifice.

"We need help," she said, "and I can't walk much further."

The boy made no effort to move, instead seemingly content to gaze at the river.

"The water's going away," he said. "When it's gone, we can walk up the sand and see if anybody follows. If the authorities come, you can be my mother, and we can be playing, like they do in books."

The boy looked at the sky, and Sara got ready to answer any difficult questions he might ask. Instead, he just returned his attention to the river.

"I think the water goes away when it gets dark," he said, "then comes back in the morning. If the man follows, it will take him away because he won't be expecting it."

Sara looked at the boy. Really they needed to make a joint escape, but this could easily lead to angry parents accusing her of kidnapping their daydreaming child. She tried to adopt a stern schoolteacher's voice.

"Where do you live, really?" she asked.

"Nowhere," said the boy without thinking.

Sara took a lot longer to consider her response. "Same place as me," she acknowledged.

The boy took his new responsibilities very seriously and, like all great explorers, climbed the highest nearby tree, to see whatever there was to be seen. When the topmost branches began to wobble under his weight, he clung on tight, while moving his head around until he found a place where he could see between the leaves.

Looking along the river, in the direction he had been travelling, he saw a bridge carrying a lane towards some woods on the far bank. A little way before the lane, on his side of the river, was a field with a lot of wigwams. He realised the natives who lived there must have shoes, for without them, walking on the lane would be impossible.

A few minutes later, the boy was still trying to work out how to climb back down, when he noticed the man he had seen earlier darting about, all the time watching the lady from behind various bushes. The boy understood the two grown-ups were playing some sort of... 'back-to-front hide and seek'. The rules seemed really complicated, but up here, high in the flimsy branches, he knew he was the boss.

"I can see you," he shouted.

The effect on the man was spectacular. He ran about in confused circles, before throwing himself against the next tree. With his arms straight by his sides, he disappeared from view.

"I can still see you," fibbed the boy.

The man broke cover and, like a rabbit who could not see where the fox was coming from, ran chaotically away. The boy thought the game was very silly.

By the time the boy returned to the ground, he was too excited by his discovery of the wigwams to get involved in whatever game the grown-ups were playing.

"I'll be back," he shouted to the lady as he hurried away to meet the natives.

Only on approaching the wigwam field did his confidence begin to wane. Some of the wigwams looked really big and were all sorts of funny shapes. Also, in his country, grown-ups always wore shoes, but here, few seemed to bother, instead choosing to keep their feet off the ground by lying on canvas beds. Then, to one corner of the field, he saw a solitary wigwam. In front of this was a metal-framed bed, with a single pair of feet resting on top. He crawled along a low hedge that surrounded the settlement to take a closer look. Slowly his confidence began to increase; in this shoeless country, the natives would find it quite hard to chase him.

"Friend," he called towards the pair of feet, while remaining on the safe side of the hedge. "I come in peace," he added.

A woman who had been lying on the bed sat up, and looked directly at him. She then said some strange words, and walked into the wigwam. A few seconds later, a man appeared.

"My wife not know your language," he said.

The woman reappeared from the wigwam and, by putting her chin onto the man's shoulder, managed to take some weight from her feet. Her toes sank into the soft sandy soil, which she seemed to like, because it made her smile.

"What country is this?" asked the boy.

The man looked confused and, when he replied, took great care over his words.

"We Norge," he said, "on holiday."

"Nirway," said the woman.

"You call it Norway," said the man.

The woman nodded, apparently unable to tell the difference between the two pronunciations. Or, perhaps they had only recently invented the word, and were still undecided how it should sound. As the lady carried on talking, the boy realised she was trying to repeat what the man said. This, he realised, was how new words got invented. Eventually, the couple stopped talking between themselves, and turned their attention him.

"My mother," said the boy, "has lost her shoe-shoes – things you put on foot-foot. She went swimming, and somebody took them, and now she can't walk because she has soft feet."

The man spoke some foreign words to the lady, then went inside the wigwam. He returned with two pieces of flat plastic with straps attached.

"Our shoes might not fit," he said, "but these general sandals should help your mother get home."

The boy reached over the hedge to take the strange pieces of plastic.

"Thank you very much," he said. Then, yet another project successfully completed, he turned on his heels to run.

Two miles downstream, Sara was gazing into the woods where the pervert was hiding. Eventually, her mind turned to the equally horrible man she had seen on her bedroom floor. She was fairly certain he had done it, though only because her 'down below' felt a little sore. Her parents would think she had done it anyway, this being the logical conclusion of finding the naked man lying on the carpet. Given how ugly he was, her parents could only think she had done it for money, or because she would do it with anybody who asked. She lowered her head in shame, not because she had done it, but because she could not remember anything about it...

…Then she realised it was all the fault of her pathetic ex-boyfriend. Six months before, when she had told him, 'we can't,' it obviously meant not yet, and perhaps find somewhere better than a field? How could he have thought it meant, 'go and give Janet your weekly allowance for a half-hour lesson behind the picture house?' It had made her romantically ill for six months, and she was sure it had taken a grade off her 'O' levels. Now, just about on track with her 'A' levels, and a man…any man…had somehow appeared in her bedroom. This, in a vodka and tonic sort of way, presumably made her think it was an opportunity to show her pathetic ex-boyfriend she was not a stuck-up virgin, like he had told all her friends. But all of this was speculation to fill a blank space in her memory. The reality was probably more gruesome, amnesia being a form of self-survival.

Cautiously, she touched her breasts, and grimaced; whatever had happened, the man had clearly thought them to be detachable accessories.

Janet, she reflected, had not even given her pathetic ex-boyfriend any discount, which she would sometimes do for those she liked. She made up for this by charging double for the over-forties. Janet had a good business head, and was now fully professional, offering her services to the rich and famous. Sara realised that if her ex-boyfriend went back now, he would be one of the customers who had to pay double, because he was pathetic, and Janet would find him rather tiresome.

Suddenly, a slight cough made Sara jump from her thoughts. After a moment of panic, she was astonished to see the boy had actually returned, and was now holding out a pair of sandals.

"Uh," she said, looking at them incredulously.

They were only a cheap throwaway pair, but at that precise moment, it seemed a miracle had taken place. She tried them on, the cold plastic immediately bringing back memories of her childhood holidays on the beach. It is where she wanted to be right now, flip-flopping along the sand, as a child, bucket in one hand, spade in the other, and no perverts folding £10 notes across their thingies.

She stood up to look critically at her feet. Normally she would not have been seen dead in such things – unless they had a reasonable label – but these seemed to match quite well with her sheet. If she walked down the street now, the older people would think she had just been to a 'happening'. A few flowers in her hair and they would think her quite…

"Wild thing," she said, doing a swivel, her feet not hurting at all.

The boy did not understand, but thought it might be something to do with her being a part-time witch. She could not be a full-time witch, because somebody who knew a lot of magic would not have needed him to sort out her shoes. He watched in horror as she picked up some buttercups, and stuck them in her hair.

"How do I look?" she asked.

Anything to do with flowers was embarrassing, so he tried to concentrate on his own achievement.

"They are called sandals," he said, "I got them from some people in the wigwam."

"That makes no sense," responded Sara. "Quite apart from anything else, why would homeless people just give you a pair of sandals?"

The boy shrugged his shoulders. "I just told them my mother went swimming and lost her shoes," he said.

"Mother!" gasped Sara. "You can't tell people that!"

"Why?"

"Because you can't."

"Why?"

"Stop saying that."

"Why?"

Sara's experience of children was very limited, but she knew once they started saying 'why', they could go on forever without getting bored.

"I am not old enough to be your mother," she said, then immediately winced.

"Why?"

This simple 'why' technique gave all children the upper hand.

"Thank you for the sandals," she said, accepting that, for the time being, the argument was lost.

The boy sat beside her. "Now it's your turn," he said.

"To do what?"

"The things only a grown-up can do. I'm hungry, thirsty, that sort of stuff."

Sara wanted to say that if they handed themselves in to the police, they would give him a lift home to his parents. However, she did not want to get the local police involved, with her father being a magistrate, and everything. When she finally got arrested, she wanted it to be out of the area.

"The other side of the river," she said, "that will be better."

The boy watched the lady stand, then walk away in completely the wrong direction.

"There's no bridges that way," he called.

"There must be, and if we go the other way, we will have to pass the homeless people in the…err, wigwam."

"When I came in from the ocean," responded the boy, "I didn't see any bridges. The first is up there, honest."

Sara stopped. She knew the seaside was too far to walk, but when the river was in full flow, travelling on a fencing panel the boy could easily be doing eight miles an hour. If he was in the water for three hours, he could have covered twenty-four miles. It did not seem credible that he was doing anything but playing river games, albeit foolishly.

"When did you go into the river?" she asked.

"I went into the ocean, many days ago."

Sara decided to be more direct, and kneeled before him to hold his hands.

"Where do you come from, really?" she asked.

The boy gave her a great big grin; this was the sort of embarrassing thing mothers did, holding hands. She was quite hopeless, but he did not care. Keeping hold of one hand, he began to pull her in the required direction.

"We don't have to stop at the wigwam," he said, "but I'm very thirsty, and you can't drink that sort of water, it tastes horrible."

He pointed to the river, which Sara thought probably contained traces of salt.

"You must never drink that sort of water," she said, "it's poisonous, I think."

"I drank a little," he replied. "In the middle of the ocean, I kept bouncing up and down, so could not help it."

Then the boy remembered the mouth-washing ceremony in his old country – the monk making him eat soap, then holding him flat to the floor, while pouring a jug of water into his mouth. It was not even himself who had said the bad word.

"But I've tasted worse," he added bravely.

Sara walked on in silence; the more this situation developed, the more complicated it seemed to get. She would have to take the boy to a police station, of course, but at the moment, that seemed particularly difficult. Finally, she decided it was too late to sort out anything tonight; in the morning everything would seem better, though in her own case, she could not see how.

Sometime later, the people from Norway were surprised to see a hippy child appearing from the other side of the hedge, then asking to borrow a bottle of lemonade for her brother, who had just fallen in the water. They wanted to help more, but she said it was fine, because he was always falling in the water. After she had gone, they smiled at each other. It was little things like this that made their foreign holidays so amusing.

Sara knew that keeping her sheet safely together really required both hands, which made handing the boy a lemonade bottle a dangerous operation.

"I need some string," she moaned, "to keep it in at the waist."

The boy reached into his pocket, then gave her what looked like a length of bailer twine.

"Magic!" she gasped in admiration.

The boy shrugged. "Always need string," he replied casually.

She had no idea why a boy would always need string, nor did she care. The important thing was that her sheet, tied around her waist, was much less prone to accidents. Then she turned to the boy and, for the first time, confidently held out one arm. She waggled the fingers, thereby proving they were now free to do other things, beyond clutching the sheet.

"Sara Brooks, fashion designer," she said. "How do I look?"

The boy had no idea what she was talking about.

"What's a fashion designer?" he asked.

"Someone who designs clothes," she replied.

"Oh," he said, none the wiser.

"Your turn," said Sara. "What are you?"

The boy looked at her suspiciously. He was always on the alert for interrogation techniques coming from all sorts of angles. On one running-away escape, he had been captured by the police, and they had got him to confess by giving him a mug of hot drinking chocolate. Then they immediately telephoned the orphanage to report him. This time, he would cover his tracks completely.

"I'm Nork," he said.

"Nork? What sort of name is that?"

He did not know; he needed to invent a word, and it had just sort of happened. Obviously, Norge had been floating about in his head, but changing the 'ge' to a 'k' was an inspiration, almost as brilliant as sticking an extra 'o' to God, to get 'good'.

"Foreign," he said, "spelled without an 'e'."

"Faraway foreign, or close foreign?"

He shrugged. "We are nearly at the bridge," he said.

Sara glanced ahead. It was a horrible bridge, all narrow and long, due to the marshy ground on the far side. If a car came when they were in the middle, there would be nowhere to hide. Instinctively, she glanced back along the river towards the place she had once called 'home'. Then she jumped closer to the boy, almost knocking him over.

"It's him!" she gasped.

The man tried to disappear behind a telegraph pole, but Nork recognised his arms.

"He's been following us all the time," he said, "I thought you were playing a game of 'back-to-front hide and seek'."

"Uh? No, he's a Peeping Tom, among other things. I obviously did not frighten him enough."

Nork looked at the telegraph pole with arms.

"He can't hurt us," he said, "we have four arms and four feet, he only has two."

"What? Oh, together you mean, but when we part, he will be able to get one of us."

Nork did not see why they would ever need to part. To give this idea a little test, he began walking across the bridge, glancing back, quite prepared to retrace his steps if she failed to follow.

Sara gazed across the bridge, towards the place her father had once told her stories about. It was his equivalent of the deep dark woods, where a big bad wolf was waiting to gobble her whole. But now, this side of the bridge had an even more sinister pervert waiting to pounce. Bravely – or foolishly – she hurried after the boy, into the unknown.

When the boy looked back to see the lady giving chase, he felt more confident about things; perhaps if he made her choose, she would always choose him.

"How much do you want to hide from Tom?" he asked, when she caught up with him.

"Who?"

"Your not-friend."

"Oh, very, but I don't see how, now he's got the scent."

"So, he's got a dog. Now they can follow our smell, that makes things a lot harder."

"No dog, and he's not really called Tom."

"I see," said Nork, even though he didn't.

"Do you want to lose Tom very much," he asked, "or very, very, very much?"

"A million verys," said Sara, "at least!"

"Then follow," said Nork, "and do whatever I say, very quickly."

After crossing the bridge, the boy turned left to walk along a gravel footpath that went into the woods fronting the river. Sara was not very impressed by this, but the threat of what lay behind was even worse. Then she realised that, according to the boy, they were walking towards the ocean.

"I hope you don't expect me to go swimming?" she asked.

But the boy paid no attention. "In a few seconds," he said, "Tom will be across the bridge, and lose sight of us as we go around the next bend. Then we run to the stream that comes down the hillside."

"Why?" asked Sara.

But the boy did not answer. Instead, a few seconds later, he started running. Not wishing to be left alone with the pervert, she gave chase. On reaching the stream, the boy jumped from some planks that crossed it, then splashed his way upwards. Given the thick woodland on both sides of the stream, he quickly disappeared from view.

Sara remained standing on the planks. The fast-flowing water was ankle deep, and not entirely free of the trailing vegetation. In short, it was the sort of place a grown-up would never go…unless they wanted to lose a pervert a million times! It was thus, after a few minutes, she caught up with the boy, who was standing perfectly still, the water swirling about his knees.

"Grown-ups don't walk up streams," he said, "Tom will not think to leave the path."

"At last, we can agree about something," she said, "but Tom might do all sorts of strange things…no, not Tom, you've got me saying it now."

"Shhh," said Nork, "we need to be totally quiet, and listen."

Eventually, Sara heard the faint sound of approaching footsteps, which got louder as they clomped onto the planks, before fading into the distance.

"Clever boy," she said.

Then, turning around, she discovered the boy was already continuing his walk upstream. Not knowing what to do, she looked towards the lower path. So which way to choose?

It only took a moment for her to associate the known path with the pervert. Taking the lesser of two evils, she splashed her way upwards, until she saw the boy sitting above the stream, his feet dangling in space. As she got closer, she realised he was sitting above a pipe, from which the stream appeared. On reaching his side, she scrambled up the grassy bank to stand on a rough track above, possibly designed for tractors.

"It will get dark soon," said the boy.

Sara thought it odd that he made such an observation without any panic in his voice.

"Halfway up the hill there's a place to sleep," he added.

"You can't know that," she said, "unless this is where you come from?"

"I saw it from the river," he replied. "It's about two miles around the other side of the hill."

Sara's main concern was still the pervert, so she followed the boy as he began walking along an increasingly rough path. More and more she thought about the place to sleep, but how?

On holiday with her parents she had never stayed in any hotel that did not have four stars, the sort where a member of staff attended a cloakroom. She looked at her sheet, and decided wearing this made entry into even a three-star hotel impossible, quite apart from which, she did not have any money. Her life, it seemed, was two miles away from a dead end.

As the walk continued, she realised the boy was the important person in this relationship.

She shook her head, as if trying to shake away the word 'relationship'. It was ridiculous to use such a word when thinking about...whatever was happening here. All that would happen next is that the boy would 'importantly' go into the hotel, and the police would come to take him back to his parents. She would somehow make her presence known, possibly by waving to a police car, while standing in the bushes, near the hotel entrance. If she was lucky, the police would let her sleep in the cells overnight. It was still a dead end to her own life, but at least it would be a warmer variation.

Having accepted her fate, Sara followed the boy until they came to a grassy clearing. Looking across this, she saw a large building of rough stone, at the far end of which, a slate roof had collapsed into the upper storey, the chimney pots lying on the ground beneath. Strangely, the boy was walking through a hole in the wall that had probably once contained a door. In the next instant, a load of sheep ran out, panic-scattering to either side of her. Cautiously, she advanced to put her head through the gap. The boy now seemed really tall, his head almost touching the ceiling. She realised this was because he was standing on wall-to-wall dried sheep dung, about two feet thick. Somehow, he did not seem worried by this, walking casually across to a set of wooden stairs that went up to a hole in the ceiling.

"Where are you going?" she whispered.

"The place to sleep," he answered.

"But there's no glass in the windows, just huge holes to let in the wind."

"That's how I knew it was a place to sleep," he responded. "If it had glass, somebody might be living here already."

Sara bent lower, then nervously put a foot onto the dung. Surprisingly, it gave the sensation of being a rather soft carpet, albeit a slightly smelly one. On reaching the stairs, she followed the boy to the floor above. This had rough wooden floorboards…and nothing else!

"I thought you said it was a place to sleep," she said.

The boy paid no attention, instead climbing a loft ladder to disappear above, after which, a lot of straw began falling through the hole in the ceiling. When the 'haystack' was quite high, he climbed back down, and began to spread it across the floorboards. This done, he looked up.

"I made the bed," he said.

Sara's mind refused to see the scattering of straw as a bed.

"I made the bed," he repeated, hoping that second time around she would 'get the joke'.

But instead of laughing, the lady just went to stare out of the window. At that, the boy gave in, and made his way downstairs, to find a place to sleep.

Sara looked through the hole in the wall, where a window had once been. Below, she could make out sections of river, beyond which was the wide, flat valley where her previous existence had been spent doing 'nice' things. Then she imagined her house, virtually demolished by 'the happening', both parents wanting to kill her for the devastation she had brought into their lives. Sending her to private school had cost them nearly half a million pounds, and this is what she had done to repay them? It would have been better for them if she had never been born!

As darkness surrounded the derelict sheep barn, Sara thought about the pervert searching for her outside, in the woods. Finally, she accepted that, for tonight, she desperately needed the boy to be by her side.

She must stop thinking of him as the boy, but somebody sufficiently important to have a name.

"Nork," she said.

There, it was official now. She turned around to smile at him, but found herself to be completely alone. Never had she known such panic. What if he never came back? She would be at the mercy of a prowling pervert. After all, there was no particular reason why the boy might not just disappear with the same lack of formality by which he had arrived. Why had she ignored him for…however long it had been?

Nervously, she made her way to the stairs with the intention of quietly calling his name, that is to say, not so loud as the pervert in the woods might hear. After descending two steps, she made out a dark form that resembled the shape of a boy. Strangely, he was sitting on the sheep dung, his back against the wall, face resting on knees. In that huddled position, he looked really small, causing her to downgrade his age to eleven. Then she remembered his legs were so thin, he was clearly suffering from starvation. Yet she had made no effort to feed him, which is probably why he was sulking, but thankfully he had not abandoned her.

"What are you doing?" she asked, in the softest voice she could manage.

The boy made an 'uh' sound, then looked up.

"Sleeping," he said.

"But you made the bed upstairs."

"You said I was not allowed to sleep with you," he said.

"Oh, I did not mean…"

Her voice trailed off. Now she had downgraded his age to eleven, it was quite possible he did not know what 'sleeping together' actually meant, and it was not a subject into which she wanted to be drawn.

"I've changed my mind," she said.

Nork raced up the stairs, and quickly made himself comfortable on the straw. After a few minutes, the lady lay next to him, and he found the courage to turn around and, by degrees, snuggle up against her back. Finally, he gave a contented sigh; he had found a mother and, for the first day in this strange land, that was good enough!

TWO

Sara watched helplessly as a camera on tripod-legs ran past her, eager to get inside her house, to show her parents the 'sheet' photograph it had just taken. Slowly, her brain became confused by the equally strange notion that she was lying on straw. Then, turning around, she tried to make sense of a boy sitting on the floor, apparently watching her.

"Are you still part of the dream?" she asked.

The boy made no comment, but offered her a bottle of lemonade. Very slowly she sat up to accept the gift, pleased to find it had been chilled. Surrealism only happens in dreams and, when she awoke, she would surely find herself in a nice, warm bed. She drank, then returned the bottle to the boy.

"It's…" she began.

"Pretend lemonade," said the boy.

"Not from the river?"

"You can't pretend that much lemonade. This comes from a stream out the back. It's in a proper lemonade bottle though."

Strangely, the concept of pretend lemonade made her feel better. Also, she felt herself to be younger, almost as if her age had regressed by two years. Certainly she had lost two kilograms in weight, which returned her 'tummy' to where it had been at the age of fifteen – completely flat!

"What did you say your name was?" she asked.

"Nork," replied the boy.

"Ah, I remember it was unusual. And where did you say you came from?"

"You spell it without the 'e'," said the boy.

"What?"

"Nork, some people put an 'e' on the end, I don't."

The boy handed her a ball of bailer twine.

"It's for your fashion design," he said. He then gave her a piece of broken roofing slate. "You can cut it with this," he added. "We'll take the rest with us, then tonight we can play conkers…after we find a conker tree."

Sara found his style of conversation rather upsetting, but after removing the word 'conkers', she realised his words actually made a lot of sense. She told him to wait downstairs and, if anybody came, to shout. After he had gone, she quickly set to work, using the slate and bailer twine to invent a basic system of needlework. After a few knots, she created something that allowed her to walk downstairs in relative safety. Of equal importance, she now had both arms outside her 'dress', allowing her to deal better with…whatever came next.

After leaving the barn, Nork led the way along a footpath that wandered around the wooded hillside, maintaining roughly the same height. Eventually they came to a meadow, where Sara stopped to replace the buttercups in her hair.

35

Nork still found this embarrassing, but he was getting used to it, so plodded on without comment. Then, perhaps a mile further on, they came to a solid path.

"Where are we going?" asked Sara.

"Breakfast," replied Nork.

Sara frowned. "If we follow the river," she said, "we might see the camera with a man hanging around its neck." To correct any confusion this might generate, she added, "Like in my dream...before the tripod got involved."

Nork looked puzzled, then just accepted that sometimes grown-ups said very strange things.

"We need to eat," he said, "the last thing I had was a cornflake sandwich...before I went into the ocean, many days ago."

"The last thing I had," said Sara, "was a slice of cucumber, in a glass of Pimm's."

She gave a horrified gasp. None of her friends drank Pimm's; it could only mean her father's cocktail cabinet had fallen victim to a screwdriver. As for the cucumber...that tended to suggest the destruction she had brought into her parents' lives extended all the way to the kitchen.

Unhappily, she plodded behind the boy until they came to a long run of fencing panels. She wanted to say something about these, then casually turn the conversation around to enquire why he used them as a method of transport. However, on the other side of the panels were gardens, leading to houses where presumably people lived. This suggested she had many more immediate problems than his method of arrival.

"Nork," she called.

He had been learning running away for two years. Did she really think he was going to be caught out by something so basic as a name test? He immediately turned around to face her.

"Yes?" he said, thereby confirming he was called Nork.

"I don't know what to do," she replied.

"I understand," he said, knowing that, once again, it was necessary for him to take control of things.

After walking a few hundred yards, he happened to look over a fence to see the most amazing thing in the whole world – a real orange box attached to some planks of wood, supported by four pram wheels. There were a lot of other things bolted on, like chrome cycle lamps, and a number plate that spelled MENACE 1.

"Wow!" he exclaimed.

Sara looked over the fence, but could see nothing of any importance.

"Wow!" repeated Nork, as if unable to believe his eyes.

A middle-aged man, who had been bending down to attend his garden cabbages, slowly stood up, then looked around to see…

"Wow!" exclaimed the man.

Nork paid no attention, his own hypnotic gaze focused entirely on the go-cart. In return, the man's attention was directed entirely towards something Nork did not understand. This caused their 'wow' statements to echo back and forth, until Sara decided to interrupt.

"Wow?" she questioned.

Just then, a middle-aged woman emerged from a garden shed.

"Would everybody stop saying wow," she said, "and explain themselves using grown-up words."

Then the woman saw a girl leaning over their fence,

wearing…not very much, and understood why her husband was doing all the wow-ing.

"Huh," she said.

Sara wondered what had happened to all the grown-up words. "Huh?" she questioned, thereby giving the woman an opportunity to explain herself.

The man, having heard his wife say 'huh,' quickly returned to the real world, one in which, if he did not immediately look away from the girl, he would be put on washing-up duty for a month. However, he still remained confused as to why such a delightful creature would be looking over his fence at eight in the morning. Then, feeling most guilty about his impure thoughts, he turned his attention to a boy, whose chin was resting on the top of the fence, beside the girl.

Following the boy's gaze, the man found himself looking at his old go-cart, last used…oh, ages ago, when he was a nipper. Sadly, his own children had no interest in 'Menace 1', instead demanding skateboards and funny-looking bicycles for Christmas. In truth, his wife had wanted to use his go-cart as firewood for many years, but he could not bear to think of it being cremated.

"You like it?" he asked.

"It's amazing!" said Nork.

"Been in the garden for the past thirty years," said the man, "so it's a bit…"

His wife then realised what the boy was talking about. "…But it's yours now," she interrupted. "We'll even give you a hammer and nails, so you can fix it."

Sara was totally confused by all the fuss being made about something she could not see. Then, without further explanation, she watched the woman pick up some junk, carry it to the fence, and drop it onto the path. Next, the woman went into the shed, returning with a sack, that she also dropped onto the path. This done, the woman turned away, and shooed her husband towards the house.

"Promise you will look after it," shouted the husband.

"Promise, forever and ever," Nork called back.

Sara had begun the day thinking that at least things could not get any worse. As Nork walked away, pulling a set of reins, she realised this had been an overly optimistic prediction. Reluctantly, she followed him to where a narrow alleyway ran between two gardens. Before she had time to fully adapt to the increasing nightmare, she found herself looking out at a busy street.

It was the most grown-ups Nork had ever seen in one place. To make matters worse, on this side of the river, they were all speaking English. When people said words like 'Norge', you could not make much sense of it, but equally, they could not turn around and say "You're under arrest." Any one of the grown-ups in this street could be a secret agent from his home country!

Nork realised it was now more important than ever to put some distance between here and the place from where he had escaped. He pulled his wagon back from the street, and set to work with the hammer and nails, making it all good and strong for the great journey ahead.

Sara took a few minutes to accept that her sheet, though tolerable when walking through woodland, did not work for a busy street. In the first situation, any accidents could be corrected without being observed. The street situation was more like one of those nightmares in which you found yourself naked, while everybody else was fully clothed.

Having decided this, she walked back to the boy who was now working on his contraption with hammer and nails.

"What are you doing?" she asked.

"Brrm-brrr," he responded proudly.

Not wishing to be drawn into any conversation that began with such a phrase, she leaned against a fence to watch his labours. After ten minutes or so, he stood up, and pulled his contraption towards the street.

"I'm really hungry," he called back, "I haven't eaten for many days."

Sara, seeing his skinny legs, thought this was probably true. Of equal importance, she had not eaten for thirty-six hours. Then, thinking logically, she realised that going 'out there' would get her arrested by the police, who would take her to the cells, and eventually provide her with food.

"Let's get this over with," she said. "You lead, I'll follow."

To her annoyance, the boy entered the street, still pulling his stupid go-cart.

"Like nobody's going to notice us," she said sarcastically as the pedestrians scattered to give them passage.

Looking back, Nork discovered his mother was paying great attention to her feet, for which he had provided the sandals. This made him feel extra brave, especially since he was holding the reins of his recently repaired wagon. Then, after a few hundred paces, he stopped, and threw the reins over a wastepaper basket, as if tethering a horse.

"What's that for?" he asked.

Sara glanced up from her feet. "Waste paper," she replied.

"Not that," he replied crossly, "that!"

Sara looked to where he was pointing – the sort of cafe her parents would cross the road to avoid. And she had to admit, in this particular case, it was quite easy to imagine all the bugs and diseases swirling out of the door, to surround her ankles.

"The blackboard," said Nork. "Is it a spelling test?"

Sara stared at the menu. "I don't understand," she replied.

Nork studied the board that contained a lot of words and numbers. He was very good at dealing with these. Indeed, he could instantly recite everything up to his fifteen times table, and even spell pterodactyl; it stopped the monks giving you the cane for being a 'stupid boy' when sitting in class.

But the way everything was arranged on this blackboard was very confusing. Not only were some of the words spelled wrongly, but the numbers had no signs telling him what he should do with them, or where the answer should go. However, in his new country, he thought such boards might be important, so asked his mother to explain them. Suddenly, his face dropped in astonishment.

"You can choose what you want!" he exclaimed.

He found such an idea impossible to believe. To him, the grown-ups in the kitchen provided whatever they thought you needed to eat.

"You don't have to eat cabbage," he exclaimed, "ever again?"

This spoken as if he had just witnessed a miracle. Then, as if doubting the truth of his new religion, he glanced at the board.

"So, if we want numbers 4, 12, 15 and two 26s, it would cost us £7.68?" he asked.

"Dunno," she replied, "you'd have to add it up." She looked at the numbers and nodded. "If I gave them a £10 note that would be OK," she said.

"They would have to give us £2.32 change," he responded immediately, as if answering a monk. He closed his eyes, waiting for a more difficult question to follow: '*If his mother had three children, and they all shared their change equally, they would each have fifty-eight pence...*' However, his mother only seemed interested in asking him the baby questions.

"Where do you get a £10 note from?" he asked.

"From a bank."

There was one across the road, but Nork thought the building looked most unfriendly.

"Are they anything to do with the authorities?" he asked.

"Not really...sort of, I suppose."

"Then you'll have to go, I'll wait outside."

She smiled. "It doesn't work that way," she said, "you have to give them the money in the first place."

"And how much have you given them?"

"Dunno...anyway, I can't go in dressed like this, they don't know me."

Nork bravely touched her hand. He was now actually facing her, all soppy, with everybody watching.

"I know you," he said, "I'll come with you and tell them who you are. I really need to eat."

Sara shook her head, but her tummy was furiously demanding food, leaving her no strength to resist as Nork pulled her forwards – fortunately without untethering his cart. Once inside the bank, she became the centre of attention, making her want to run, but the boy held her hand so tightly, there would be four legs to organise. To her surprise, when she got to the counter, the man gave her a great, beaming smile.

"Can I help you?" he asked, a pleading look in his eyes.

Sara had seen that look many times before, but only when gazing at a cinema screen, when the handsome actor fancied some lady or other. She let out an embarrassed giggle.

"I'd like some money, please," she said.

"Anything else?" asked the man.

She smiled. "No, just the money, please," she said.

"A £10 note," said a chin resting on the counter.

The man looked at the boy.

"He's my brother," said Sara, "down for the week."

Nork thought having a sister was the most sissy thing he could ever imagine, and refused to acknowledge the word.

"She's the famous Sara Brooks," he said, "fashion designer."

The man looked embarrassed. "Don't know much about clothes," he said, "but I like what you are wearing. We still have to wear a shirt and tie. That seems much more…"

"Comfortable?" suggested Sara.

The man was trying to get the courage to say 'sexy', but thought such a remark might get him hauled before his stuffy manager. He forced himself to think about the grey world of banking, now interrupted by a nipple pushing against the white cotton. She was not even wearing a bra, just this beautiful creation that he believed would fall to the ground, if only her little brother pulled the right bit of cord. He felt a bead of perspiration form on his brow.

"ID?" he said.

She shrugged. "Still working on the pockets," she replied.

Nork listened to all the things you had to say to get a £10 note, which seemed very complicated. The man wanted her address, security code, date of birth and, finally, a telephone number. Strangely, it was the man who provided the telephone number on a bit of paper that he handed across with a £10 note. Nork watched everything that was going on, until his mother took a buttercup from her hair, and passed it to the man. Nork frowned. There were thousands of them in the field they had recently passed, but the man seemed delighted with the gift.

The cashier watched the girl walk away, each step allowing him to see further down her body.

"Oh God, sandals," he moaned as they made flip-flop noises across the stone floor. It was the sexiest thing he had ever seen, and within the confined world of banking, probably the sexiest thing that had ever happened. And for a brief moment, he and the girl had been the centre of attention, their names entwined. Proudly, he ticked the box on the payment slip that indicated he had been able to identify the customer from personal knowledge. Then he turned to look at his co-worker.

"Sara Brooks," he said, "she's a famous fashion designer."

The lady at the next window looked at the girl, who appeared to be on her way home from a toga party. Why it so devastated her colleague, she had no idea. Then the boy's chin came to rest on the counter again.

"She's my mother really," he said to the man.

When Nork heard the lady at the next window laugh, he went to tell her the same thing. Then he looked around to see if there was anybody else he could tell, but his mother was scurrying out of the door, so he ran back to take his rightful place by her side.

With the exception of the 'mother' thing, Sara walked back across the road feeling much better about life. Her effect on the man was obvious, and he had liked her sandals. Soon her hunger would be gone, and the rest of the day was theirs

– hers, after she had worked out what to do with the boy.

Once inside the cafe, Sara realised her parents had been right to classify such places as biological weapons. Added to this, all the men were staring at her, their mouths open to reveal munched-up food. Some went further, to include a display of false teeth.

Looking on the positive side, Sara realised food poisoning would get her a free ride in an ambulance to a hospital, where she would be fed. In consequence, she told Nork to order breakfast, then hurried to hide herself in the darkest corner.

At the counter, Nork ordered beans on toast, which he knew to be the best breakfast in the whole world. After giving the counter-man the £10 note, he held out his hand for the change. Dropping the coins onto the counter, he slid them across to his free hand, like he had been taught in class, though where he came from, the money was plastic, and only ever used to teach sums. At the end of the lesson it had to be given back to the monk, it was never actually given away to get stuff. Even more confusing, here the coins were all made of metal, and it took him a little while to recognise their value. When he was certain he understood the foreign money, he looked up.

"I need another eighty-seven pence," he said.

The man shook his head, but otherwise paid no attention.

"Ten pounds minus £6.84 equals £3.16," said Nork.

Nork put the coins back on the counter, partly to make certain he had not made a mistake with the funny-looking money, but also to explain to the counter-man how he could work it out, by using his fingers.

Sara, frustrated by the delay all this chatter was causing to her food, left her hiding place, and nervously came to stand beside him.

"Children," she said, apologetically, "can't take them anywhere. I'm afraid you will have to explain it to him…very quickly, so we can be fed."

The man looked a little flustered. "Oh," he said, after scratching his head, "it seems I charged for the beans twice."

"Beans are forty pence," said Nork. "Two times forty equals eighty, minus it from anything, cannot come to eighty-seven pence."

Then a very old man left his table, and shuffled towards the counter. His worn-out clothes were decorated with so much darning wool, Sara immediately recognised him to be a tramp, and instinctively stepped sideways to give him three feet of personal body space. Then, her extensive knowledge of wardrobe matters made her realise that the suit had once been of the highest quality.

Nork took a less critical view. The man was holding a cane, like the monks always used on boys who got their sums wrong.

"The boy is quite right," said the man, "if beans are forty pence they cannot adjust the price by seven pence, unless you start dividing up the beans."

Sara blinked. His voice carried real authority, his words not at all slurred by drink, as she had imagined.

"A lot of people are not very good with sums and spelling," said Nork. "If he gives me a piece of paper, I can show him how to do it, so you won't need to cane him."

The old man looked at him. "Well I never!" he exclaimed. "A boy with a proper education. Can you multiply thirteen by twelve?"

"A hundred and fifty-six," responded Nork automatically.

"Good, good, and spelling too, I presume?"

Nork nodded, and spelled pterodactyl.

"We never had those when I was a boy," said the man, "but I shall take your word for it." Then he turned to the man behind the counter. "You look a little hot," he said, "anything wrong?"

The counter-man took a pound note from the till, and slid it across the counter.

"There you are," he mumbled.

A woman at a nearby table gasped with horror. "The boy was right," she hissed to her friend.

Nork tried to pick up the pound note and replace it with thirteen pence, but the old man immediately put his cane in the way.

"Double or quits," said the old man.

"I made a mistake," said the counter-man, "OK?"

"A very convenient mistake," said the old man, "and you know how gossip travels in a town like this. I wonder how many customers you will have tomorrow, all sitting here, doing their sums with the change you give them."

"I could throw you both out!" snapped the counter-man.

The old man recovered his stick from the counter, and leaned on it heavily for support.

"Go on then," he said, "or you could do double or quits, like I first suggested."

Nork looked between the grown-ups, unable to know what to make of it. He was astonished the counter-man who kept making mistakes had so far avoided getting the cane.

"What's double or quits?" he asked.

"It's a gamble," said the old man, "something you should never do unless the odds are in your favour."

"A coin tosses evenly," said the counter-man, "and boys can't gamble."

"I was thinking more of a quiz," said the old man. "Call it a hunch, but I think this boy has had a proper education, like my own, back in the 1920s. For every spelling mistake he finds on your menu board, it's double; if he finds nothing, then you get to keep your precious pound, though perhaps, your lesson has been learned, and you will never try to steal from a child again."

"The board's spelt right," responded the counter-man defensively, "anyway the kid won't know any different."

The old man rummaged about in a trouser pocket, and after much searching, eventually found a 50p coin. Then he looked down to the boy.

"This is my gamble," he said, "if you can't find anything wrong, I will give the man this precious 50p." He then pointed his stick to the menu board behind the counter. "Do we agree?" he asked.

The counter-man realised all his customers had now realigned their chairs to face the counter, as if watching a play. He looked at the board. All the words seemed blurred, but even if there was a mistake, it would not cost him more than thirteen pence…or something. Truth was, he was completely confused by the situation in which he now found himself. The only important thing now was to get rid of the old man and the boy as quickly as possible.

"Go on then," he said.

Nork focused all his attention on the board.

"Butter has two Ts," he said, "and cabbage has two Bs. Spagetti's not right, but I don't know why, because I always call it 'worms' cooked in tomato sauce. I can spell that if you like. W O R…"

Nork had never heard such laughter. By the time he got

to 'M' he gave up trying to shout above the uproar.

After the audience had settled, the old man gave a nod of approval.

"I did not say you had to spell them," he said, "merely point out if it was wrong, which, you have done. Spagetti's got an 'h' missing, incidently. So what is one pound times two times two times two?"

Nork did not understand where the pound came from, but that was not important. "£8," he said, thereby answering the sum he had been given.

"Sod off," said the counter-man.

The old man brought his walking stick down on the man's head.

"Women and children are present," he said, "now pay up, or I'm going to the newspapers!"

The counter-man knew he had lost control of the situation, not helped by a man in his early twenties leaving his table and walking to the counter. He was carrying an important-looking briefcase, the sort the food hygiene inspectors used to make themselves look important.

"Look no further," said the new arrival. "I'm from *The Daily Herald*, and yes, this situation makes a quirky page-filler."

Sara quickly retreated to the shadows; if the press were involved, she needed to hide. The journalist, apparently disappointed by her retreat, turned to the counter-man.

"£8," he said, "then perhaps I might accidentally forget to file this part of the story."

"That's press brutality," said the counter-man, "I could report you to someone."

"You could," said the journalist, "it all depends whether you want to make the front page of my newspaper tomorrow."

The counter-man made a grumbling noise, then raided the till for a handful of coins, which he slid across the worktop.

"That's all you're getting," he snapped.

Nork realised this was similar to what had happened in the bank, so scooped the coins onto a plate, and took them across to his mother. He then removed a buttercup from her hair, and returned to give the much-valued gift to the counter-man. Again, the whole cafe audience erupted into laughter, which soon became a round of applause.

The journalist took a few steps towards the girl, stopping abruptly to take a sharp intake of breath, her wild ginger hair and sexy dress both sending a dangerous level of hormones surging through his body. But more important than this, he knew 'posh birds' only came to places like this when they were looking for a 'bit of rough'…which he was always happy to provide. This one though, seemed a bit special. Most probably she would want to play 'oh no' games before dropping her knickers. Also the boy was rather standing in the way of his general progress. He gave him a £10 note.

"Perhaps you could go and buy your mathematics friend a cup of tea, or *something*," he said.

Nork quite liked the idea of buying the man a cup of tea, because it sounded really grown up. What 'something' might be, he had no idea – beans on toast, probably.

The journalist, having impressed the girl with his generosity, advanced to where he could see down the top of her dress. The secret shadow of her breasts made whatever else might be happening in the cafe irrelevant.

Sara looked at the official-looking man with a briefcase. She could not think how to respond to his questions, so let him ramble on until Nork returned to the table. A moment later, the counter-man arrived, and placed two enormous plates on the table. Sara looked at the plate nearest herself.

According to her parents, beans on toast were like illegal drugs, taken secretly in dark rooms, when nobody was watching. Only by serving them as part of a full English breakfast, could their working-class origins be tolerated. Even then, it would be a few beans on wholemeal bread, not two enormous bean mountains, the toast beneath being implied, rather than visible. As to the grubby fingermarks around the edge of the plate, these gave the impression the food was ready to fight back.

"Breakfast?" she questioned.

The counter-man did not answer, instead hurrying away, no doubt in fear of the boy's ability to extract money from him.

Sara's etiquette lessons had not dealt with a situation like this, but improvising, she used her knife to avalanche the beans from their mountainous summits. This allowed her to begin excavating from the sides, the fork now appearing less like a shovel, and more like a tool from which she could take delicate nibbles…or many ordinary nibbles, as it turned out, this being her first food for thirty-six hours.

The journalist realised feeding time was a good excuse to get himself a coffee, and consider his next move. Then he remembered he had just given the boy his last £10 note. Indeed, he even lacked the bus fare to get home, leaving him with a six-mile walk…unless the boy gave him the change he had been expecting. But the boy was totally preoccupied with the beans on toast, and to interrupt him now would make it look like he was a desperate man who did not have the bus fare to get home. Then the journalist looked towards the old man to discover he was equally preoccupied with beans on toast…plus two eggs, and many sausages.

The journalist knew there would still be change, but how could he ask the boy to produce it, without looking mean? Reluctantly, he came to accept that getting inside this girl's knickers might cost him the full £10.

After Sara had consumed the last bean, she remembered the journalist was waiting to interview her, but why? She was only famous for being the breakfast companion of a boy whose ability to spell and add up marked him out as a genius. She was certain the man was expecting something more interesting than this in return for, presumably putting two meals on his expense account.

"What's the story about?" she asked.

"We do a fashion page," he said, "but this part of the world gets to hear little about what is going on in Paris."

Sara's mind raced back to her walk-in wardrobe at home. This did have many items that originated in Paris.

"About fashion?" she asked.

"You will have to explain it to me," responded the journalist. "Our fashion editor is the only one who understands clothes. Let me think. Where did you buy the dress from, and why have you come to our town?"

"It's not a dress," replied Sara, "it's a…desert robe."

"And that's what people are starting to wear in…?"

"…In the Summer collection, yes."

Suddenly, there was a blinding flash of light. When the cafe reappeared, Sara realised a man on the next table had attacked her with a camera. The boy had vanished, so it was just herself who had been imprisoned on film.

"If you want to buy the photograph for your fashion

pages," said the horrible man, "I live at number one, Railway Cottages. Reckon £10 should just about cover it!"

Sara felt a tug on her sheet, and looking down saw the boy hiding beneath the table.

"I can't have my photograph taken," he said.

"Neither can I," she whispered.

"Is he a spy, from the authorities?"

Sara shook her head. Then she realised the fashion editor of the newspaper would immediately understand the true situation, and pass the copy to the department dealing with 'Sheet Girl Visits…wherever we are'. The fact that her father only read the *Financial Times* was irrelevant. Other people, his secret enemies, would take great delight in bringing 'The Sheet' story to his attention.

The boy crawled from underneath the table and, keeping his back to the camera, walked towards the door. He returned a few moments later with the sack containing the hammer and nails. After sliding the mountain of coins into this, he once again retreated.

"Thank you for feeding me," he called to the journalist as he left the building.

The journalist watched the girl race after the boy. Instinctively he put a hand into his empty back pocket. "Sod it," he said.

On reaching the outside, Sara realised her run had caused the sheet to become significantly less than a 'desert robe'. To make her 'clothing accident' worse, many of the cafe customers had followed her outside to see what would happen next. She supposed having the press involved had made her public property – a public who now gathered around, leaving her with no obvious escape routes. Then she saw the horrible man with the camera staring at her, goggle-eyed.

"You are destined to be famous," he shouted. "There's a club in town where you could get free drinks all night in return for dancing about on the tables!" Then he started to raise the camera.

Into this nightmare, Sara heard Nork saying something about 'it taking a passenger'. She looked down to see he was sitting in his cart contraption, which she realised was pointing slightly downhill. Never had the lesser of two evils sounded so attractive. She clambered into the box, which made her audience cheer. She decided there were many things about being old that she did not understand; partly, if you grew up in the war, you had an obsession for orange boxes and dried egg powder.

"Get us out of here!" she whispered.

"Yes, Mother," said the boy loudly.

The audience gasped at the sudden change in plot.

"Your son!" gasped one presently.

Sara closed her eyes. *The world does not exist*, she thought. Then she felt a bump, followed by a swaying seat, and ultimately the wind playing with her hair. Peeping through spaced fingers, she realised the crowd had vanished, as indeed had the houses. Ahead, the lane fell steeply towards the river. They were going too fast for her to leap out; instead she dropped her hands to grab the sides of the box.

"Fine," she screamed, "you can stop now!"

"Grrrr-zoooom," said Nork.

He touched the front axle, and the vehicle leapt from the pavement to take to the road.

"Screeech-zoom," he yelled for the benefit of his mother,

who he thought might not understand about engines. Then his own tummy started to get nervous, but the lane was almost straight, and if he showed his mother how brave he was, she might like him even better. Soon he was travelling at rocket speed. However, his racing car was solid, the wheels true, and well attached. His mother was screaming with delight; this hill could go on forever; it was the happiest time of his entire life! Amazingly, he had to admit, day two in the new country was turning out to be even better than day one.

Suddenly, there was a flash from the top of a pole. A spy in the air; he had not been expecting that! Then he remembered the way he had let his guard drop with the previous photographs, and resolved to be more careful in future; this country had cameras everywhere!

Towards the bottom of the hill he gently applied the brake to stop by a footpath sign. It was very noisy, because his mother was screaming really close to his ears. He leapt from his car and ran a little way up the footpath, where he stopped, waiting for his mother to become quiet. Then he realised all the buttercups had gone from her hair, so he climbed a fence to pick some more assorted flowers. On his return, he presented them to her, but she seemed lost to another world, so he bravely put them into her hair.

"You set off a speed camera," she said quietly.

Nork smiled. Grown-ups hardly ever praised him, and this was the first time his mother had done so. She repeated the statement three or four times, and each time, he thought of something brave, yet modest, to say.

Shakily, Sara extracted herself from the box. "Menace 1," she said, "it will be on the front page now."

It suddenly occurred to her that she was no longer Sara

Brooks, but a magistrate's daughter, activating a speed camera, dressed in a sheet! The boy's voice came into her nightmare.

"With a son," she added.

The boy beamed at her, throwing his arms about her waist, pressing his face into her side.

"We need to go," he said, "Tom's chasing us again."

Sara spun around. The pervert was a long way up the hill, and seemed to be flagging, but his apparent determination only reinforced the idea that he was running after her. She allowed Nork to pull her onto the footpath, slightly annoyed that he was putting an equal amount of effort into dragging the reins of his go-cart with his other hand. After a short while, he stopped to inspect a fence. Slowly he walked on, then miraculously dropped to his hands and knees, and reappeared the other side of the barrier. He then pulled the cart through.

"Hurry," he said, "the man is after us, we need to hide!"

Reluctantly, she followed. "He'll find the hole too," she said.

"He's a grown-up," said Nork, "he won't know where to look."

Sara frowned. "If you have never been to this…country before," she said, "how did you know there was a hole here? Is this where you play with your friends?"

The boy looked bewildered by her rambling statement that so clearly contradicted itself.

"Railway line," he said, "river, and I saw children in the town. There's always a hole in a fence, where a hole needs to be."

For the first time, Sara looked around, to realise she was trespassing on British Railways property.

"It's naughty to play on a railway line," she said weakly, and slightly confused as to why she was here.

"We're not playing," he said, "but waiting for a train." He pulled both herself and the cart over to some bushes. "And hiding," he added.

In truth, Nork had never seen a train, but he had read books about them, and knew a signal with a flat arm meant the train would have to stop. Then, on hearing the rails making a clicking noise, he looked along the line with mounting excitement. A moment later he became tremendously disappointed; it was not puffing smoke or hissing steam, just sort of rattling towards them.

"Coughs and sneezles spread di-esels," he moaned.

As the seconds ticked by, things improved. The train appeared to grow in size, and squealed to a halt, with the carriages towering high above him. He emerged from the bushes, dragging his cart. With some difficulty, he climbed a little ladder to reach the door.

"Stop!" screamed Sara. "What are you doing?"

The operation needed all his concentration, so he allowed his mother to protest; she would not be heard above the noise of the engines. After opening the door, he pulled up his go-cart by the reins, then looked down to make sure his mother could manage the ladder. To his surprise, she was still in the bushes.

"Hurry," he shouted, "diesels do not need to stop very long."

Sara came out of the bushes to talk him down, but looking up, saw he was lying on the floor, with a hand reaching towards her. What she wanted least was to be on the train. What she wanted even less was to be left alone on a railway track, with a pervert looking for her. She concluded that climbing up was, once again, the lesser of two evils. In a trembling nightmare, she ascended to sit on the carriage floor. Nork dragged her feet inside, then closed the door.

Having boarded a train in such a manner, Sara naturally assumed Nork would now try to comfort her, or at least attempt to distract her from the traumatic circumstances. But, what he actually did was walk into the main carriage, pulling his cart behind him, as if there was nothing to worry about.

Nervously she peered after him; if anybody had seen them climb onboard, they pretended not to notice. Anyway, the carriage was pretty much empty, its few occupants busy reading newspapers, or semi-dozing with their eyes closed. Nork was now sitting in a window seat, the cart between the seats. Whatever she did, the ticket collector would be drawn to her strange costume. She decided safety in numbers meant it was better to have the two odd people in the same place. She sat beside Nork and waited for…whatever was to happen next, which happened to be a train whooshing by on the other track, after which, she felt herself starting to move. Nork had his nose pressed to the glass.

"There's Tom again," he said.

Sara looked out of the window to see the pervert gazing through the fence. It was only a brief moment, but a good one. Nork gave him a goodbye wave, then turned to smile at his mother. He had won, Tom had lost!

Sara had so many questions to ask the boy, she could not think where to begin. He seemed to know an awful lot about trains, fences and spelling, but besides this, appeared very poorly educated. For instance, he believed he had crossed an ocean on a fencing panel, yet clearly this could not be so. Then she realised fences were a common theme.

"They must have fences where you come from," she said. "You arrived on one, and know about all the holes they contain."

Nork looked at her suspiciously.

"Found it in the ocean."

"So you were playing on the beach, and…?"

Nork hated telling fibs, but if the grown-ups of his new country realised he had only lost sight of land for a few hours, they might be able to trace his escape backwards. But if they thought he had drifted across an ocean for many days, they would think he had come from America or Africa. Then, after much searching, they would shrug their shoulders. 'He must come from nowhere,' he could imagine them saying. And that suited him just fine.

It worried him that his mother was uncomfortably close to the truth, so confined himself to staring out of the window, while pretending not to hear her questions.

"OK," said Sara eventually, "tell me later."

Then, more importantly, she turned her attention to the aisle, down which a ticket collector would soon arrive. Perhaps half an hour passed before she realised ticket collectors only made their way along the carriages after a station stop. Now, he or she was probably sitting in the buffet car, drinking tea.

This line of thought was interrupted by Nork who, no doubt becoming bored by just looking out of the window, curled up on the seat to put his head on her lap. She knew it was wrong, but some instinct made her reach down to run a finger through his mass of tangled hair. Then, by degrees, she drifted into a world of dreams – wild dreams of being famous, and big-dipper-go-cart rides.

Eventually this reduced to a half-dream, in this case, the image of her father sitting on the opposite seat, reading a newspaper that treated her sheet photograph as front-page news. Desperately, she tried to reach across to grab the paper, but her arms were not long enough. Then the words 'all change' entered her world, and slowly she opened her eyes to look out of the window. To her surprise, she saw a busy station platform. Her journey had come to an end, the sort of conclusion where she was certain to be arrested.

She gave Nork a gentle shake. "It is over," she said.

Nork looked up. "What?" he asked.

"They won't let us out of the turnstiles without tickets," she said. "And, anyway, we are in the middle of a big city, a place I cannot go. We are now truly stuck."

But Nork did not seem to care. He stood up and walked towards the door, pulling his stupid go-cart behind.

"Did you not hear me?" she shouted. "We are in serious big trouble."

But Nork paid no attention. On reaching the platform, he walked across it, then boarded a train waiting at the far side. This forced her to give chase. A lot of people turned to look at her as she leapt wildly onto the platform.

There was nothing else she could do but follow Nork onto the next train, and explain that he could not do this, which seemed rather silly, because he already had! However, Nork listened politely, then shrugged his shoulders.

"I thought you said they would not let us out of the station barriers," he said.

"Well, yes…"

He looked puzzled by her confusing talk, but it did not really matter, because the carriage had already given a jolt, and the platform outside the window was now sliding by with increasing speed. This allowed him to think about more important things…

On the previous train, the authorities could have traced him back to the river, and from there, the ocean. Having now put a station gap from where he started, he felt almost safe. Indeed, after much consideration, he felt sufficiently relaxed to curl up on the seat and place his head on his mother's lap, hoping she would play with his hair again, because it felt nice, in a soppy sort of way; but he did not care, he had found a mother, and that was quite an achievement for only his second day in his new country!

Sara was panicking. Having just left a station, a ticket collector would surely appear at any moment…But it still came as a terrible shock when she heard a voice saying, "Tickets."

"Shhhh," she said, "you'll wake the boy."

"Tickets," whispered the man.

She tried to think quickly.

"I've got no pockets," she said, "the boy's got them in his sack. Can you get them next time?"

"No," replied the man unhelpfully.

"So you want me to wake him up, and start him charging up and down your aisle on his cart thing?"

Nork was only pretending to be asleep. After listening quietly to all the talk, he lifted his head to look at the man, who seemed rather cross. His mother had given him the hint of what he must do, so he stood up to touch his cart.

"Brrrm-brrrr," he said.

The man jumped between the seats. "No," he said.

"Is that the only word you know?" said Sara indignantly. "He only wants to play racing drivers, it will be OK."

"I'll get you thrown off," said the ticket collector.

"Fine," said Sara.

"At the next station."

Nork tugged at the man's arm. "What time is it?" he asked.

"Time you sat down," said the ticket collector.

"I thought you wanted us to leave," responded Sara, "make your mind up."

"I want you to…I want…" babbled the collector.

Sara realised that as Nork had squeezed by, he had pulled her sheet, displaying the top of her breasts. The man was now staring at these, apparently hypnotised. It was then that she finally understood the truth of her new situation…

In her old life she always wore respectable clothes, and the few boys who noticed her were more interested in her mind, and her ability to play chess at a competitive level. She now realised that her first boyfriend had gone off with the tart Janet because she would show her breasts to anyone who gave her 50p. Now it made her most indignant to realise that girls were expected to display themselves, as if at a cattle market. Did they not understand she had an 'O' level in Physics, and could easily apply Newton's Laws of Motion to the go-cart in the aisle?

But scientific knowledge would not get them a free train ride. That, it seemed, relied entirely on her breasts. Instead of adjusting her sheet, she looked towards Nork, who was now sitting in the driving seat of his cart which he had positioned to point down the aisle. She noticed the brake was on, but clearly the official had no experience of the technology involved.

"Newton's First Law of Motion," she said, "states that

a moving body continues moving at the same speed, in a straight line, unless acted upon by an unbalanced force."

The ticket collector seemed more interested in her breasts.

"It means," continued Sara, "that if the train stops, he will go hurtling down the aisle at eighty miles an hour, something your humble legs are not going to stop."

"It's a bet," said Nork, "I'm going for the world speed record!"

"It's for a good charity," continued Sara, "so most people are happy to give him 10p for every mile an hour he reaches. Nork, show the man how much money you got last time."

Nork reached into the box to recover his treasure sack. From it, he first produced a hammer.

Sara quickly improvised. "The last place had a very steep hill," she said. "We needed tools to get the money from aggrieved debtors, who were thinking more along the lines of a sponsored go-cart push in the region of two miles an hour. But, given your advanced knowledge, perhaps you would like to sponsor him for a penny a mile."

"You cannot be serious!" snapped the ticket collector.

Sara shrugged. "Maybe not," she said, "but that's not going to stop him shooting down the carriages when the train stops. That is governed entirely by the laws of physics."

Sara realised the ticket collector's eyes had moved from her breasts to focus entirely on the hammer, nails and all the money.

"Come on, Nork," said Sara, "the train's not going to stop just yet, get some sleep before your big moment down the ski jump."

Obediently, Nork pulled the cart back from the aisle, and, after curling up on the seat, put his head on her lap.

"Snore," he said.

"It seems time is going backwards," said Sara to the ticket collector, "just to give you a second chance. Perhaps you might now go for the easier option of pretending not to see us?"

She then lowered her head, closed her eyes, and also said, "Snore."

"Zzzzz," added Nork more loudly.

"Zzzzz," imitated Sara, more concerned with getting her acting right than increasing its volume.

The man kept talking about tickets, but with decreasing confidence. His two illegal passengers just kept saying 'snore' and 'zzzz', interspersed with giggles.

"I'll be back just before the station," said the man, "then we'll see who's laughing!"

Nork was very pleased with himself. He had made his mother giggle, and got rid of the ticket collector. Then he looked out of the window to count the passing telegraph poles on his fingers, while also counting to sixty in his head. This train was only travelling half the speed of the first. Still, it was moving away from the city that his mother did not like, and for that, she was sure to like him better.

Eventually, the train stopped at a place that looked remarkably like nowhere in particular. Sara noted they often did this, but could never quite work out why. Possibly it was a courtesy service, so that people had a general excuse for being late for work.

Looking out of the window, Nork saw the same landscape, but without any of the complicated ideas suffered by grown-ups. To him, there were no houses or ticket barriers, so all their problems had been solved.

"Our stop," he said, grabbing the reins of his cart, and dragging it along the carriage.

Sara raced after him to stop him doing anything silly, but he was too quick, and had already opened the door. He jumped down, and pulled the cart after him.

"We can't just get off!" she protested.

"Why not? We just got on. Anyway, this is where we need to be, and there are no ticket barriers."

He held up his hand to help her down.

"No," she said firmly.

"That Fat Controller lives at the next station," he replied, "and he's not a very nice man."

"That's why I need you here," she pleaded, "not because of the Fat Controller, because…"

It suddenly occurred to her that the next stop could be in the middle of another very large city. On her own, without tickets, thousands of miles from anywhere she knew…the boy was right, this is where they needed to be. Civilisation, when it came, needed to be in small measure, and approached on her own terms. Carefully, she backed down the emergency ladder and, slightly bemused, stood beside Nork.

"Now what?" she asked.

Nork seemed totally unconcerned by the situation, and casually climbed up to close the door.

"Goodbye, train," he said.

After returning to the ground, he walked to a low wire fence and, using a post, leapfrogged over the top.

"Isn't there supposed to be a hole somewhere?" protested Sara.

"No need, you can use my cart as a stile, if you like. I've left the brake on."

Sara felt the need to move away from the train and the ticket collector, who would probably be so incensed by their escape, he would pull the communication cord, so they could be arrested for trespass. Reluctantly, she used the cart to step over the fence.

"Guess we are legal again," she said, "nobody can prove we were on the train."

Nork reached across to bring his cart into legal territory. "Not now they can't," he said.

Sara smiled. The not-very-nice ticket collector would think he had been hallucinating about their ride. He might be searching the train for hours, before accepting they had just vanished in a puff of smoke. As if to admit defeat, the train gave a jolt, then accelerated away.

For the first time, Sara took a good look around. What had seemed quite pretty from the window now appeared to be an endless wilderness of rolling hills. In the distance were some really big mountains with pointy tops…too big to be English!

"Do you have any idea where we are?" she asked.

She knew the answer, but wanted to hear Nork confess that he had brought her to a wilderness so vast, they were certain to die trying to cross it.

"Of course," said Nork, "I was counting the telegraph poles when we were on the train. Not all of them, but mostly we were passing thirty a minute. The sun was always behind us, first a little to the left, then a little to the right. We are now 5,400 telegraph poles from where you found me, and that means we are at the North Pole."

Nork realised his mother was not very good at 'getting' jokes, even good ones. This one even had the extra advantage of distracting her from the fact he had no idea where they were...

But that was not important. What mattered was that a distance of 5,400 telegraph poles made him feel almost safe from the authorities.

"The North Pole," he repeated as he walked away, smiling and nodding, to indicate how happy he was with the world.

"Scotland," mumbled Sara to herself. "How did that happen?"

THREE

Sara's actual experience of mud was very limited. However, her theoretical knowledge was quite good, having studied the subject as part of her World War One poetry course. Also, she had once seen quite a lot of it when viewing the hippopotamus enclosure at her local zoo.

Now, standing on a small patch of gravel, she watched Nork disappearing into a great wilderness of the stuff. Strangely, he was still pulling his stupid go-cart, presumably pretending it was a tank, crossing No Man's Land in the manner of a World War One soldier. Thankfully, the way the mud squished up to his knees meant he would soon need to turn back, so there was no need for her to follow.

In order to pass the time, Sara allowed her gaze to wander left, where a cliff face rose directly from the bog. This, she decided, represented death by falling.

Looking to the right, she saw a depression in the landscape caused the mud to disappear beneath a lake. This clearly represented death by drowning.

Turning around, she looked in the direction of the railway

line, now a few miles distant. This represented death by starvation, unless she stood on the tracks, waving her arms in the hope a train would stop. Most probably, this represented death by being flattened!

Realising she was surrounded by death, she decided to wait until Nork returned to her patch of gravel, after which they could talk about being trapped, and the various ways in which they might die. But turning away from the railway, she discovered Nork was still marching onwards, like a soldier, believing in *the old familiar lie, to die for one's country is grand*.

She must stop thinking about World War One poetry; her situation was obviously far more desperate. Nork was not coming back! This forced her to think the unthinkable… onwards, into the Valley of Death!

Nork sensed he was starting to walk slightly uphill; this confirmed when the mud became drier, eventually allowing grassy clumps to form. Looking up from his feet, he saw a short hillside rising to a domed summit, beyond which the sky looked bright and sunny. He walked onwards, hoping that whatever lay the other side would answer his mother's earlier, rather repetitive, question of 'now what?' But where was his mother?

Turning around, he saw she was still in the middle of the bog. She obviously found it a fun place to play, but this suited him fine, because it would give him time to work out a plan. But, on reaching the top of the hill, Nork found himself simply looking at a lot more mountains.

Now what? he thought; obviously not something he could say out loud to his mother.

When his mother arrived, she was talking to herself. "Are

we there yet?" she asked. "No," she continued. "Why not?" she asked. "Because we're not…"

Nork looked at her strangely. "Are you OK?" he asked.

"Fine," she replied, "just conducting a normal child-grown-up conversation, in which it seems I have to speak both parts."

Nork had no objection to having a mother who was quite mad. Indeed, he quite liked it because it gave her a sense of fun that was completely absent in the other grown-ups he had met.

Sara looked down at the mud that vaguely represented the shape of her feet. A few days ago, such a catastrophe would have been beyond her comprehension, but now? Well, she just accepted it. Then she looked up to study the landscape. As expected, it was completely devoid of civilisation.

"Now what?" she asked.

Thankfully, Nork had remembered that when grown-ups had nothing interesting to say, they always talked about the weather.

"Nice weather," he said, holding out a hand to catch the sunshine.

"Nice weather," retorted Sara, "what's that supposed to mean?"

"It's not raining," suggested Nork.

Then he walked away, before his mother could ask him any more difficult questions.

After walking for about fifteen minutes, Nork was surprised to find himself looking at a high chain-link fence. Though he had no experience of this variety, he felt certain it was unlikely to have any holes. More importantly, he must not let his mother know the difficulty had surprised him. After racing towards it, he pushed his cart upwards to hook the front wheels over the top. Then, using the soap box as a ladder, he stood on the front axle, and jumped over the top. Now, on the far side, he waited casually, ready to fake disbelief if his mother protested. As it happened, she was still more interested in talking to herself than observing the world around her.

"Oh," she said as she got closer, "and the weather's quite nice as well since you ask."

Then she saw the fence, and stopped abruptly. Looking left and right, it seemed to go on forever. How Nork came to be the other side, she had no idea.

"Very funny," she said.

"What?" he asked.

"That," she said, also determined to state the obvious.

When Nork made no response, she gave a little cough.

"Excuse me," she said, "both sides of the fence are wilderness, so why do I need to be over there?"

"Going back simply returns us to the railway line," he replied, "and there's no water, and when it gets dark, no shelter."

"Which begs the question, how?"

Nork thought long and hard. He knew precise instructions about where to put her feet, and how to leap from the top of a chain-link fence would not help. This was something she needed to work out for herself.

"There's one very easy way to climb it," he said. "Pretend you are ten years old, playing on the climbing frames."

"But I am not."

"You were once. Pretend the farmer is chasing you for stealing an apple."

He picked up a stone, and pushed it between the wires.

"A pretend apple," he said, "and the farmer is just coming up behind you now, with a dog."

"Makes no difference, I still prefer to be on this side."

"Because you have forgotten how to pretend."

Sara looked at the go-cart hanging by its wheels. She gave it a pull, and was surprised to find it quite solid. Nork seemed to have forgotten she was there, just assuming she was willing to leap from six feet in the air, wearing only a sheet.

"I am ten years old," she said, "and running from...Nork."

"Yes."

"This is very embarrassing," she said, "but I want you to come over here."

Nork stood up and, carefully putting his toes between the links, managed to jump clumsily over the top.

"Now," said his mother, "I want you to come running from over there screaming..."

"What?"

"You must promise never to tell anybody about this."

"OK, if it gets you over the fence."

She looked around. "The bottom-biting monster," she mumbled.

Nork coughed with embarrassment. "Bottom-biting monster?" he responded.

"Yes, one of those. If I am to pretend to be ten years old, then you have to pretend to be a BBM."

"And bite you?"

"Well, you sort of run up, making a growling noise, like a real monster, and yes, in this case, if you catch me, bite."

"That's a very hard game of pretend," said Nork.

"That's a very high fence to climb over," she replied.

Nork knew talking about bottoms was not a mouth-washing offence, but any mistake, and it could easily become so. If this game went wrong, he could be in ever so much trouble. Still, his mother needed to get over the fence, so he slinked away.

"Now," he shouted when he was well hidden.

"The BBM never gives a warning," she called. "...Oh hello, Mr Toad, have you seen Mr Badger today?"

"Still now," shouted back Nork.

Nork waited in his trench, listening to his mother babble on about animals. How soldiers found the courage to go into battle, he had no idea. Then he pretended a farmer was chasing him for stealing an apple. He jumped up.

"I am the bottom-biting monster," he yelled, "grrrrr-grrrr!"

His mother screamed and leapt into the air. Her first sandal touched the bottom of the soap box, the second the top.

"Arrrrgggghh," she screamed, "go away!"

Nork was so astonished by her agility that he kept on coming.

"A bottom to bite!" he yelled.

"You don't have to do it," yelled Sara. Oh God, he had actually forgotten he was pretending! Then, remembering her six-year-old self, she clambered onto the axle to avoid the teeth that had spotted her bottom, and were heading straight towards it. She threw herself into the air, tumbling to the ground with all the decorum of a youngster on the other side. Then she rolled forwards, screaming with laughter.

Nork pressed his face to the fence. It was the first girl-game he had ever played, and he had lost. He thought it was surprisingly frightening.

Fortunately, his mother was too busy giggling to notice how clumsily he was getting his cart over the fence. It wobbled alarmingly, and he seriously began to think it might be himself who needed help. Finally, he managed to lower his cart, and jumped down after it. This, he decided, was a very silly place to put a fence. It could serve no useful purpose, other than to…

Ah…to stop grizzly bears wandering about the mountains eating people. However, it was still a very silly fence, because there were no signs saying on which side the animals lived.

Turning around, he found his mother watching him. He had never seen such a look before, but some instinct told him it meant she liked him better. It was sort of embarrassing and nice at the same time.

"Now I've told you one of my secrets," she said, "it's your turn to tell me one of yours, something from before I met you."

Nork had no interest in talking about his old country, so trudged up the next whale-back of land without comment. At the top, he stopped abruptly.

A long way below, a great lake shimmered in the sunshine, its far bank rising in rocky spurs to become a 'proper' mountain with a pointy top. Lower down, many rivers raced into deep gorges, making it impossible for any mountaineering expedition to reach it. Where the ground eased, pockets of forest had taken hold, individually nothing more than domestic-sized woods, but collectively a wonderland of tree-climbing, for a great explorer like himself, who would somehow get there…by canoe, probably. Having decided this, he sat on the heather waiting for his mother to catch up. He wanted to act casual, so she would believe this was all part of his clever plan.

Sara arrived and sat beside Nork. Her attention was then drawn to what lay below – a meadow, down which a thin track wandered towards a loch. Civilisation, she decided, was within her reach.

"How far do you reckon it is to the settlement?" she asked.

Nork had no idea. "Awesome," he said, so as to keep his answer slightly vague, but tending towards 'a long way'.

Sara realised 'awesome' meant a distance his legs found intimidating – further than they could walk tonight anyway, which was all she really needed to know. Then, feeling the need to rest, she lay back on the heather and closed her eyes. To her surprise, she found herself smiling as her thoughts returned to the bottom-biting monster. The last time this had been part of her life, she was about six, and her older brother was chasing her around the garden, pretending to be a BBM. And now this adventure with Nork was making her feel younger. With some difficulty, she accepted that today had been quite fun, except for the mud that had now welded itself between her feet and sandals.

Outside her own private thoughts, she heard Nork babbling happily to himself. His imaginary friends had come to play. A few tears began to appear in her eyes as she remembered her own, more innocent childhood.

"Mooo," said Nork.

"Mooo," repeated Sara, thinking how funny it had been on the train when they had played the snoring game with the ticket collector.

"I like cows," said Nork.

"They have pretty eyes," she said, "though I always find them rather frightening."

"Moooo," said Nork, possibly adding an extra 'o'.

Sara felt a cloud pass across the sky. She was actually sunbathing, or had been until the sun went in.

"To make friends with a cow," said Nork, "you need to sit down, then they think you are smaller than them, and don't run away, snort."

"That was a very good snort…err, don't tell me, you are actually talking to a cow."

"Why else would I be saying moo? If they were pigs, I would be saying oink."

"They?" she questioned.

Slowly, she opened her eyes to discover a big, hairy face looking down at her. Either side of its head were great, curly horns. The fear was too close to let her scream; there were thousands of them, all gathered around to inspect what had invaded their territory.

"Don't move," she whispered, "then they won't attack."

Nork reached across to distract the main aggressor by tickling behind its ear. The beast seemed quite pleased by this, and looked towards the boy.

"If you don't frighten them," he said, "they will lick your arm, and it tickles really nice."

Sara then realised the cows did not have udders; a simple flick of the head would send a great horn into her body. She could imagine all the blood gushing out. Annoyingly, Nork seemed more interested in the huge shaggy beasts then her own survival. Even more annoyingly, they seemed to be queuing up to be tickled behind the ears.

"This is more dangerous than you think," she whispered, "believe me."

"No it's not," said Nork. "Now we are friends they will

follow us when we walk off. Obviously we are not going to hurt them. That one there needs a tickle."

In a terrified gesture of friendship, Sara stretched out a hand. Strangely, the beast seemed quite nervous of it.

"Nice cow," she said, it clearly being silly to remind them that they were actually 'men-cows'.

Slowly she stood up, causing the beast to step back while it became accustomed to her new height. Now, she could fully appreciate their ragged, hairy appearance.

"Aberdeen Angus," she said, "they have a reputation for being good-natured, I think."

Nork stood up and went around patting them all on the head. One of the animals lunged at her but, when she screamed, it backed off with a snort.

"Help," she said weakly.

Nork reached across to take the assorted flowers from her hair and, putting them on the flat of his hand, held them out for inspection. He giggled as the beast sniffed at them, and finally lifted them gently away with its tongue.

"I think they like me better than you," he said. "If you want, I can meet you at the bottom of the hill."

He walked away and, sure enough, the beasts ambled after him. Minutes passed while she let her panic subside, and the next time she took a proper look around, found herself completely abandoned.

"So much for friendship," she mumbled.

She held out a thumb and, when it blotted out a complete animal, she began to walk sideways in a way that maintained the 'thumb-cow-sized relationship'.

Eventually, a few animals held back from the Nork-led procession, to munch mouthfuls of grass. As the last devoted follower stopped, at what she imagined to be a particularly tasty clump of grass, Nork looked back.

"Goodbye, cows," he shouted, while giving them a wave.

After changing his line, he came to walk beside her.

"They said we can come back to visit them whenever we want," he said.

"They were bulls," gasped Sara. "Did you not look underneath?"

"Why?" asked Nork.

"Because...err..."

It occurred to Sara that Nork did not know the difference between men-cows and lady-cows. If he did, underneath would have been the first place he looked – well, after the horns, maybe. Then she remembered what he had said about sleeping together. This boy had not been told the facts of life.

"Never mind," she said, "though perhaps you would just tell me one thing: did you come from an all-boy environment?"

"I came from nowhere," he said.

"I see," said Sara, "that explains a lot. Tell you what, if I accept you were delivered on a fencing panel, as a brand-new boy, will you never again tell anyone that I am your mother? It's too complicated to explain, but that's the deal, agreed?"

Nork gave a sniff of disapproval.

"From now on I am your big sister," she continued, "agreed?"

"Uh," responded Nork.

"Guess that's the best I'm going to get, that I am your uh-sister. Well, I suppose it makes it sound rather genuine."

She then decided that it was better to be cruel than kind.

"If people think I am your mother," she said, "the

authorities will come to take you away. As my brother, nobody's going to worry too much."

"Uh," repeated Nork, which he thought was the only sensible response to having a sister. Well that, and stepping two feet to the side, to keep some distance between them.

Just before reaching the loch, the path turned the right, after which it became more like a cart track. This allowed Nork to speed up, the go-cart bouncing behind, with most of the dried mud spinning from the wheels. After half a mile or so, he stopped to stare down at a narrow-gauge railway track that crossed the cart track. Looking left, he saw the railway continued on to a wooden jetty that extended perhaps twenty feet into the lake. There were no boats moored against it, but he still walked to the end to recover a loose length of rope from a bollard. Turning around, he saw that after crossing the cart track, the railway line went into a cutting between two rocky walls. He made his way upwards, to see if it went anywhere interesting. It did! Excitedly he hurried back down to tell his mother what he had discovered…but where was she?

After walking back along the cart track, he saw his mother sitting on a fallen tree. On reaching her side, he held out the rope.

"For your fashion design," he said.

But his mother did not look up. "I can't walk any further," she said, "this is where I am destined to…"

She did not finish the sentence, for how could she explain to a young boy that complete exhaustion takes away the will to live?

"I've found a place to sleep," he said, "it's really good, and it's got beds and everything."

Then he tried to pull her upright, but without success.

"We have just crossed a hundred miles of mountains," she said. "No more pain, just leave me!"

"I can't," said Nork, "because if it rains, you will die of cold, unless a passing policeman finds you and takes you to the station, where he will give you a mug of hot drinking chocolate, pretending to be your friend, so he can betray you to the authorities. But that was before I learnt about escaping properly. Wait here."

Sara always struggled with Nork's jokes. And in any event, for a 'don't go anywhere' joke to work properly, she would have to be tied to a tree.

A little later, she looked up to see a go-cart pulling up beside her. Nork spoke to her in the manner of a very strict schoolteacher, albeit using a lower octave.

"Get in," he demanded.

She had no pride left, and after collapsing into the contraption, felt herself rattling about, until the improvised pram stopped just before some railway lines.

"I can't pull you up the hill," said Nork, "but it's not far to walk."

Sara thought all the jiggling about in the cart must have re-awakened some survival instinct, because using the sides of the soap box, she pushed herself into a standing position.

"One step at a time," said Nork, "then tomorrow, after you have slept, we can have another wonderful day…Mother!"

FOUR

Sara was struggling with the peculiar notion that she was gazing up at a ceiling made of corrugated iron, an illusion made more surreal by the metal appearing to be within touching distance. In the hope of seeing something more sensible, she rolled over...only to fall from whatever she had been lying on. A moment later, she crash-landed onto whatever was below.

Confused and bewildered, she sat up to discover she had fallen from a bench made of two railway sleepers, their ends set into opposing stone walls. Ah! She remembered that bit; 'sleeping on sleepers,' Nork had said, after he had brought her to this place. But last night, after her army assault course across the mountains, she had been too exhausted to consider such things. Her only thought had been to lie down as quickly as possible.

Now, looking around, she realised the 'room' was a little under six-feet square, having no windows, the only light coming through a gap in one wall. She absolutely refused to think of this as a doorway, since it did not have a door that could be closed. To either side of the gap, were two railway-sleeper benches, which she absolutely refused to think of as beds.

After sitting up, she looked between her legs to discover she had landed on an earth floor which, she supposed, was where all the insects lived. Standing quickly, she discovered the corrugated-iron ceiling was, indeed, extremely low.

In order to bring some normality into her life, she said, "Ouch," then touched her head in a gesture of sympathy. Finding no bump or blood, she bent low and walked through the gap in the wall to reach the outside. Here, any normality quickly vanished, because she appeared to be standing beneath a great amphitheatre of towering rock walls. After blinking several times, everything still looked the same, so she concluded it must be real.

So, she thought, *I have just spent the night in an air raid shelter-type hut, its previous use presumably being a refuge for the quarry workers who needed to shelter from all the dynamite explosions. How much more weird can things get?* The answer came quite quickly, because a railway line emerged from a cutting to her left, heading straight across the quarry floor, to disappear inside a hole in the rock wall to her right. All of these observations implied the tunnel went…well, to whatever was inside the mountain.

Having sorted out her immediate surroundings, she began to think about her poor body. Nervously, she tried swinging her legs to see how much pain the muscle fatigue would generate. Surprisingly little. Then she remembered the mountain of beans on toast the boy had placed before her in the cafe. This, she realised, had become an army of calories, all marching through her body, searching for a place to offload their energy – not very feminine, but at that precise moment, the ability to walk seemed more important.

Clever boy, she said to herself.

Then she thought about the way he had led her across a wilderness of shaggy bulls, with great big horns. Suddenly, the name Nork sounded rather appropriate. It could easily belong to a Norse god, who had been sent to guide her through all the challenges of an epic journey. Then she remembered how, when she had collapsed semi-conscious onto a fallen tree, he had dragged her forwards to the quarry…no, it was much worse than that! He had pulled her along in his go-cart, in much the same way as he might bring a sack of potatoes back from the shops. After the surge of embarrassment passed, she looked around to see where he was. He needed to be here, by her side, because only he understood the ways of the wilderness.

*

Deep within the mountain, Nork's outstretched hand came against an iron rod. Feeling about, he realised the way ahead was barred by a number of these, each one going into the ceiling a little way above his head. Kneeling down, he felt them disappearing into the floor. Iron bars would not have been put in such a place unless there was something really good the other side.

Between the wall and outer bar was a gap. Given his experience of fence holes, he knew that if his head could fit through, then his body could wriggle after it. He smiled; these bars had been designed to keep out grown-ups, not eleven-year-old boys who needed to go exploring.

Standing on the other side of the bars, he looked back

to see the entrance as a pinprick of light, making him feel slightly less brave. He decided to go no further without a torch, so wriggled back. Then, copying his method of arrival, he placed his feet on opposing rails of the railway, and slid them forwards, this time heading towards the light.

As he approached the entrance, his mind returned to his mother, who had been fast asleep when he had left their 'house' this morning. Remembering that she had not laughed at his joke about sleeping on railway sleepers, he frowned. He had even repeated it three times, without success.

On leaving the tunnel, he saw his mother standing in the middle of the quarry. She immediately hurried across, and threw her arms about him.

"Thank God you're safe," she said, "I don't know what I would have done, being here on my own."

"Mother," he said.

She let him go, and turned around, arms folded.

"Sister," she said.

He also turned around, with his arms folded; a sister who wanted to do hugging things was the most sissy thing he could ever imagine!

Sara realised that however unfortunate her situation might be, she needed to be brave, and take control of things. She walked away, down the railway track, this presumably being the way she had arrived. Indeed, after a few minutes, she found herself standing on a path that ran parallel to the loch. Then she saw the go-cart, parked as if it were a car. Remembering she had used the contraption as a taxi, she once again became overwhelmed by embarrassment. Idly, she imagined pushing the contraption along the jetty, so it would float away from her life forever.

After a few minutes, the boy came slouching down the cutting, to stand three feet away from her.

Sara pretended to be cheerful. "It's a gravity railway line," she said. "In the old days, it would have been used to get stone from the quarry to the boats. Do you think we could try it, using your go-cart?"

Nork ignored the statement. "I'm coming back to explore," he said, "when we have a torch."

Sara let the word 'we' pass without comment, which seemed sufficient to return Nork to his normal, cheerful mood. Anyway, she had a far more urgent problem to deal with – that of finding breakfast...or more precisely, finding the money to buy breakfast. When she mentioned this to Nork, he merely shrugged.

"I counted the money this morning," he said, "we have £22.32."

"That's not possible," she responded, "I only got £10 from the bank."

"The man who liked doing sums told me to keep the change from his breakfast. And then, when I went to the counter, the man became all nervous as I started to explain how to do his sums properly. He told me to go away, and leave him alone, forever, so I still have the £10 note."

Sara realised the boy was a money magnet. The approaching breakfast would be the fourth time he had saved her life.

After two miles or so, Sara saw a house at the side of their lane. Soon after that she was on a busy pavement, where she noticed all the men were stopping to stare in her direction. However, she was too hungry to give it any regard, and hurried into what she thought might be the high street. In any event, it was the road that went up the hill from the harbour, and seemed to be the place where all commercial activity took place. On reaching a cafe, she stopped.

"You're the one with all the money," she said to Nork.

All the way along the path, Nork had been waiting for her to say that. His reply had been well rehearsed.

"Now we're together," he mumbled, "it's our money."

"Together…" gasped Sara.

"Together," he interrupted, before she had time to spoil it by pretending not to be his mother.

Sara accepted the word 'together' might be necessary for another day, so turned her attention to the cafe, peering through the window to see if it had any dark corners. Only then did she notice the reflection in the glass – two ladies of about sixty, standing behind them, both staring at her with utter disgust. Unable to control their indignation any longer, one of the ladies let out a snort of derision.

"You should be ashamed of yourself," she said. "I wouldn't let no daughter of mine walk around like that, this is a respectable town. When I was your age, we used to wear proper clothes."

"She's a fashion designer," said Nork.

Sara realised that a number of men had stopped walking by, instead pretending to look at things, or just generally hovering while trying to make distracted conversation. Learning from her previous mistakes, she put an arm around Nork.

"My brother," she said, "brother, brother, brother. Love them, or hate them, they just can't be anything else."

Sensing Nork was going to say something awkward, she put a hand over his mouth.

"My brother's doing a sponsored go-cart push from John o' Groats to Land's End," she said, "though possibly the long way round."

The old woman who had produced the snort, eyed her suspiciously.

"Nonsense," she said, "dressed like that, you'll catch your death of cold."

Sara frowned; she could not get the hang of conning people. Nork removed her hand from his mouth.

"It's true," he said, "and here's the go-cart to prove it." He fished a handful of coins from his hammer sack. "At the last village we got this much," he added.

"Ah," said the woman, at first taken aback, but then smiling.

"And who is doing all the pushing, I wonder?" she asked.

"I push," he replied, "except down hills, when I drive."

"I push sometimes," retorted Sara. "I pushed up that big hill, while you were asleep."

The woman who had been bending down to examine Nork straightened.

"They're doing a sponsored go-cart push," she shouted at her companion.

"What?" replied the companion, who must have been quite deaf.

"Sponsored go-cart push," yelled the first woman.

Suddenly, a man who had been drooling against a lamp post broke from the herd. He came across and held out a 50p coin. She smiled; he was trying to give it to her, not Nork, the previous money magnet.

"Sadly, I have no pockets," she said.

Nork lifted the hem of her sheet, and held it up to his chin.

"My sister collects the money sometimes," he said.

Before Sara realised the true horror of the situation, the man had dropped the coin into her canvas pouch. This activated the herd instinct of the other men, who all surged forwards to take a closer look. Coins began dropping into the sheet, and she did not have enough hands to correct the extra strain the weight was putting on her safety knots. Either the sheet would pull from her shoulders, or things would otherwise just start coming undone. The old woman who had snorted seemed to understand this, screaming out the appropriate warning. The announcement was enough to turn the trickle of money into a mad panic of emptying pockets. Sara realised that she had become like one of those coin machines at the fair, each man believing their penny would be the one that sent everything over the edge!

Then, besides the horror of the situation, a little devil spoke to her – only Marilyn Monroe had ever managed to be so famous by standing over an air vent with a lifty-up dress! That was not particularly rude, yet it appeared to drive men crazy, the photograph reproduced a million times. Getting carried away in the heat of the moment, she tried to exclaim in her silliest voice, that her dress would be falling off if they did not stop. The result was predictable, though fortunately only with regards to the money.

When all the pockets had been emptied, the audience stood around, disappointed, and wondering what to do next.

"Thank you," she said, "thank you all ever so much."

With both hands clutching her collecting sheet, Sara backed through the cafe door, and retreated to the darkest corner. Here she let the sheet lie across a table, and swept the coins over the edge. Then she stood back to admire her wealth.

Nork followed, pulling his wagon behind – wagon, he had realised, was a far more grown-up word than go-cart. As to whether it should be parked inside the cafe, he gave less consideration. Left outside, somebody might steal it. Then he looked towards his mother, to find her smiling at him.

"Now who's buying breakfast?" she said proudly.

"Me," said Nork. "If the people looking through the window think you are using their money to buy food, they will say we are naughty people."

"I doubt that," said Sara.

But Nork was already at the counter. *Perhaps he has a point*, she thought, things were complicated enough without going to prison for fraud. Then she sat down to count her money.

"The mean lot," she mumbled to herself. The penny piles stood like skyscrapers above a few low-rise buildings of 10ps. The 50p pile might just about be considered as a single bungalow. She felt certain such a coin distribution was not an indignity Marilyn Monroe would have suffered. Then her status dropped even further, as Nork returned to present her with a plate of beans on toast.

Looking at Nork, she realised he was eating his meal as a sandwich, requiring both hands, with one set of fingers supporting the soggy bit of toast in the middle. Most of the beans went into his mouth, with just the odd one falling back to the plate. She then realised her own hunger was too great to mess about with cutlery. With extreme guilt, she picked up the toast to take a bite. A moment later she was overwhelmed by the delightful sensation of munching a mouthful of calories.

Mr McTavish liked to keep himself informed about what was going on in his town. He only missed the arrival of the 'go-cart kids' because he was too busy finding out what was going on in his hotel, which he considered to be even more important. Looking through a two-way mirror into the staff quarters, he saw a well-rounded cook squeezing a handful of fat between her fingers. In her free hand, she held a packet of biscuits that she had stolen from his dining room. She would undoubtedly lose the battle of will, a weakness that gave her a fine figure for a woman of fifty-three.

Why he so liked to watch Cook in her bottle-green knickers always confused him; possibly it went back to his school days, when she had slapped him across the face, after he had asked her to drop her pants in the secret corner of the playground. It was a reasonable instruction, since he was the son of the Laird. Now, in these changed circumstances, he could frequently see her dropping her knickers, which surely represented justice. Indeed, it was Cook who had given him the inspiration for the two-way mirrors. His secret building work to convert all possible rooms had taken five years, but it had proved a wise investment ever since.

The basement corridor in which he now stood had once led to a set of stairs that went up to the staff quarters in the attic. It had been sealed off by his grandfather in the 1890s, so as to isolate male and female servants. By the time the ancient country retreat was converted into a hotel, this corridor, together with the associated stairs, had long been forgotten. If he had told the fire officer about it, the expense of building a spiral escape on the outside of the building could have been saved. But knowledge is power, and keeping a careful eye on the guests in the back bedrooms had many unexpected advantages.

Annoyingly, Cook did not drop her knickers today, instead pulling up a black dress that she wore to make her hips look narrower. To add insult to injury, she then ate six of the biscuits…which he had paid for! Feeling most cross by the injustice, he slid the security panel closed – essential so as to present a wall of wood if any of the mirrors got broken.

After sliding the panel bolts closed, he turned on his torch, and walked through the otherwise total blackness to the stairs. These took him to the third floor where he pushed a revolving bookcase – an unnecessary gadget, because the staff would never go exploring his private apartment, but it made him feel clever and important.

He walked across his bedroom to fix a nice malt whisky. Then, tumbler in hand, he made his way down the official stairway to see what was happening in the rest of the hotel. On reaching reception, he saw two new arrivals checking in. They paid little regard to procedure, instead talking casually about some kids pushing a go-cart all the way from John o' Groats to Land's End. He was very experienced at judging guests: the woman was adventurous, and had amazing breasts, while the man preferred doing it with the light on.

"Room 22," he said to the receptionist, "and a bottle of complimentary champagne."

The receptionist knew this meant the room price went up by £8, though she had no idea about the significance of the room number. They all had full-length mirrors on the wall.

Continuing to speak with their annoying English accents, the couple thanked him.

"No, thank you," he replied. "You are here for the fishing or shooting, I suppose?"

"How dreadful," said the woman, "of course not!"

McTavish forced a smile. "How nice," he said, "I am trying to get a golf course built on the land behind the town, to stop that sort of thing. Don't you think animals are so nice to look at?"

He found the English strange, but felt certain it was the sort of thing they wanted to hear.

"You mentioned something about a go-cart?" he added.

"A sponsored push. What a lovely way to spend the Summer holidays, and all for charity. Such nice children."

Her male companion frowned. The way his mind had imagined what her body might look like, if only her dress blew away in the wind, was still making him feel guilty. Tonight, he would have to make extra-special love to his wife, just to say sorry…inside his head.

After leaving the hotel, McTavish asked a few pedestrians about the 'go-cart kids'. Next, he went into a telephone box to call his local newspaper friend. McTavish then made his way to the cafe where the children were last seen. At the door, he stopped for a sharp intake of breath. The girl sitting near the go-cart had 'room 22' flashing above her head, but not even the most amazing film star in the world was more important than charging a stuck-up English couple £60 a night. After all, he could hardly sell the photographs. The boy was a side issue, who would eat little, and probably come to do something useful…eventually. He walked towards the girl, and sat down, without being invited.

"I'm Mr McTavish," he said. "I own the big hotel at the top of the high street."

"Hello," responded Sara, "you are the sort of person I have been hoping to meet."

The boy stared at him – hardly the inspection you expected when simply joining somebody at a dinner table. McTavish tried to ignore the peering eyes.

"I hear you are doing a sponsored go-cart push for charity," he said. "I think I might be of some assistance."

"You might," said Sara, "but I feel the word 'big' before hotel means it's too expensive, though perhaps you could recommend a cheap bed and breakfast place?"

McTavish was a businessman, and all common sense told him there was some profit to be made in this.

"Nobody seems to know what charity you are collecting for," he observed casually.

"That is because we did not say," said the girl. "People just see the cart and keep giving us money."

"Cart? Oh yes, I expect it does help. Pushing it all the way to Land's End, I hear."

"Yes, the long way round."

The cafe door opened again, and another man came to sit beside them.

"I'm from the local paper," he said. "Mr McTavish informs me you are…well, he didn't make much sense."

"Yes I did," interrupted McTavish, "it's for charity."

"Oh," replied the man, "that bit's fine, but I spoke to some people outside, and they reckoned you walked in from the old quarry track. A go-cart push across the mountains, from that direction, is simply too amazing."

"Wagon," said Nork crossly. "And yes, we did it, we passed a lot of cows."

"And a deer fence?" interrogated the journalist.

"We climbed over that," said the boy, "it was right in the way of everything."

Sara interrupted. "How local is local?" she asked. "I mean your paper."

"Not very," smiled the journalist, "it goes most places."

"Down south?" she persisted, nudging Nork to warn him it might be necessary to run.

"Sure does. We even have a newsagent in Edinburgh, and two postal subscribers in Glasgow."

"Wow, that far! Proceed. Your paper will let the people down south know we are coming."

"You still haven't said what charity you are collecting for," interrupted McTavish.

"Animals," said Sara. "We run an animal shelter."

"Yes," said Nork, "unwanted pets. Do you know if any of the cows we passed are unwanted?"

McTavish shook his head. "Hardly the sort of thing I can get involved with," he said, "but as it happens, I'm on the committee of a similar sort of thing – the Fishermen's Friendly Society – and we look after the families of all those lost at sea."

"But we're on the side of the fish," protested Sara.

"I can't have raving animal rights protestors staying free of charge at my hotel," said McTavish, "but the Fishermen's Friendly Society…around these parts your popularity will hit the roof."

"Free of charge?" enquired Sara.

"I don't know if we have any rooms free, but there's certainly a spare staff unit."

"With a bath?"

"Of course, it's where the residential staff live."

"What did you say we were collecting for again?" she asked.

"The Fishermen's Friendly Society."

"And we are no longer on the side of the fish?"

"Definitely not."

She looked at Nork. "You got that," she said, "four legs good, flippery things bad."

Nork nodded, while the journalist got out his pad to scribble it down.

"That's Nork without the 'e'," said Sara. "He's my brother. My parents had very funny ideas when it came to names."

Desperately, her mind raced on to what was coming next.

"And you are?" asked the journalist.

"It's too embarrassing," she said, "just call me Jane."

Nork looked at Sara. "Jane?" he questioned.

She smiled. "Yes, dear brother. Now I believe nice Mr McTavish is going to give us somewhere to sleep." She looked at the man. "I take it that 'we' means we both have somewhere to stay? My brother is very keen on the word 'we'."

"Staff sleep two to a room," responded McTavish, "one is completely empty."

"And there is an endless supply of beans on toast?"

"Indeed."

"Any more questions, Nork?"

Nork looked miserably at his feet. He knew 'nice McTavish' was a silly use of the English language. A far better name would be 'Fish Face'. Anyway, Nork liked the house in the quarry, where he had his mother to himself. Slowly, he came to see that his life was starting to go wrong; what he had now was a stupid hotel, a sister named Jane, and a man called Fish Face who wanted to get in the way of everything.

"Fine," said Nork reluctantly, knowing it to be a lie.

Then he watched Fish Face go to the counter, returning with two plastic bin sacks. He scooped the money already collected into the first sack, and gave it to Sara.

"For your animal charity," he said.

Then, without asking permission, he used the second sack to line the orange box on the go-cart.

"Whatever you were thinking of collecting," he said, "multiply it by twenty. Let people throw their money into the cart as we pass."

Without much enthusiasm, Nork followed the others outside. McTavish put the brake on the wagon, and stood on the planks to give himself extra height. He then gave a short speech about brave fishermen, a cause most dear to his own heart, and the centre of a charity go-cart push all the way to Land's End. To a round of applause, he gave Sara a personal cheque for £20. On doing this, the journalist took their picture, after which a few people came forward to throw money into the wagon… not coins, but actual notes! After this, Nork began to feel better; pushing the wagon made him the centre of attention, and all expressed astonishment that they had crossed the mountains to approach the town along the old quarry track.

Presently, the crowd drifted away, and McTavish marched them back to the hotel. Sara thought the bin bag contained at least £200, well worth walking about in a sheet for a couple of hours.

Once inside the foyer, McTavish took the bag from the orange box. Sara got the impression this now belonged to the 'fishermen', without any loose change falling in her direction. McTavish then prised the reins of the go-cart from Nork's fingers, and passed them to the receptionist.

"The cart can go in the old stables," he said, "see to it. We will need it again tomorrow."

McTavish then told the receptionist they were his guests, staying at his own personal expense. He then led them to a door behind the desk. Nork tried to look backwards towards his wagon, but things were happening too quickly. The next thing he knew, his mother had taken a firm grip of a hand to lead him down some stone stairs. At the bottom, he looked ahead to see a low, arched corridor. A little way along this, Fish Face opened a door, and Nork found himself staring into a room with two single beds.

"This is where your staff live?" asked Sara.

"Some," said McTavish. "There's a common room at the end of the corridor. We've got five live-ins at the moment."

"And the bath?" asked Sara.

"Next door to the common room."

McTavish sat on the bed as if he owned the place, which of course he did, but Sara still felt it a wrong thing to do without asking.

"I shall organise some more fundraising tomorrow," he said. "We have ten towns and villages in the borough, I think we shall do them all."

Nork wanted to get away and explore, but could not work out if permission would be granted. His mother clearly had an obsession about baths. After a moment's thought, he decided to get the inevitable torture over with as soon as possible.

"Can I have a bath?" he asked, partly hoping that such an astonishing request would distract his mother's attention from Fish Face.

To his disgust, his mother looked at Fish Face to see what he thought.

"Of course," said Fish Face, "you need to be nice and clean for fundraising."

Nork backed away, desperately hoping this did not mean bath days happened more than once a week.

Once inside the bathroom, Nork quickly located the soap and towel, but could not find the rule to measure the legal three inches of hot water. Looking into all the cupboards, he found a lot of complicated stuff, of which he had no understanding, but nothing in the way of a measuring stick. The bath rule had been with him forever, its use strictly enforced by the monks. He could never imagine taking a bath without it.

On returning to the bedroom, he discovered his mother appeared less happy than when he had left. This pleased him; her only source of happiness should be himself!

"I can't find the measuring stick for the water," he said.

McTavish looked at him, and smiled. In his childhood, he could remember his father expecting the servants to use measuring sticks. As far as he could remember, it had run to the end of the private household in the 1950s, but he never thought he would get away with it on his hotel staff. This was his chance to show the go-cart children how generous he was.

"There is absolutely no limit to the water," he said, "or how hot you want it. Have a bubble bath up to your nose, if you want!"

Nork stared at him with such astonishment; McTavish thought he had been overgenerous. Obviously, he was going to deduct administration expenses from their charity collection, but would it pay for all the hot water? Then he remembered Jane had been starting to get difficult about the fundraising, and relented.

"A nice hot bath with water up to your nose," he repeated, "now run along and play."

McTavish turned from the boy to look at Jane. Her face had softened, and her whole posture now conveyed gooeyness.

"OK," she said, "your fundraising system sounds fine. Ten o'clock tomorrow morning, we'll be ready."

"Good," said McTavish, "we understand each other."

He stood up, and after giving a short bow, left the room.

"We can have as much water as we want?" stammered Nork.

Sara looked at him thoughtfully. "Which only begs the question," she said, "can I bags first?"

"Whichever would please you most," he answered.

"Me baggies first."

"In which case, can I go and explore?"

"Of course! For at least an hour, I should think."

Nork decided the day was starting to get better, not so good as day one, but tolerable all the same. He decided the best bit had been waking up in the quarry house to see his mother sleeping on the opposite bed. Also, the bath intrigued him; to be surrounded by hot water, and not to have the upper half shivering, was the strangest custom of this new country he had yet encountered.

After climbing the stone steps, he returned to the reception desk, where he asked how to get to the stables. This led him to discover a secret way into the hotel without coming through the posh entrance, with its thick carpet. A whole world of muddy feet now became possible. Indeed, everything upstairs became irrelevant; he could now confine himself to the back-yard entrance, and the dungeons below.

There were no horses in the stables, just three cars and

his wagon, parked in the fourth bay. He went to look at it, and say sorry for dragging it over the mountains. However, it had been built to carry two people at incredible speed, and seemed quite undamaged by the experience. Tomorrow, he would get some cleaning materials to make it look nice, but for now, it could rest, while he went exploring by himself.

*

After closing the bolt on the heavy oak door, Sara turned to the Victorian cast-iron bath on its four ornamental legs. She ran the back of her fingers along the rim, as if it were a religious icon.

"As much hot water as I can ever use," she whispered to herself.

McTavish might have unusual ideas about charity, but besides this, his understanding of a lady's needs were quite wonderful. Next came the other thing of which she had been dreaming. Stepping onto the bathroom scales, she closed her eyes, hardly daring to look.

"Ten or less," she whispered, "please let it be that."

Slowly, the dial appeared through semi-closed eyelids. Moving her head to the right, the needle seemed to be hovering below ten, but deep down she knew this was cheating. She took off her sheet and let it drop to the floor. The dial hesitated, then twitched just a little.

"Yes!" she exclaimed, throwing her fist triumphantly into the air.

The result was alarming, the dial briefly recording her as twelve stone. Then it rebounded to eight, before settling back to a gnat's whisker under ten. It was enough; given her increasing leg muscles, she had probably lost all the wobbly fat from around her middle.

Stepping off the friendly scales, she turned to face the full-length mirror. As expected, the podginess had gone. She resolved never to let the dial go above ten again for, as she knew only too well, eleven was alarmingly close.

Turning her attention to the bath, she realised the big Victorian taps had knobbly projections, designed to be toe-operated. Steaming water was soon gushing out of them which, given the nature of her recent misfortunes, foretold of a heavenly experience to come. If Nork tapped on the door in less than two hours, he would be told to go away. Toe-operated bath taps could sustain perfection forever!

Soon, she sank into the hottest water it was possible to have without burning. Aches and pains floated away as her entire body gave a contented sigh. *Thank you, Mr McTavish,* it seemed to say. *Whatever happens to me in future, you will always be responsible for the most ecstatic moment of my life.*

Dreamily, her mind floated forwards to her new life; after the bath, McTavish had promised her dinner, and later, she would have a nice warm bed, all to herself. As to the sheet, it was unfortunate that McTavish expected her to wear it at all times, but as he had forcibly pointed out, it was only her fashion design that made her famous, thereby drawing the crowds when they went fundraising. Anyway, now the friendly bathroom scales 'spoke' to her nicely, being the centre of attention worried her less. It was, she realised, quite lucky that her parents had not yet got around to adopting the new fashion of duvets. Walking into town clutching one of those around her body would not have resulted in half the adventure!

*

After leaving the hotel, Nork wandered down the high street, to sit on the harbour wall. With his legs dangling over the side, it was a good place to daydream about all the exciting times to come. Occasionally, he looked at the boats. This morning, when they had first arrived, they had been bobbing up and down on the water, but now they were mostly sitting on newly exposed mud. This meant the water was connected to the sea, which would be useful if he ever needed to escape from the authorities. Thinking of this, he got up with the intention of exploring all the ways it was possible to leave town in a hurry…not the way he had come, because that only went back towards his starting point, but towards the sea. However, once outside the town, he became distracted by all the trees that needed to be climbed. Then he saw a load of deer, all wandering around to munch grass. Soon he was lost to a daydream of local adventure, that only came to an end when it got dark.

On returning to the hotel, he knew that having so much fun was bound to make the grown-ups shout at him for something or other; it was just the way of things. However, using the side entrance, he made it to the dungeons without being seen. On reaching his door, he opened it just a fraction.

"I'm sorry…" he began.

Then he realised his mother was not in. Looking towards his bed, he discovered a note propped up against his pillow:

'*You obviously found some good things to do. Have gone to have dinner with Mr McTavish. I've checked that*

there's a good supply of beans and toast. If you ask Cook
in the end room, she will make it for you.
Love Jane.'

He read the words with tears in his eyes. His mother had actually written him a letter, and made certain he had food to eat. Then she had used the word 'love'. He put the letter under his pillow. Tomorrow, he would buy a bag to carry such possessions, and perhaps some pens and paper to write a letter back.

Slowly, he walked along the corridor, torn between the need to take a bath, and the desire to eat beans on toast. He stood between the two doors, trying to decide. This world was so unusual, it might even be possible to sit in the bath eating beans on toast at the same time. Nobody seemed very keen to stop him doing anything much. In the end, he decided to try the bath first, then, when his mother returned from dinner, he could be sitting on the bed, all nice and clean. He frowned. '*Dinner,*' she had written. She was even crazier than he had thought. It had been dark for an hour; even he knew it was teatime.

Nork enjoyed his bath, especially the tingling sensation it made to his skin. Less good, he used the wrong type of soap that made him smell of flowers. After it was over, he self-consciously shuffled towards his room, embarrassed by a cleanliness that was unnatural for a boy.

Approaching the door to his room, he was surprised to hear voices. He stopped to listen; his mother had at least six visitors, and with himself smelling of flowers! The fact that his mother pretended to be his sister made it even more embarrassing, so he shuffled back and forth, before finally deciding to knock. After hearing his mother shout, 'come in,' he nervously poked his head around the door. She appeared as an angel, with a face glowing in a halo of light. To his astonishment, there was nobody else in the room.

On a shelf, two feet away from his head, a box had appeared. He had never seen one before, but the monks of his old country had warned him about them. They turned the brain into boiled cabbage, in much the same way as cigarettes turned the lungs into black treacle. But he knew grown-ups often did things they shouldn't. He reached across to pull the plug that connected the box to the wall. It stopped talking, and the light went out.

"Hey," said his mother, "I was watching that."

"They turn the brain to boiled cabbage," he said, "you shouldn't."

"No they don't."

He had no intention of arguing. Quite apart from turning the brain to boiled cabbage, the monks had told him it was illegal to watch them. He picked up the box, and carried it to the door. When he looked back, he saw his mother staring at where it had been; her brain was already starting to turn to boiled cabbage. Taking advantage of her temporary mental absence, he put the box on his shoulder, and carried it up to reception.

"We don't need this," he said. "Ah, but don't bother, I will take it to the stables myself."

After dumping 'the box' by his wagon, he returned to his mother, whose mouth was opening and closing, as if unable to speak of his brave deed. She was still staring at the shelf where the boiled-cabbage machine had been. So, kneeling on the bed, he put his face in the same place. He gave a broad grin.

"I can talk just as well as the box," he said. "Would you like to hear some jokes?"

"You stole my television!" she gasped.

"I'm not allowed to watch them," he replied, "they turn the brain to…"

"…Boiled cabbage, I know."

To his relief, she suddenly broke from her trance to focus on his face. "I've been exploring," he said. "Would you like to hear about what I found?"

"No, I want to hear what Kirsty was going to do when she found out about Kim."

Nork realised the boiled-cabbage machine was already making his mother talk gibberish.

"I've found some really good trees to climb," he said, "and…"

"Mr McTavish gave me that television," interrupted his mother. "What have you done with it?"

Nork felt himself getting upset. Fish Face was getting in the way of everything. Even when he was not there, his mother wanted to look at the box he had given her. Then he noticed the big fluffy slippers on her feet, which he suspected were a present from Fish Face. He was in charge of getting things for her feet, and now his sandals had been discarded, pushed under the bed. He tried hard not to gulp at his misfortune. Two people were trying to take her away: Fish Face, and Kirsty from inside the box. In desperation, he bent forward so she could smell the flowers, and see how clean his neck was.

"I had a bath," he said. "I'll have one every day, if you want."

Sara looked thoughtful. "Can I assume the television is safe and well?" she asked.

He looked at her miserably. He had been exploring new lands, and she had not asked him if he was safe and well. All the television did was go to sleep in the stables, and she worried about that instead. The two acts of bravery were not even comparable.

Seeing his miserable face, Sara softened. "But everybody watches television," she said.

Nork felt like crying, so merely shook his head.

"What, never?"

Then she realised Nork was looking at her with big-child eyes that, for some unfathomable reason, appeared to be on the verge of tears. It made her feel guilty, especially since he had brought her across the mountains, to this place of safety. Instinctively, she put her arms around him.

"It turns the brain to boiled cabbage," he mumbled, "please don't look at it again."

"Well, not tonight it seems. So what shall we do now?"

Nork liked the feeling of having his face close to her shoulder.

"Why can't I tell people you are my mother?" he asked.

"Because…"

Sara realised telling a boy the facts of life was impossible. Indeed, given their current situation, probably illegally rude. She pushed him away, then took the easy grown-up option.

"Because you can't," she said, "let that be the end of it, or I shall walk away, and leave you at the hotel, on your own, forever and ever!"

She winced at the cruelty of her words, but she needed to resolve the matter, once and for all.

*

In the secret darkness watching them, McTavish's mouth dropped in astonishment! The slag, she must have done it when she was thirteen, probably in the playground, after dropping her knickers. How many boys since?

So thirteen, that made her twenty-three now, not the schoolgirl he had first imagined. But, he had heard fashion designers spent their whole lives trying to look young for the camera. Then he remembered how, earlier, when she was standing on the bathroom scales, she had thrown aside her designer dress, to reveal there were no knickers underneath to remove!

The whole of his body gave a shudder. Twenty-three years was old enough to make her want a more mature man, like himself. Carefully, he closed the security panel behind the mirror, and rushed to his room to attend to his truly massive erection.

FIVE

Nork had a problem with names; his mother had too many of them for him to remember. As to calling her 'sister', that was just too ridiculous for any words yet invented.

On the way to his first official fundraising event, Nork bounced about in the back of a pickup truck, with all the names getting jumbled up in his head, yet he knew he must always say the right one at the right time, which was really difficult. Added to all this, Fish Face kept calling his wagon a go-cart, when these were something children got for Christmas. Wagons were used by brave cowboys to travel across America!

After the pickup truck came to a halt, Nork climbed out, then lifted his wagon over the side. As he set it down on the dusty gravel lane, Sara got out of the cab, and stood blinking.

"We are in the middle of nowhere!" she exclaimed.

McTavish explained it was exactly the place where they needed to be, because if they arrived at the settlement, hot, sweaty and possibly staggering, it would increase their sympathy donations. Pointing along the lane, he announced he was going ahead to proclaim their arrival. Without further explanation, he then drove away.

Sara looked around to discover she had been abandoned at the lowest point of a deep valley. To either side, the unfenced lane was surrounded by a great bog. Looking up, she saw the pickup truck zigzagging its way up the steepest hillside it was possible to imagine.

Nork, meanwhile, looked at Sara's feet, pleased to discover she was wearing his sandals, and not the fluffy things Fish Face had provided. This was almost as good as what had happened this morning…

When he had gone to the stables to collect his wagon, the place where the boiled-cabbage machine had been left was now an empty space. It was a miraculous triumph! Miraculous, because it had been left next to his unlocked wagon. Even if the burglar happened to want a boiled-cabbage machine, he would surely have loaded it onto his wagon, to drive it away. Nork had still been looking at the empty space, when his mother arrived.

"It has been stolen!" he had proclaimed, pointing to the empty space.

He tried explaining about his unlocked wagon, but she just told him not to be silly, whatever that meant. Then Fish Face had come in, and overheard what they were talking about. He was very cross, and said Jane would never again be given another television to lose.

Absolute success! thought Nork, very secretly, thinking his mother might not agree.

Now, as he plodded up the hill, his mind wandered deeper into the problem of a burglar who liked to steal boiled-cabbage machines, but did not want his wagon. The whole situation did not make any sense. He only knew that something was very wrong, but it was impossible to know what.

Sara spent a long time looking at the hill, up which Nork was pulling his stupid go-cart. Her only thought was that tonight, yet again, she would not have a television to watch.

After the fundraising was over, McTavish drove them back to the hotel, where they all went their separate ways – McTavish upstairs with the sack of money, Sara to the bathroom, Nork to where he thought it would be possible to get food, since this morning he had overslept, so had missed breakfast.

It was Nork's first visit to the staff common room, so he opened the door just a fraction to look nervously inside. His attention was immediately drawn to a boiled-cabbage machine in the near corner of the room. Two grown-ups were staring at it, mesmerised. His success with the first boiled-cabbage machine told him what needed to be done, but he was not brave enough to take this one to the stables, so he merely went across to unplug it, then turn it around, so the glass screen faced the wall. As before, he immediately became the centre of attention, which he liked. He then explained about the boiled-cabbage effect, before going on to talk about the mine shaft he had explored the day before. Suddenly, a lady sitting in the armchair slapped her hands together with delight.

"Well I never," she exclaimed, "what a remarkable child!"

Nork looked at her, to discover she was so round she completely filled her armchair. She had a lot of wrinkles, which told him she was very old. Thankfully, all her wrinkles were arranged in a smile.

"I'm Cook," she said. "I assume you are the boy called Nork?"

The man sitting in the next chair was still gazing at the back of the boiled-cabbage machine.

"This is Mark," said Cook, "he's a waiter in the restaurant."

Nork found this very puzzling. Where he came from, men did not have first names. Mostly they were called 'sir', but if this caused confusion, it was possible to call them Mr Tomkins, or whatever. Why this man had a first name, he had no idea. Even more confusing was his pastime of waiting in the restaurant. What was he waiting for? Indeed, what was a restaurant? Nork knew a lot of words because of his spelling, but had never come across 'restaurant' before. Being slightly nervous of men, he asked Cook about it, who responded with laughter.

"With you as our visitor," she concluded, "we really don't need the television to entertain us."

Nork understood that being a visitor made him very important. To let Cook know he understood this, he gave his chin a serious scratch. It was then a remarkable idea came to him – that all men secretly had first names, and that because he was a visitor, Cook considered him a grown-up, who was allowed to know such things. What else did grown-ups do in secret? It had always puzzled him that he had never seen them playing marbles. Perhaps he could bring the subject up, just to test things generally.

"Would you like a game of marbles?" he asked, looking around the room to indicate he was expecting to find some.

"Grown-ups play marbles on a table upstairs," replied Cook.

Grown-ups play marbles secretly, thought Nork, *and they have told me about it because they think I am a grown-up visitor*. Then the man who waited in the restaurant finally looked away from the television.

"Uh," he said.

"Marbles," repeated Cook, "you know, on the table, with those stick things."

"Marbles!" exclaimed Mark. "That's snooker."

"Same thing," said Cook, "but I've got something much better."

Cook stood up, and went to rummage in one of the cupboards. Mark turned to Nork.

"Snooker is a wonderful game," he said, "you can play it for years and still not be able to spin a ball properly."

"Marble," corrected Cook.

"I can spin marbles," said Nork, "it makes them go in a circle."

"Exactly," said Cook, "same thing."

Before Mark could contradict her, Cook returned to the table with a big red box.

"Monopoly," she said, "now here's a game we can all play."

Nork looked at the box with excited eyes. He liked doing new things. "The snooker room might be free," Mark protested, but Cook overruled him with a slap across the back of the hand, telling him to behave.

A little later, Nork was excitedly collecting the game's pretend money from Bond Street, when the door opened.

"What a pig of a shift," said a voice behind him, "number 18's got paws like an octopus!"

"Octopuses don't have paws," said Nork, "tentically they have tentacles."

"…With paws on the end," said the lady who walked into the room, then turned to look at him.

"Oh," she said, "we have a visitor…"

Nork decided she had only recently become a grown-up;

you could tell from her complete lack of wrinkles. Also, she had a lot of black hair falling behind her shoulders, while those who were properly old did things differently. Fish Face, for instance, had a bald patch on the top of his head, while Cook wore a frilly white hat, like the ones he had seen in the pictures of olden days.

"Good heavens," said the lady, "you're playing Monopoly." Then she glanced to the back of the television. "So, it's true," she said, "the boy who doesn't like televisions actually exists. I heard you threw Jane's in the loch."

"No," said Nork, "I hid it in the stables, and it got stolen."

The lady reached out to shake his hand, which he understood was something grown-ups did.

"I'm Stephanie," she said, "pleased to make your acquaintance."

He liked the touch of her hand; it was all soft and friendly. He thought her wide eyes suggested she would like doing exciting things, like tree-climbing and exploring mine shafts. Then Mark interrupted his thoughts.

"Footy's on in ten minutes," he said.

Nork watched as Stephanie went to the boiled-cabbage machine, picked it up, and left the room.

"I think you might have started something," said Cook, "though I must say, Stephanie's always been a little unusual, in a nice sort of way."

When Stephanie returned, she was carrying a bag of crisps, which she gave to Nork. She then took a book from one of the shelves.

"Count me in for the next game," she said, before falling backwards into an armchair, "but I should warn you, I play pretty mean."

Strangely, Mark seemed happier for the second game, now that Stephanie was playing.

*

McTavish sat in his room to count the takings from the day's fundraising. £206.83 was not enough. After removing his personal cheque, and £60 to cover accommodation expenses for the go-cart kids, he was only left with £106.83. Oh, and £60 for the lost television. OK, he had seen it in the stables and brought it up to his room, but that was not the issue. Nobody had seen him carrying it, so the burglar theory would never be questioned. All of these adjustments meant the day's takings now stood at £46.83. Essentially, he needed the total payment to the Fishermen's Friendly Society to be over £10,000. That would get him on the front page of the local newspaper, and pretty much guarantee that in the forthcoming elections, he would become a town councillor. So why had his fundraising idea gone so wrong?

Then he remembered Jane's breasts, and the way they remained firm as she had climbed into the bath. They were perfectly designed for making public appearances. Tomorrow, he would tell her to make some modifications to her fashion dress, just to display a hint of what they might look like if they accidentally escaped. No, he would only talk about the dress, not the intended consequences!

Nork thought some fundraising events were better than others. Once, at a golf club, he only had to push his wagon into a big room. Sara...

He would never get the hang of thinking of her as Jane. Sara was his mother, with whom he had shared a great adventure. Jane had become a different person, who was more interested in worshipping Fish Face...

Anyway, at the golf club, he had walked into the big room, with Sara walking beside him, occasionally clutching at her newly designed dress. Then, on the stage, Fish Face had given a long speech about all the brave fishermen. Eventually, to the accompaniment of clicking cameras, Fish Face handed Sara a cheque for £100. The chairman of the golf club immediately responded by presenting her with a cheque for £110, after which the money seemed to be coming from all directions.

After a short while, Nork had found himself being taken away by a nice lady who worked in the kitchens, where he was fed and watered, like a carthorse of olden days, he thought. However, there was no more wagon-pushing that day, and just before midnight, he was collected in the pickup truck and taken back to the hotel.

When Nork was not fundraising, nobody worried about what he did. However, his leg muscles ached most of the time, so he rather lost the urge to go exploring. Besides, in a country where he was allowed to come and go as he pleased, much of the fun was removed; out of bounds needed a fence to make it exciting.

After the day he met Stephanie, Nork invariably found somebody to talk to, or play a game with. In order to be liked, he sometimes helped Cook peel the potatoes, and when this became boring, he overcame his fear of the upstairs to help Stephanie make the beds; and once, secretly, she even taught him how to play snooker.

Fish Face soon stopped fundraising every day, because he was elected to become a councillor and run important things. However, Nork realised that Fish Face now accepted him as a grown-up, because he was expected to work, not as a hobby, but properly, often peeling potatoes for two hours solid, or scrubbing the stone floors with a huge broom. Kitchen porter, Fish Face called it, adding it was only necessary for him to do twenty hours a week, so long as Cook gave good reports of how hard he was working.

When Nork was not working, he tried to get Sara to spend time with him, but she seemed more interested in doing things upstairs, so he turned his attention to becoming friends with Stephanie. Then, one afternoon, she suggested that he borrow her library tickets, just in case the interesting things became less interesting, in the days to come.

At the library, the lady behind the counter took a sensible approach to his chin resting on the counter. Given his celebrity status, and slow method of leaving town, she reckoned it was safe to let him take books away, though annoyingly, insisted on calling him 'Stephanie', just to keep things in good order.

Nork waited to be given his book. *Of course*, he thought, *she cannot do this until she knows how old I am.* He decided, in a situation like this, he should use his pretend age of eleven.

The lady did not question him about it, merely led him to a bookshelf that went on forever.

"This is our teenage section really," she said. "If you find it too hard, there's a children's corner over there."

Then, she walked off and left him.

"Excuse me," he called after her.

"Shssss," she said, "not so loud."

"Sorry," he whispered, "but you have not told me which book I can have."

She frowned. "You want help to choose?" she asked.

Suddenly, a wild idea flashed across his brain. Surely it

was not like the cafe, where you could choose whatever you wanted? They only had twenty-two types of food listed, so they still sort of decided what you had. If he had been presented with a shelf of twenty-two books…well, perhaps, but here there were millions of them. You could never read so many books when you were eleven; all the ages must be jumbled up together.

"Can I read that one?" he asked, pointing to something by Charles Dickens.

"Don't know, bit hard."

"I'm allowed to read him, he writes about children."

"Not always, and his words are so long."

"No they're not."

He said the word he had recently learned, and later looked up in the dictionary.

"Restaurant," he said, before spelling it out loud.

"Remarkable," she said.

So he spelled remarkable, which made her laugh – quiet loudly, he thought. Then she reached up to present him with a book.

"*The Famous Five*," she said, "it's all about children." She then led him past thousands of books. "*The Lion, the Witch and the Wardrobe*," she said, "different, but good."

Next she took him across the whole library, to where the grown-ups went.

"*The Lost World*," she said, "it's all about going to find dinosaurs."

Nork looked at the three books loaded into his arms.

"And I can read all these?" he asked.

"No harm in trying."

Suddenly, he pointed to a book at random.

"Could I read that one?" he asked in disbelief.

"You only have three tickets, so you'll have to put one of the others back if you wish to take it away."

"But I could, if I wanted?"

She looked at the title. "Of course," she said, "but I don't see why you would want to, not even I've heard of the author."

She picked up the book, and flipped through the pages, saying bla, bla, bla.

"You're better off with a Catherine Cookson," she said, "but I'd start off with *The Famous Five*, just to see how you get on."

In his old country, books had not been written for a long time, and mostly dealt with chimney sweeps and the like; boys needed to know about such things in order to realise how lucky they were to be part of modern times. *The Famous Five* 'book', he discovered, was just too amazing; it actually encouraged you to go out of bounds, a strange choice, given that here it had no meaning, except for the hole in the mountain, which still needed exploring beyond the bars. But not yet; first he needed to find out what happened when the dinosaur hunters landed in South America, which was rather useful, given that his work in the kitchen meant his muscles were too tired to do much running around. Now, after his shift, he preferred to just sit, and travel the world through books. Then, on finishing a book about chimney sweeps, he found himself staring at the armchair in the alcove of the common room. The surround looked remarkably like a fireplace. Going across, he gave the low roof a push. It offered no resistance, proving to be a mere piece of plywood balanced on rough stone. Taking it down, he looked up the chimney, which, even in this world, he thought must be slightly out of bounds.

Then he thought about the olden days, when a boy would have been up there, with a brush, hoping a grown-up did not come in and light a fire.

After moving the armchair, Nork began to experiment with getting off the ground. It was very difficult, but eventually he managed to place one foot on either wall, and carefully began to climb. The shaft of light from the entrance soon dwindled and, looking between his legs, he could see the flagstones waiting for him to make a mistake. It would be a hard landing, but fortunately the chimney narrowed again, its stones now laid in a clumsier fashion, so as to provide better footholds. After twenty feet or so, he stopped to marvel at the children of a previous age; he was less than halfway to the top, yet already it was quite hard to see. To wriggle even higher, with a candle balanced on his head, would be incredibly brave. Instead of going higher, he stopped, closed his eyes, and played a game of pretend chimney sweeps in his head.

Stephanie walked into the common room and made herself a cup of coffee. She then noticed the armchair had been removed from the fireplace, a sheet of plywood resting against it. Little trails of soot came flurrying down, and below there was quite a pile. Looking up would clearly be silly, unless she wanted a black face, so she bent down to shout at the back wall.

"Is that Nork?" she called, already knowing the answer.

There was a scratching noise, but no reply.

"A very large squirrel then?" she called.

Everything became silent. She inspected the armchair, and decided it was safe to sit in.

"Is it good?" she shouted.

Clearly, the chimney explorer found this a difficult question.

"Do squirrels like hot drinking chocolate, I wonder?" she said. "I made this by mistake, now I want a cup of coffee."

She went across to the gas stove to make a mug of drinking chocolate, and presently the trails of soot were accompanied by a rustling noise. She listened intently and decided it was getting louder. Returning to the chair with both drinks, she awaited the arrival of some feet. Eventually one came to dangle.

"Good heavens," she said, "I never knew squirrels wore shoes."

A second foot hovered for a moment, then both dropped to the flagstones. This time, quite a lot of soot came down, to make a pyramid on top of Nork's head. Without doubt, it was the blackest child she had ever seen.

"Heavens above!" she exclaimed. "It is the chimney monster!"

Two eyes blinked at her, making her laugh.

"You are not cross?" said Nork guiltily.

"Why should I be cross, it's not my chimney, though heaven knows what Mr McTavish would make of it."

Nork came forward in what could potentially be a gesture of friendship.

"Stop!" she demanded. "Getting into the chimney was quite easy, getting you out is a major challenge."

Nork jumped back, and she handed him the mug of drinking chocolate to keep him in place.

"It was quite hard," he protested, "you have to put one foot there, the other on the metal spike, and the first handhold is right up there."

He pointed up the chimney.

"But you are the chimney monster," she said, "such things are surely easy for you. I was thinking more about Cook not finding out; you are quite covered in the evidence. Soot, you see, is bad for you, it makes the skin go all wrinkly, and your ears grow big, like those of a rabbit."

"No it doesn't," said Nork, "though I suppose it's a bit itchy."

"That will be the skin wondering if it should start to wrinkle. I think we should get you into the bath, and make some attempt to remove the evidence, before Cook starts setting chimney-monster traps."

Nork looked at her thoughtfully. "What's a chimney monster?" he asked.

"The scary thing that stops children going into chimneys, but, of course, you know he doesn't exist because you have been to look. However, Cook doesn't know it's only pretend. She would be quite alarmed to see a trail of soot across the floor; to her, a chimney monster would be on the loose. Shall we try and keep it a secret?"

Nork nodded.

"Right," said Stephanie, "I do not think we can avoid a trail to the bathroom, but there you must remove all the evidence, especially behind your ears, unless you want them to start growing. Pass your clothes out, and I will put them in the washing machine, but, if the next lot of sheets are ever so slightly grey, you must never tell. With drying, it takes about an hour – about the time it should take you to get clean, I imagine."

They got away with it, for when he returned from the bath, he was spotless, and found all the soot had gone from the floors as well. Strangely, the following day, Cook hesitated before sitting in her favourite chair, and he almost imagined she looked towards the chimney. But she smiled at him, so she could not have really known; she was just checking for chimney monsters, and he had only just noticed.

SIX

Nork thought starting work was like arriving in a new country – very difficult to understand. Indeed, after most shifts, he returned to the common room and, like any other grown-up, collapsed into an armchair to gaze blankly up at the ceiling, trying to make sense of everything.

What Nork found most confusing about his new life was the way Cook insisted on giving him 'proper meals', as she liked to call them. In truth, the only food he fully recognised was porridge, which she always *made* him eat for breakfast… at least until he realised he could add as much milk and sugar as he wanted. After this, breakfast became his favourite meal of the day. However, he still found it difficult to understand why some of the older staff only put salt in their porridge. He tried it once…never again!

For two days a week, Cook used her time off to stay with people she knew. To cover this period, she showed Nork how to make beans on toast, or otherwise raid the food cupboard, as he thought necessary. This made him see that throughout his previous life he had always been hungry, which is why, as he had tramped across the mountains with his mother, he had not given the lack of food any thought. To him, it was just normal.

All of this confusion, yet it still only covered the things relating to his tummy. For his life in general, where to begin? When he had told Stephanie about all the confusion of arriving in a new country, she had looked very sad.

"It's more like arriving on a new planet," she had replied. "But you are a brave astronaut who, after you have learned to understand the space aliens who already live there, will do all sorts of wonderful things."

She had then examined him more closely, exclaiming that his cheeks now looked less hollow, and his tummy had lost most of its inwards curve. According to her, this meant he was turning into a fine young man. She had then put a finger and thumb gently around his upper arm.

"Give it a month," she had said, "and your body will grow all the muscles needed to cope with a four-hour shift, which means we can go exploring together on our days off, if you want?"

He could not imagine his muscles growing, but decided it was OK to pretend.

After two weeks, he came to see work was a good thing; it got him fed, housed, and accepted as a grown-up. Just to emphasise this, he stopped drinking hot chocolate, instead making himself cups of coffee, pretending to like it, at least for the first week, after which, it became true. Then, to his complete astonishment, what Stephanie had said about his muscles growing also came true! He could do a four-hour shift, hopefully with a coffee break, then afterwards, think, now what? When he told Stephanie about this, she had responded with a serious nod.

"I'll ask Cook to synchronise our next days off," she said, "it will be fun!"

He had pretended to know what the grown-up word 'synchronise' meant, then, on his next visit to the library, he found it in the dictionary. He decided it was a word he liked, especially after he had memorised the spelling.

Three days later, Nork was walking down the high street on a synchronised day off with Stephanie. She was carrying a rucksack, which meant they were going on a proper mountaineering expedition. However, she would not say where they were going, instead telling him the importance of keeping secrets.

"Thing is," she added, "talking about secret things in the hotel is…well, McTavish generally finds out what has been said. He's obviously got spies on the payroll, but I can't imagine who. Anyway, if you ever want to tell me anything secret, make sure we are away from the building. Likewise, I am now going to show you some secret things, about which you will never talk to anyone, not even your sister."

Nork realised that on saying the word 'sister', Stephanie had turned to study his reaction.

"I understand you better than you think," she said. "Even when you were the chimney monster, because that's the sort of mischief I would get up to at your age."

Nork was still trying to imagine Stephanie climbing chimneys, when she took his arm, and led him onto a projecting harbour wall. Looking ahead, Nork realised it went nowhere; surely, she was not going to jump into the water at the end? Then, halfway along, she stopped, and kneeled down to pull the canvas cover from a rowing boat. Nork looked in astonishment as she stepped onboard and folded the canvas underneath the middle seat.

"We can't just steal it," he stammered.

"If I thought you were the sort of boy to go around stealing stuff," she said, "I would not be spending time with you. This is my boat. You sit in the middle of the back seat, if you trust me, that is."

Nork did as he was told. Within a few minutes, they were a long way from the shore, Stephanie swinging the oars with ease.

"It's not a fast boat," she said, "made for the sea, hence very wide and safe, at least if you understand the weather and tides. My father taught me to row it when I was five. By the age of eight, his only rule was that I must always remain in sight of land."

Nork decided this was even more exciting than exploring holes in the ground.

"Thing is," continued Stephanie, "we lived on a very isolated hillside, with no road access. This boat was the only way we could get to town, so learning to row was just part of my early life until…"

Stephanie pulled in the oars, and let the boat drift.

"When I was six," she said, "my mother died. After I recovered from the shock, my father sat me down for a grown-up talk. He asked whether I wanted to continue living in the mountains, or move into town. I did not hesitate, I was too much of a country girl to face the outside world."

Nork struggled to hold back the tears. Then, completely forgetting he was a grown-up, he fell sideways to rest his head on Stephanie's legs, so she could not see his watery eyes.

"Please don't ever go away," he mumbled, "ever."

Stephanie gazed towards the town where most of her teenage years had been endured. Then, instinctively, she reached down to stroke the hair of the small boy. What had she got herself into? And how did this fit in with her increasing determination to tell McTavish exactly what she thought of him, preferably over the public address system, before running out of the hotel for the last time?

"Anyway," she continued, "after my mother died, I took her place for cooking and keeping the cottage clean. As the years passed, this became easier, until I was thirteen…that was when my father went out on his normal fishing trip – only this time he never came back. It took me two weeks to accept his not coming back was forever. Then, after a month, the food store was empty, so I was faced with two choices: tell the authorities, who were certain to send me to an orphanage, or go to see McTavish, who I knew was happy to use child labour."

She stopped stroking Nork's hair and, picking up the oars, continued to row.

"So you see," she said, "while the other staff just accepted you as Jane's brother, I looked at the situation more critically. Thing is, Jane speaks with a very posh, public school accent – certainly with elocution lessons. You speak…well, I don't understand English accents, but I am certain you did not grow up in the same household as Jane. All I want to say for now, is that if you ever want to talk about anything, I will understand."

Nork remained silent, content to keep his head resting on Stephanie's legs, to hide his tears.

"Well," said Stephanie, some time later, "we are here."

Looking up, Nork saw they were in a little inlet, and before he could take it all in, Stephanie had moored against a wooden landing stage. After securing the boat, Nork climbed out to find his legs all wobbly. He then followed Stephanie up a winding woodland track for about a mile, after which he came to a sunlit clearing. Directly ahead was a quarry wall, perhaps thirty feet high.

"My father," she said, "had a strict rule about my upbringing after my mother died. I was to spend no more than twenty hours a week looking after domestic things. Sound familiar?"

Nork looked away. Part of him wanted to tell Stephanie all about his days at the orphanage, but an even bigger part remained fixed on the idea that his life began on the day he met Sara…who had now turned into Jane.

After a short silence, Stephanie continued talking.

"His second rule," she said, "was that I spend at least twenty hours a week reading educational books. Homeschooling, they call it. If you decide to use McTavish to provide your food and accommodation, I will expect you to do the same."

She winced; this implied she was taking responsibility for him, made even more committing by his enthusiastic nod of acceptance.

"After forty hours of work and study," she said, "I often ran wild. To me going up a chimney seemed a perfectly reasonable thing to do. At other times, I would go places with my father, often coming here, where he taught me rock climbing. All these things abandoned when I was thirteen, possibly forever, until you came along, to remind me of the joys of having a wild childhood."

Nork looked along the vertical quarry wall.

"It's not possible," he said.

"Remove the 'not'," responded Stephanie, "and I would agree with you completely."

She then walked across to an old, rusty dustbin. Lifting the lid, she recovered a rope. After tying this around her waist, she reached into the bin to recover a lot of straps and complicated bits of metal stuff. Nork could not help giggling as she put him into a harness, which went around his legs and waist. She then tied the other end of the rope to him.

"All safe," she said, "see you at the top."

After walking to the rock, she rubbed her hands together, as if to say, 'don't mess with me'. Nork watched in astonishment as she climbed a narrow crack, using just her fingers, with her feet spaced either side. At the top she disappeared.

"Right," came her voice after a few minutes, "I'm tied to a spike, climb when you are ready. I'll bring you up on a tight rope."

Nork walked to the rock, then looked up. Suddenly, he realised why he had never seen grown-ups climbing trees. After a certain age, you transferred to rock climbing, and did it in secret places like this! This meant Stephanie considered him a grown-up, who went to work, and no longer had any interest in doing baby things. Then he frowned. This rock was vastly harder than any tree he had climbed, but then again, he had never wanted to impress anybody so much as he now wanted to impress Stephanie. Reaching up, he jammed his fingers into the crack and pulled up as hard as he could…

Nork could not remember how many climbs he did, or how long it took. Only when completely exhausted did he sit down with his back against the rock. Stephanie sat beside him, and opened her rucksack to produce a picnic.

"Was it fun?" she asked.

"Best ever," he said.

Yet again, he fell sideways to rest his head on her lap. This time Stephanie looked skywards to imagine her father looking down on her. He would have been impressed by her efforts this afternoon. Not because she had climbed anything particularly difficult, but because she had taken care of a small boy, in the same way he had once looked after her. And perhaps this afternoon, she had returned to her carefree days of childhood, so cruelly abandoned when she was thirteen.

*

Nork's adventure with Stephanie had used up so much energy that he found going to work the following day quite exhausting. She told him this was a normal part of being a grown-up, and he would soon get used to it. She then sat across the table to teach him algebra, as part of her twenty-hours-a-week education rule.

"You need to be healthy in both mind and body," she had said. "Give it a few days, and it will all seem quite normal."

As always, what Stephanie said proved to be true. The following Friday, he was sitting in the common room, overflowing with so much energy that doing nothing made him very cross. Then, through boredom, his gaze focused on the Monopoly cupboard. He decided it looked rather like a fireplace with doors.

After walking across, he opened the doors, to discover the top easily pushed up. Even better, on one shelf there was a torch, and he shone it up the shaft to see what it looked like. The lowest bit was clean stone, and above, it was lined with wood, some of which had been painted white. After wriggling onto the top shelf, he ran his hand around the shaft and, though it came out dusty, there was no soot. On an impulse, he pulled the cupboard doors shut, then stepped up to stand on the timber frame. In order to fully enter the world of pretend, he dropped the false ceiling back down. This, he decided, was his *Lion, the Witch and the Wardrobe* game, even though it was not actually a wardrobe, and the only activity involved standing in the dark. After a few minutes to think about things, he shone his torch up the shaft. There was no soot, so Cook would not get cross if he went higher, to where he could see a rope hanging down the shaft. After all, nobody would have put a rope there if it was not meant to be climbed.

Stephanie had shown him how to bridge up between opposing walls, so he found it quite easy to reach the rope, and give it a gentle tug. There was no effect, so he hung from it. High above, there was a creaking noise, as he slowly dropped back down, to stand on top of the cupboard. After letting the rope go, it immediately went back up to its previous height. For this, whatever game it might become, he needed to use both hands.

Taking some string from his pocket, he tied the torch around his neck, then climbed back up to the rope. Once again, hanging from this returned him to the ceiling, but this time he did not let go, instead climbing on the spot. Finally, the creaking noise ceased, and he started to ascend. What the rope was attached to, he had no idea, because the torch was pointing down. However, this meant he knew how far he would fall, if the rope came free. After climbing as high as he dared, he held on very tight with one hand, using the other to shine the torch upwards. By going another five feet, he could step onto a ledge, which answered the question as to why the rope was there. That ledge, he decided, was there so boys could do the bravest dare ever done.

His heart began to beat faster; this new adventure was starting to get really good! He climbed until he could step onto the ledge, then let go of the rope. What happened next was really confusing. The rope shot upwards, and there came a great whooshing noise. He dropped to his knees, and held his hands over his ears. Then came a cracking noise, followed by a mighty gust of wind. Next, an almighty crashing sound echoed up the shaft. He waited for whatever came next, but there was just an eerie silence. Minutes passed, yet all remained quiet. Slowly, his fear subsided to a normal level of excitement, allowing him to crawl to the edge of his shelf, and point his torch down the shaft. The bottom had become very awkward, with splintered planks of wood all mixed up with a tumble of rope. He managed to make out a pulley wheel, with a rusty bolt sticking up. His climbing rope had vanished.

Though climbing back down might be possible, it was hardly desirable. Quite apart from anything else, there was so much debris at the bottom, he would have to shout for help to get through. If Cook thought a chimney monster was scary, heaven knows what she would make of people who set about this sort of thing – a tunnel-demolition monster, he supposed. Shining his torch about his platform revealed it to be about six-feet square. At the far side, a rough timber frame went almost, but not quite, to the ceiling. To this some rough boards had been attached to the far side. He easily climbed the frame to look over the top. To his astonishment, he discovered the other side had a landing, with a flight of stairs going up to his right. Directly ahead was another set of stairs that went down. He immediately realised this was a really good game of out of bounds, the challenge being to get back to the common room without alerting Cook to the damage he had caused. So long as she did not try to lift the Monopoly cupboard ceiling, she need never know.

Squeezing over the top of the wall, he hung for a moment to think about things. This side was very smooth, so there was no way back. Finally he decided that his tunnel demolition had been so complete, there was no way back anyway, so he let go, to drop silently onto the landing.

Upwards obviously went to the posh part of the building, so could be ignored. Cautiously, he walked downwards until he came to a long corridor, which he imagined to be part of the basement. He flashed his torch about, but discovered nothing exciting, which he thought rather unusual for things below ground.

Walking along the corridor brought him to a door at the far end. It gave the appearance of guarding somewhere important, which made him quite nervous of what might be on the other side. Partly, he was in the world of pretend, but equally it could be a real dungeon, with skeletons lying on the floor. Finally he decided it was an outside door, that would probably take him onto the street. From there, he could sneak back through his normal entrance, without telling anyone how naughty he had been demolishing the shaft above the Monopoly cupboard.

He tried the door, which proved to be as solid as it looked. Then he noticed a big iron key hanging from a rusty hook, hammered into the stone wall on his right. He decided it was OK to mess with, so tried it in the lock. It made a clunking noise and, after a complete turn, could be removed.

After a few minutes to gather his courage, he pulled the

door open, to see...nothing. That is to say, nothing but an empty cupboard. He then noticed a big hole in the floor. Shining his torch down this revealed a very rusty iron-rung ladder, that disappeared into the depths of the Earth. Even for him, this was too far out of bounds.

Returning to the main passage, he looked along the right-hand wall. He now realised it contained a lot of bolts and hinges, though strangely, no obvious doors. He wandered along, until he found the biggest hinges, then slid open the opposite bolts. Taking the rough timber frame between his fingers, he pushed, then gently pulled. When the wall swung towards him, he found himself once more in a game of 'lions and witches', except now he was looking into a strangely familiar bathroom, but from a completely baffling perspective. He poked his head in, or would have done, had his nose not squashed up, while his head made a banging noise which, a moment later, proved quite painful.

As the stars faded, he looked into the bathroom, then carefully reached out his hand. His fingers pressed against something solid, but there was no obvious reason why it should be so. However, he was fairly certain he was no longer in the Monopoly cupboard, playing a game of pretend. Without any explanation about what he had seen, he closed the wooden panel, and shut the bolts. He then wandered down the corridor, opening and closing things to the same effect. He was quite able to look at the world he knew, but only through an impenetrable barrier. It made him quite nervous to think he might be trapped in a special time bubble, from which there was no escape.

Suddenly, he became aware of a shuffling noise, and listened intently to whatever was coming. Quickly, he realised what was really happening. This was the most out of bounds it was possible to be, and something was coming down the stairs to find him. He turned off his own torch to disappear, but soon realised this was not good enough. The chimney monster, or similar terror of his imagination, was coming to get him. He crawled along the floor until he felt the hole, then stood up, to pull the dungeon door shut behind him. The iron key was still in his pocket, and he managed to lock away the terror that had now stepped onto the stones, where, only a minute before, he had been standing. He waited for a dreadful hammering on the door, though for all he knew, whatever was coming to get him was quite able to walk through solid wood.

Eventually, his fear abated enough to let him feel the keyhole, then put an eye towards it. Being such a big mechanism, he could easily see the length of the corridor, to behold a sight that made his flesh creep. In the sombre glow of an open panel stood a dark, hovering figure. Nork's early memory of the 'bogeyman' returned. Throughout his early childhood, this meant a 'man' who frequently waited in dark places, to surround him in the cloak of death.

Nork realised that if he could see the light through the keyhole, the bogeyman would see his torch shining the other way. In complete darkness, Nork lay on the floor and dropped his legs into the hole. His feet then found the iron-rung ladder that would take him to a place so out of bounds it was impossible to imagine. However, it had the advantage of not being where he was at the moment.

Doing everything in the dark, while trying to remain silent, was so hard it took him ages to get himself properly onto the ladder. Then, testing each rung with his leading foot, he descended into the unknown.

After a long descent, a foot made a splashing sound. A moment later, it got very wet. His next step down left him standing on something solid, with the water almost reaching his knees. Here, with his arms at full stretch, his fingers were just about able to touch the rocky walls and ceiling of what he assumed to be a tunnel.

He decided he could go no further without light and, though he felt certain this would travel up the shaft, and through the keyhole, he could think of no other way to proceed. He pulled the torch over his head, and pushed it up his jumper. After clicking the switch, his jumper began to glow, revealing that he was standing in a slow-moving river. Uh? Rivers go across fields and stuff, not underground!

Then he remembered the bogeyman, lurking up above. Compared to this, the river was not important, merely something through which he had to wade to get away from the shaft down which he had arrived. Slowly, using the glow of his jumper, he waded a hundred paces into the tunnel, a number that made him feel a bit safer. He then removed the torch from his jumper to shine it directly ahead. This showed the tunnel went slightly downwards, as did the river, which seemed to make sense.

Eventually, the loose stones covering the floor became more level, allowing some of the river to disappear. He had very little understanding of underground rivers, so mostly this was guesswork. Anyway, as he walked onwards, the roof kept going downwards, therefore getting lower. Eventually, he was bending down, then crawling, and finally wriggling flat on his tummy, with his mouth only a few inches above the water. Here, he stopped to shine his torch through whatever came next, which happened to be even lower. However, he could hear a waterfall, which sensibly meant the stream would soon go downwards. He turned on his back and, keeping his face a few inches from the ceiling, wriggled onwards. Soon, the water was making his ears go cold, and twice he thought it might get into his mouth. Then he realised that while wriggling, he needed to keep his mouth closed. After this, when his body demanded he took a breath, he would stop, and with his nose touching the roof, suck the air into his lungs. Then, without warning, the low roof disappeared, allowing him to sit on a rocky shelf, over which the water tumbled.

Shining his torch upwards revealed he had entered a massive cavern. Sadly, he was about halfway up one of the walls. Looking over the edge of his shelf, he saw the rock falling steeply to the main floor. It was not possible!

Then, Stephanie's voice came to him. "Remove the 'not'," she had said, "and I would agree with you completely." She had then showed him how to do impossible things.

After shining his torch about, he dropped his feet over the side and, letting go of the ledge, jammed his fingers into a narrow crack. After a few minutes he was standing at the bottom, a place where he even allowed himself to say, "Wow, bostin!", a phrase that came back to him as a dull echo.

Looking around the great chamber, he saw many tunnels disappearing into the rock walls. Which one to choose? Then he noticed a set of railway tracks emerging from one of the tunnels, to end in the middle of the chamber.

So, he thought, *if this is where the rails end, they must begin somewhere else.*

After walking to where the rails ended, he thought it unwise to enter the tunnel while still carrying the evidence of how naughty he had been; even in this country, demolishing the shaft above the Monopoly cupboard would surely get him told off. Removing the iron key from his pocket, he placed it beneath the last few inches of track. To make certain it would never be found, he placed a stone slab on top. Then he walked along the rails into the tunnel, until he was forced to stop by a set of iron bars. Instinctively, he wriggled through the gap on the extreme left. Turning off his torch, his eyes eventually detected a pinprick of light. There was no magic about this place; he had simply discovered the old mine workings.

By the time Nork stepped into bright sunshine, his fear, and to a large extent his childhood, had left him. Certainly he now understood the bogeyman did not exist. Then, looking towards the hut, where he had once expected to spend his life with his mother, he now saw nothing of interest.

Walking back to the hotel, he began to think how exciting his future life was going to be. Then, on entering the building, he realised his face might hold traces of mud, so he went straight to the bathroom to remove all evidence of his exciting afternoon. Undressed, and just about to get in the hot, soapy water, he became seized with panic; this room had a doorway to the other world! Turning, he realised the strange angle from which he had seen the bath was from inside the mirror. He had sought sanctuary in the place of the demon, a beast that could – or might not – be there. Not knowing if he was being watched, and if so, by what, generated an overwhelming panic. He could not even face being in the same room as the 'gateway' to the 'other place'. He picked up his clothes and fled naked into the corridor. Here, he dressed quickly and, just in time, pulled up his shorts before Stephanie came down the steps. She looked at him standing by the bathroom.

"You OK?" she asked. "You look as if you have seen a ghost."

He could say nothing, so shook his head, before running into his own room.

"Baths are not that frightening!" she shouted after him.

Then she looked at the hot, steamy water. She knew it had not been used, because Nork still had lots of mud on his face. Thinking it a shame to waste such an opportunity, she went inside.

Nork sat in his room, but only for a moment. The mirror looked down on him accusingly, causing him to dive underneath the bed. Then the truth dawned on him. This place was a 'special prison' for children who, like himself, kept running away; it was a place where he could be watched! Spies were everywhere; Stephanie had already told him about them, and now they would know how naughty he had been, demolishing the shaft above the Monopoly cupboard. They would know everything about what he had done, and where he had been. He was in big trouble. But, if he moved quickly, it was not too late to save himself.

Accepting the true situation, that his ex-mother no longer wanted anything to do with him, he wrote her a quick 'goodbye' note. He then ran to the common room to collect what he needed for crossing the mountains. Next, he raced up the stairs to load his wagon with food, together with any other items he was able to grab. As far as he could tell, the fishermen people had got £20,000, because of all his wagon-pushing, yet he had seen none of it! Somewhere, somebody owed him a ball of string, and other sundry items that he would need to reach his next country.

SEVEN

Unaware of Nork's letter waiting on her bed, Jane walked onto the landing stage where McTavish moored his yacht.

"Hello?" she called.

McTavish poked his head from a hatch in the foredeck.

"Don't be so formal," he said, "make yourself at home, I'm only getting the champagne."

Jane expected the yacht to be cruel, like the bathroom scales that now told her she was saying goodbye to a size 12 forever. While her trademark was a well-designed sheet, the 'size-14' issue could remain a well-guarded secret, but the yacht would know. Then, by swinging its mast like the gigantic needle, it would tell the world of her recent sinful behaviour in the restaurant – but thankfully the yacht was sufficiently large to be discreet, even if the All-England Rugby Squad stepped on board.

When Jane saw a table on the front deck had been set up with eight champagne glasses, she relaxed. McTavish might not be straightforward when it came to fundraising, but he was obviously more serious when it came to impressing rich people. The idea he might fancy her was clearly the result of her own foolish pride. This cruise was, and always had been, a celebration to announce the fishermen's fund reaching £10,000.

Taking McTavish at his word, Jane went to explore below decks. Here she found three rooms and – whoops! – she closed the door of the end cabin very quickly. Such a large bed, and so many mirrors; it was clearly somewhere she was not meant to be. Having no interest in the door marked 'engine room', she returned to the deck, where she discovered McTavish emerging from the hatch, carrying a box of champagne.

"I need to keep it locked up," he said. "Some of my charity trips are not so civilised as this rather select gathering."

Jane looked at the glasses on the table. "If we are to have one bottle each," she joked, "you will need eight bottles. That case only has six!"

"I am navigating," replied McTavish, "and need to keep a clear head. The banker and his wife are teetotal."

"I was not serious," interrupted Jane. "Two glasses and I shall be quite giggly and, with so many important guests attending, one must not appear silly."

McTavish nodded. "I'm sorry," he said, "it's just that some of my charity events get carried away with the champagne. Once, they got through four cases in an hour. Quite legless, which on a yacht, I have been told, can be somewhat confusing."

McTavish put half the champagne into three ice-filled silver buckets.

"There's a bottle on the table already chilled, if you want," he said. "I'll just go and see what's happened to the others."

Jane had already noticed the bottle, and did not need a

second invitation. She was well accustomed to undoing the wire and waiting for the pop. Tonight, she would have four glasses, but not in a way the guests would exactly notice. After filling a glass, she gulped it down to consider the bubbles, then refilled it, so as to take more gentle sips when McTavish returned.

Suddenly, it registered that McTavish had his own private telephone cubical on the side of his jetty. He must be very rich. It was clearly rude to ask what his yacht was worth, but she could not imagine any change from £100,000. The man himself was probably a millionaire, if only because his wallet was very selective when it came to parting with portraits of the Queen, even those on a postage stamp!

McTavish returned from the telephone box, scowling and grumbling under his breath.

"Silly cow," he growled, "she's teetotal and still manages to fall off a stepladder while changing a light bulb!"

"Who, what ladder?" asked Jane.

"Wife of the golf club chairman. You would think with all their money, they would employ somebody to do things like that."

Jane took a thoughtful sip of champagne. "That still leaves thingy," she said.

"The golf club chairman's chauffeur had been organised to pick everybody up in the Rolls; he ended up doing the hospital run. The others were all waiting at home, until I telephoned. It will now take them an hour to get here."

Suddenly, McTavish stamped around in two annoyed circles.

"It's an excuse," he said, "it's nothing to do with waiting at home. When they realised there was not a free chauffeur ride, it meant they could not all get blind, stinking drunk…"

He stopped mid-sentence. "I'm sorry," he said, "I was quite forgetting myself with a girl present. I shall just go and turn off the engines, then walk you back to the hotel."

Jane frowned in annoyance. Why should she let those who were unable to change a light bulb spoil her fun? A yacht, her own private cruise of the loch – with all the champagne going flat. McTavish wasn't much better; if he was not going to impress the Lord Mayor, or somebody equally pompous, he wasn't interested. A girl! He had called her 'a girl', not a person more suited to moving in his circles, unless it was to raise funds. And, coincidently, get him elected to the council. He owed her big time; no way was she going to let him wriggle out of his moral obligation so easily.

"That's it," she snapped, "we just go home?"

McTavish looked at her sheepishly. "What else can I do?" he asked. "There are appearances to think of."

Jane looked at the two ropes wrapped around lumpy things on the deck. Taking a courage-gulp of champagne, she stomped back and forth to throw them ashore. McTavish seemed quite frightened by her temper tantrum, doing nothing to stop her as she set his yacht adrift. She took another glass of champagne that he would consider to be number two, unless he could see through the dark glass to observe the bottle was half-empty. She pulled a chair to the front of the boat, and sat down.

"It's not my fault the silly cow can't change a light bulb," she said, "take me to the sunset!"

To her astonishment, McTavish obeyed, going into the wheelhouse to guide the vessel into the gentle waters of the loch. She sighed contentedly – a private cruise on a lavish yacht, attended by her own personal captain. Hic!

Stephanie had always been careful to hide her moods from Nork, but on meeting him outside the bathroom, her smile had been very hard to manufacture. However, her scamper down the steps had startled him, and she had no wish to make his fright any worse by telling him that McTavish was a slimy toad whose fingers had…yurk!

No doubt Nork would have responded innocently by saying toads did not have fingers, but some other appendage that…only a boy could think of. So, she had remained calm, made a polite greeting, and eventually come to reflect on his thoughtful nature, which seemed to include preparing her a bath, the instant one was required.

Once sitting in the bath, all the hot bubbles helped her mind float away to an idyllic place where, on her last day of work, she was picking up the microphone of the public address system…

"…Good evening, ladies and gentlemen," she would say, "please listen carefully to the following announcement. McTavish is…"

So long as she waited until he was in the loo, she would have at least ninety seconds of glorious fame, before he came running around the corner to dive for the plug socket. She could then leapfrog the counter and be gone forever…

Or at least that is what she had dreamed about until Nork arrived, and made everything complicated. How could she abandon him now? It would mean him working as a child slave for the next three years. Only on reaching the age of fourteen would a small degree of pocket money be involved. Thinking about this allowed her to view her own life from a better perspective. For herself, McTavish had been through three phases: useful, nuisance and, more recently, problematic.

The useful phase had only applied to her first few months of service, when he had kept her fed, and housed, while she learned to cope with the death of her father.

The nuisance phase had begun when he had started to take an unusual view of her knees. Apparently, they belonged to him. General avoidance, combined with running away, had proved adequate to deal with this.

The problematic phase was a recent development. In this, he seemed to believe his 'property rights' extended all the way up to, what he disgustingly referred to as, the 'knicker line'. It was almost like the Plimsoll line of his stupid boat; it was legal to reach it, only becoming improper if he went higher without gaining special permission, which, strangely, he seemed to believe would be granted if he kept asking.

His new belief that he was behaving correctly, so long as he did not go inside her pants, meant her response of wriggling and running away was no longer adequate to deal with the increased hostilities. It was merely something to which she had become accustomed during his knee-fixation period. However, her fantasy response of leaving both job and accommodation at the same time needed careful planning, especially since it had to be tied up with her announcement on the public-address system.

As the bath water cooled, she began to think about Jane, who she considered very naive to go out on McTavish's yacht. It would bring her back in tears. Alternatively, she could be very calculating, and destined to spend the rest of her life centred around champagne, for there was no doubt that if she satisfied McTavish's 'personal needs', he would keep her on a semi-permanent basis. Then, as she moved within his circle of important acquaintances, it was only a matter of time before she picked up some old guy, more generous than McTavish, who would provide for her long-term comforts. If that was what she wanted, then McTavish was a pretty good place to begin, depending on how tightly she could shut her eyes while he was actually doing it!

After Stephanie had finished her bath, she went to the staff room to make herself and Nork a toasted cheese sandwich... or would have done, had the food cupboard not been empty. McTavish stopped £10 a week for what he called her 'subsistence food, provided free of charge'. A curious notion, she had always thought, but it sort of worked, because without fail, you could guarantee the communal food cupboard kept you alive, so long as your taste-buds did not require much stimulation. Indeed, Nork had so overdosed on beans on toast, that he was now actively seeking new foods, of which tomato sauce sandwiches, with a few chips, were currently his favourite. And now the cupboard was bare. OK, there were some potatoes and cabbage, but promoting the idea of bubble and squeak to a small boy was not possible. It sounded rather like mice cooked in washing-up liquid, but you could still see the cabbage, so he would not be fooled that easily. Given the food-cupboard crisis, she decided it was better to take Nork down to the ice-cream parlour, then pander to his nutritional requirements tomorrow with something less severe, like carrots!

In response to knocking on the door of his room, there was no reply, but as a maid, she was quite accustomed to walking into empty rooms without any particular reason. On the bed, she noticed a letter which, being a maid, it was her duty to read. The first words of the letter surprised her: '*Dear Mother...*'

This was clearly nonsense, but nonetheless important, if that is what Nork truly believed. In any event, it proved her theory that his upbringing had been sufficiently isolated to leave him unaware of biological reproduction. Ah! This would account for his idea of televisions turning the brain to 'boiled cabbage'. Wherever he came from, the people in charge obviously thought boys needed to be shielded from the evils of the wider world, which clearly necessitated a complete ban on televisions. Saying they were the invention of the Devil was obviously not scary enough to terrify a small boy into submission, but anything to do with boiled cabbage, that was seriously bad!

Now Stephanie was certain Nork had originated from a secluded institution, the only remaining mystery was how he came to be associated with an upper-class prostitute who, according to the letter, did not want him any more.

After reading his note, she went upstairs to check the go-cart situation. As expected, it had gone. After hurrying back to Nork's room, she took a notebook from her pocket, and quickly scribbled a sentence:

'*Have gone to find your son. Will bring him back, if that is what he wants, otherwise have a nice time with McTavish.*'

This done, she placed her note alongside the one Nork had written, then turned around to remove the sheet from his bed. Going to her own room, she changed into her outdoor clothes, before heading to the dining room, where she rearranged the guests' complimentary biscuit tray into something more minimalist, and less chocolate-coloured.

After leaving the hotel, she walked to the outskirts of the town, where an old cart track left the main lane to begin a wandering climb into the mountains. After three miles, the track narrowed to a path of well-worn stones, made by the hooves of pack donkeys, who established the trading route before recorded time began.

However, the romantically inclined walker, who hoped to wander idly forth, lost to poetic dreams of a bygone age, was nowadays likely to suffer a rude awakening, because the 'donkey' route was now accompanied by tyre ruts, weaving from side to side, thereby avoiding the large boulders that lay either side of the main track. Then, apparently in 'the middle of nowhere', they were quite likely to come across an old Land Rover parked on a patch of scrubland. Only beyond that was the donkey route allowed to wander romantically into the high mountains, untroubled by civilisation.

Opposite the side of the track where a Land Rover might be parked was a small stone cottage, with a slate roof. This was now owned by the most rugged member of the local mountain rescue team, who went by the name of Jim.

Jim never wore any clothes that were not designed for the extreme outdoors, be it great woolly jumpers, or thick tartan shirts. Lower down was even more eye-catching, his boots being the toughest it was possible to buy, and rumoured to be size 12. Above these, thick woolly socks generally went all the way up to his knee-length breeches. However, in hot weather, he would sometimes roll the socks down, thereby displaying enormous lower-leg muscles.

Stephanie could see the logic of his clothes, because it meant if he was called out, he could immediately go into the craggy mountains, without even stopping to say, 'hold on a sec, I'll just put me boots on'. What she found more confusing was the way he had recently started to come to the hotel for coffee, whereas the harbour cafe was less than half the price, possibly due to the tables and chairs being made from rough-sawn timber. The other confusing thing about Jim was his main employment – that of a local fireman. Doing such a job, it was reasonable to assume that he would go to work wearing the standard uniform. How he got away with his own clothes, she never knew, though perhaps one of the people he had saved from an early death was sufficiently important to let the local fire officer look the other way as Jim jumped down from the fire truck, wearing his breeches.

Stephanie reached Jim's cottage feeling well invigorated by the walk up the winding mountain track. The front door was made of rough oak planks, hammered into place using old wrought-iron nails. Also nailed to the door was a sign stating, 'Emergency Mountain Rescue Shelter'. She felt certain this was an unofficial arrangement, but like everything else about the man, extremely logical; an exhausted individual walking out of the mountains would come to this 'rescue cottage' first. In Winter, its existence could easily mean the difference between life and death.

Stephanie's banging on the door brought no response, other than a lot of barking from the inside. She guessed this would be coming from Sherpa Tenzing, a great Pyrenean Mountain Dog, whose ability to follow the faintest scent made him quite famous locally.

"Woof," she called back.

Having formally announced her arrival, Stephanie opened the door, where Sherpa immediately placed his front paws on her shoulders, and brought her crashing to the floor, so he could better lick her face. In response, she pushed three chocolate-covered biscuits into his mouth.

"Do you remember me?" she whispered into his ear.

"Ages ago, when I was a scraggy kid, I fed you biscuits, while your man was telling me off for roaming the mountains on my own. I didn't need rescuing, I only sat down to give you a great big hug, like this…"

She sat up, and threw her arms about his neck.

"…But after five years," she continued, "I don't expect 'your man' remembers anything about it, so let's keep it a big secret between ourselves."

"Woof," replied the dog. He always remembered humans who fed him brown-covered biscuits. He gave her a good sniff, so he would remember her scent if they ever met again.

After a few minutes, Jim came into the room via the back door. Seeing her sitting on the floor making a fuss of Sherpa brought him to a sudden halt. He then stood quite still, with his mouth open.

Jim had first become aware of this girl's existence about two years ago, when it was most improper to do so. Hence, on that occasion, he had looked the other way, and tried to think about harmless things, like putting out fires or climbing mountains. But, more recently, he had started taking his coffee breaks at McTavish's hotel, where sometimes, completely by accident, he might catch a glimpse of her going about her work. Sometimes, he even managed to accidentally say hello. Of course, he knew it could not lead anywhere, but being within twenty yards of her radiating, gentle personality put him in a good mood for the rest of the week. During such periods of good fortune, he would often go for solitary walks in the mountains, then sit on some distant summit, to contemplate how lucky he was to live in his nice little cottage, surrounded by so much beautiful scenery. It was on one such expedition that something quite amazing occurred to him. In five years' time, his age difference to the girl's would hardly raise an eyebrow! Could, one day, she become his wife?

But two weeks before, something even more amazing had happened. When taking his coffee break, he had heard Mark, a waiter in the restaurant, call out, 'Stephanie,' and the girl had walked towards him. Now, he knew her name! Things were heading in the right direction. In three years' time, he might be able to take her for a coffee at the harbour cafe, away from her work…and now, here she was, sitting on his floor, apparently having become best friends with Sherpa.

Stephanie wondered how a man given to long bouts of silence could work for the fire service. Rescuing people from burning buildings must involve a lot of complicated talk. Then she realised that visiting this place took determination, so she could hardly claim to be just passing.

"I need to take Sherpa for a little walk," she said.

"Why?"

"Because I like taking dogs for a walk."

"But he takes humans for a walk."

"Certainly hope so, because I'm not exactly certain where I need to go."

She thought he seemed unaccustomed to girls knocking on his door, asking to borrow his dog.

"Oh, I was just passing," she added, just to obey the conventions of an unexpected visitor.

As soon as Sherpa allowed Stephanie to stand, they headed out of the door together. Jim grabbed his anorak, and gave pursuit; it was not how he imagined their first date would be, but it was a start…three years ahead of schedule.

At the front of Jim's cottage, Sherpa was given the sheet

to smell. After running about for a little while, he looked at Stephanie, apparently awaiting further instructions.

OK, she thought, *Nork did not come this way*.

She could not imagine him setting off in the direction he had arrived, because that would take him closer to whatever he was running away from. Following the rules of logic, she began walking back down the track, therefore, in the general direction of the hotel. Jim walked behind, uncertain as to his social position within the threesome.

"Looking for someone?" he enquired.

She knew 'looking for someone' meant he would have to put it in the rescue log, and at the moment that was too difficult.

"Just browsing," she said.

Jim had a good understanding of mountains and putting out fires, while females left him completely baffled. However, Stephanie had not actually told him to go away, so he thought following her down the track, on this most pleasant of evenings, was probably acceptable. In an hour's time there would be a sunset, and by then she would surely need to sit down to talk to him.

A mile down the track, Sherpa said, "Woof," then trotted across to re-smell the sheet. Without further hesitation, he set off up a footpath that branched away to the side. Stephanie quickened her pace to keep up, while Jim had absolutely no idea what was going on.

"You can't go up there just browsing," he called, "it's the main pass across the high mountains to the next settlement."

She decided not to tell him that when she was a scraggy thirteen-year-old, wearing a maid's uniform, he had already given her a lecture about health and safety, bla bla bla. The important 'person' in this relationship was Sherpa, who knew where they needed to go, and had clearly remembered her from their previous meeting.

Jim gave pursuit, hoping not to meet any of his mountain rescue colleagues as he went into the wilderness without a rucksack of survival equipment.

*

Nork found running away much easier this time; he had a map, the money he had saved from his spelling tests, and a wagon overloaded with food supplies. He also understood the world much better. After crossing the mountains, he would survey a new settlement from a distance, then approach with extreme caution. What he was looking for was a pre-hotel sort of Sara, just to organise the grown-up things. Possibly somebody who already had a number of children. Then he could blend in without attracting too much attention, and the 'mother' would need less training. He would not be much bother, and so long as she took him rock climbing, he could sort the rest out for himself.

His face set into a frown. The person he most wanted to be with was Stephanie, but she knew about the spies at the hotel, and accepted it as something that was meant to happen. He could not risk going back to see her in the child prison, because they might lock him up in some dungeon or other. Now he knew about the 'other kingdom' behind the mirrors, he would rule nothing out.

He had left the 'prison' with the hope of crossing the pass before nightfall, but the wagon kept getting stuck on the increasingly rocky track. When the early settlers had crossed the Rocky Mountains, he reasoned, they had horses, so the humans could sit on their wagons to look at things, without any effort being put into their legs. However, on reaching an emergency shelter, he decided he had travelled far enough for day one. Tomorrow, he would cross the pass at daybreak and, if the track was good, he could drive down the other side, like he had once done with his 'mother', before catching the train.

The shelter was good, with stone walls and a corrugated iron roof, all covered with earth. The ceiling was not high enough to let him stand up straight but, sitting cross-legged on the floor, there was plenty of room for him to spread his belongings out. He then went back outside to unload his wagon. He had stolen some blankets from the hotel cupboards, but they had thousands of them, and did not seem to use them any more. He had also stolen all the food from the staff room, but this was necessary to keep him alive. Feeling very guilty, he picked up the saucepan that he had also stolen, then went to the mountain stream to fill it with water. Slowly, he came to understand he was a criminal on the run, an outlaw, like those of long ago, who had crossed the Rocky Mountains to escape the sheriff.

After collecting the water, he kept himself busy gathering wood and bits of dry grass to start a fire. It all worked as expected and, by using the stones around the fire to balance a saucepan, he managed to boil some water. Now, he was really following the cowboy stories of long ago – making coffee, and hot baked-bean sandwiches. Never before had he known such happiness. He knew that tomorrow might be bad again, but as Stephanie had once told him, life was like that when you were all grown up.

*

Jim stopped, and called for his companions to do the same. Now he had seen the smoke rising from near the rescue shelter, he was formally required to be on duty, which made him feel in control of things, something he had not felt while following Stephanie up the track as a 'browsing' companion.

"Smoke," he said. "It's probably nothing, but I need to check it out."

The serious mountains did not begin until around the next spur, with this glen representing a sort of boundary. Casual walkers often brought a picnic up here, but rarely ventured further. Exhausted climbers, retreating from the mountains, sometimes crawled to the shelter, knowing the serious difficulties were behind them. Stephanie studied Jim, who had suddenly become all formal.

"I thought this might happen," she said. "I expect you want to tell him off for coming into the mountains on his own."

"What?"

"It's what you do. I imagine you have a form to fill in, concerning his irresponsible behaviour."

After a moment to consider the situation, she decided the only way to solve the problem was to confuse him. She approached, stood on tiptoe, and kissed him on the cheek.

"You're not on duty any more," she said, "now we are just a couple out for a walk."

It was the first time she had ever tried to kiss anyone, so she rather imagined it a clumsy attempt; indeed, Jim was so tall, she had not even been on target, instead locating his lower jaw. Then, feeling guilty by her forward ways, she stepped back.

"Follow me," she said.

Jim had never known such happiness. He followed the goddess of perfection to wherever she was going. Only slowly did he become aware of his wider surroundings, and was pleased to discover they were still heading towards the column of smoke, though more in a closing circle. Then his leader sat down.

"We can watch the sunset together if you like," she said.

"There's a boy," he said, "by the shelter."

"Seems happy enough. I'll go and talk to him when he's finished his supper."

She kept Sherpa happy with a chocolate biscuit. Then she turned to Jim.

"Now," she said, "this is most important. For the rest of the day you must completely ignore your obsession for filling in forms. In fact, if you ever report any of this to the authorities, I shall hate you for the rest of my life, because if you do, it will make the boy take flight, possibly faster than we can catch him. Do you understand?"

Jim was so overwhelmed by her gentle voice, that he paid little attention to the actual words. He nodded; he was still too busy thinking about her kiss to organise any coherent answer.

*

Nork stared into the flames and, by dropping slices of bread onto the hot stones, made some toast. He reckoned that given another month he could survive well enough in the mountains without a grown-up. And, when he arrived in his new country, he would not be recognised; it would just be like arriving in California with a wagon.

"Hello," said a voice from the shadows.

He jumped up, spun around, and backed away, all at the same time.

"I've got a gun," Nork gasped.

"I come in peace," said the voice, "though I'm very hungry. Have you any toast to spare?"

Nork got his thoughts more organised, and peered into the gathering gloom.

"It's you!" he gasped.

"And I've brought a friend, and a dog, if we can join your camp?"

A dog came across to lick him and, having found the source of the scent, sat down to await further instructions. Then a man appeared, and shook his hand.

"Don't get many wagons up here nowadays," he said. "Where are you going, soldier?"

Nork found this man-to-man talk rather confusing, but he sort of liked it. He quickly decided this man was completely different to Fish Face.

"West," he said.

Stephanie had expected Jim to say nothing, or to clomp in with his size-12 boots to talk about fire regulations. Instead, he was saying precisely the right things.

"Your wagon won't make the pass," he said. "From around the next spur, there are boulders as tall as yourself."

Stephanie knew that running away was foremost in Nork's mind, turning back a well-hidden notion.

"Perhaps," she interrupted, "I could have some of that fine toast, and Jim could go and collect some more firewood."

Reluctantly, Jim did as he was told, while Stephanie sat cross-legged before the fire. She knew making Nork forget that he was supposed to be running away required care, and that persuading him back to base was best done over coffee.

The toast was mostly burnt or uncooked but, in context, it tasted appropriate. The conversation drifted back and forth until Nork seemed at ease.

After Jim returned to make up the fire, he sat beside Stephanie to talk about deer, eagles, and how to predict the weather – safe things that he knew would not get him sent away on firewood duty again.

"So," said Stephanie presently, "here's me trying to escape across the mountains, when I see your smoke, and think, he's got a wagon, which I have not. Sadly, I can never go back the way I came, because of McTavish, and his horrible ways, horrible hotel, and horrible everything."

Nork nodded. "It's a secret prison camp," he said.

"I know," she replied, "but now we have escaped, so don't have to worry about it any more. Sadly, if you can't get your wagon over the mountains, what are we to do for food?"

She gave Jim a friendly nudge in the ribs.

"Oh," he responded, "I really don't understand what is happening here."

He looked at Stephanie for clues.

"I know," said Stephanie, "why don't me and Nork find somewhere to hide? Then, when we have rested, we can load up some backpacks to trek across the mountains on foot."

"You could, I suppose."

"But where are we to go until then?"

"My place?" offered Jim.

"If you think such a hideout would not be found by McTavish and his spies, then yes…please!"

Nork looked at them both thoughtfully. He realised they were talking grown-up speak, modified for his benefit, but the basic principle seemed sensible enough. He got up, and squeezed between them. He put one arm around Stephanie, but was less certain about the man. He knew a lot of good stuff, but that did not mean he was not a spy sent to guard the pass. Unlikely, he thought, but he was beginning to discover grown-ups did a lot of unlikely things.

"Hot drinking chocolate and cream cakes back at the hideout then?" suggested Stephanie.

"Until two hours ago," said Jim, "I was out in the back yard, waiting for my porridge to cook. None of this was expected, so I'm afraid my cupboard is completely bare of visitor treats. Rats! I left the porridge on the stove, it will be burned to a cinder by now!"

"I've got food," said Nork. "We could stay here, and move on in the morning. With two of us, we could carry the wagon over the difficult bits."

"No," said Jim, "if the weather turns nasty, we could be stranded. If we are to cross the mountains, we will do so properly – boots, waterproofs and sleeping bags."

Stephanie looked at him seriously. "I hope that's not a false promise," she said. "It would be quite wrong to tell Nork something you do not intend to see through."

"Of course, if the boy wants to cross the mountains, I will take him. But, we will have to do it properly, on Saturday, because it's a two-day trek, unless you're hardened to it? And I expect the boy will want to stop to look at the deer I was talking about."

"His name's Nork," said Stephanie crossly.

"Sorry."

"It's OK," said Nork, "a lot of people have a problem with it."

Then he twisted a finger in his ear to have a good think. After meeting Fish Face, not having a man-parent seemed a really sensible idea. But now, he could see Jim was completely different. He always seemed to be smiling, for one thing, except when he looked at Stephanie, when his face went all strange. However, he had not yet made a snorting noise, like McTavish, which seemed to be a good sign. From this, he concluded, it was not in his interests to have two potential parents arguing over his name, so he stood up, and repositioned himself on Stephanie's other side. Accidentally, he sat very close, so bumping them closer together.

Stephanie was surprised to find herself crashing into Jim and, when she tried to recover, nobody seemed willing to give way. Nork had braced himself with a foot, while Jim gave the impression he was made of stone.

"Crossing the mountains," said Jim, apparently with some difficulty, "would be better with three."

Stephanie nodded. It was less committing than saying yes and, until she had worked out whether she had definitely left the hotel forever, she was happy to go along with it…for now.

"I would be grateful," she said, "if we could stop at your place tonight. I really can't face McTavish at the moment."

Nork thought this sounded OK, so before anyone changed their mind, he got up to switch on his wagon headlights. Then he went around the back to cast a professional eye at the tail lights.

With some embarrassment, Jim realised it was the only

light they had between them.

"The moon will rise in an hour," he said, "so we'll move out then. Your wagon headlights will alert the spies to our presence."

"Quite," laughed Stephanie, "and we did leave in such a hurry."

"To browse," responded Jim. "Did you find what you were looking for?"

"Perhaps," said Stephanie.

Nork turned off the lights as quickly as possible.

"Do you think they were seen?" he asked.

"Against a black mountain, even a torch would stand out for miles, but I don't suppose they paid it any regard. However, had you started to drive on the rough path, they would appear to be flashing, and then you might attract all sorts of interest. The international distress signal is six flashes of about one-second duration, repeated every two minutes. Though with all your exploring, I expect you knew that already."

Embarrassed by his lack of knowledge, Nork sat down, so as to keep Jim and Stephanie together.

"What about in daylight?" asked Stephanie.

"Six blasts of a whistle," said Jim.

Nork remained silent, hoping to give the impression that he knew this already. Then he noticed a few stars were starting to appear in the darkening sky. In order to regain some credibility, he explained they all went around in a circle.

"Except for that one," said Stephanie. "It always stays above the North Pole, while the others circle around it."

Using her finger to point, she explained how it could be located.

"So if you are ever lost on a clear night," she said, "you will know which way is north, and hopefully won't need to make your six flashes on a torch, to be rescued."

She then lay back to watch the stars making their nightly appearance. Nork was less embarrassed about doing soppy things now, so lay beside her, also to gaze upwards. Jim took this to mean he had permission to do the same, then accidentally reached down to hold Stephanie's hand. The unexpected accident caused Stephanie to frown; half the ladies in the town went wobbly at the knees whenever they saw Jim walking down the street, so why on Earth would he want to make a suggestive contact with her – a girl who never wore makeup, and had her hair cut by Cook, with unpredictable results?

After a moment to consider things, Stephanie decided that her hairstyle explained everything. Jim just wanted to show friendship, after all, somebody in their late twenties would not be interested in a teenager, who only ever wore the clothes provided by the hotel. Except for the anorak and the boots. Together they had cost her six months' pocket money, but to walk into the mountains in a maid's uniform was just too silly for words, as Jim had once told her when she was a scraggy kid. But thankfully, now it seemed he had forgotten the encounter.

As if to confirm a friendship arrangement, Stephanie instinctively reached down to wrap her fingers around Nork's much smaller hand, though this was a secret just between themselves and the stars.

EIGHT

The yacht hardly moved on the still, black waters of the loch. Even the Moon held its mirror image, unless a fish broke the surface to cast a circle of ripples. In a hypnotic champagne trance, Sara gazed at all this, and thought it the happiest moment of her life.

Annoyingly, the tide turned, causing the yacht to drift slowly about the anchor chain to face the wrong direction – wrong because it meant she was looking away from the all-powerful Moon, to see the first trace of sapphire blue rising in the eastern sky; this perfect night was coming to an end. Selfishly, she thanked the important people for not turning up; every celebrity needs a few hours away from the pressures of socialising to relax with their own thoughts.

When the sky indicated the sun was about to rise above the horizon, she left her sitting position on the hard wooden chair, and stood up to have a good stretch. Then, as she tried to massage some life back into her bottom, there was a long moan, seemingly from another world. McTavish had not interrupted her pleasant thoughts since dropping anchor;

only now did she remember he might be somewhere about. Massaging her backside was neither dignified nor advisable. Joining his higher social circle meant it was necessary to remain proper at all times. Embarrassed, she considered the possibility that he was actually on the deck, and had witnessed her indiscretion. She let her arms fall loosely by her sides, as if it had happened by accident. In two minutes, he would have forgotten all about it, and she could turn around, in all probability finding herself alone. After all, McTavish had seen this view a hundred times before; most likely he was downstairs asleep, or perhaps making breakfast.

After the embarrassment faded, she turned around, more concerned with finding breakfast than anything a man might accidentally have seen. After two paces she stopped, uncertain as to the nature of her vision. McTavish, reasonably enough, was sitting on a chair in front of the wheelhouse, also admiring the tranquil dawn. Unreasonably, or at least strangely, he was not wearing any clothes. Involuntarily, her gaze descended to the thing she should not be looking at. It was the most astonishing biological deformity she had ever seen.

Eventually, her confused brain remembered that some people considered clothes to be an inconvenience when viewing nature. Astonishment and horror then combined to form a single gasp; his 'biology' was pointing in completely the wrong direction for this to be the case.

McTavish stood up and walked to the champagne table.

"Sorry about Nessie," he said, "it's got a mind of its own sometimes."

He came across to hand her a glass of champagne, but she was too mortified to move. Bowing at the waist, he reached across to curl her fingers around the glass.

"Can't stand too close," he said, "Nessie's always hitting things. This morning I turned about in the shower and knocked a whole load of stuff off the shelf."

Sara finally recovered from the shock of the unexpected encounter, and jumped back with a scream. The glass fell from her fingers to shatter on the deck. McTavish seemed unconcerned by this, casually walking to the wheelhouse to get a broom, and returning to sweep the broken glass over the side. The fact that he simply ignored his nudity made things very awkward. She could neither force him to dress, defend herself, or, it seemed, fully ignore the shelf-clearing monster.

"Oh," she said weakly.

Then she realised the name of his biological absurdity probably meant he did a lot of nude sunbathing on Loch Ness, and thought his… 'thingy'… to be of equal importance.

McTavish's smile broadened. "A gasp and an oh," he said, "how very polite. I could not repeat what some ladies say when they see Nessie for the first time! You must, of course, ignore him."

"I will," she mumbled.

She turned sideways, until the problem was at the edge of her peripheral vision. McTavish stepped forwards to stand beside her.

"We have been very lucky with the weather," he said.

Sara realised that if McTavish was a male stripper booked for a hen night, he would be very popular, so long as he did the personal stuff with somebody else whom you did not like. The problem here was that she was on her own, and the only escape route involved swimming a great distance.

McTavish tried to pretend he had a deep, manly voice, but

since it had risen half an octave, it was quite obvious to Sara that his mind had gone back to his excitable youth.

"A shame we are not on Loch Ness," he said, "you might even see the monster on such a fine morning."

When Sara made no response, he turned to face her.

"Sorry," he said, jumping back, "I sometimes forget how far Nessie sticks out."

Sara finally found the courage to stare directly into his eyes. Cold, deceitful eyes, most noticeable because they were surrounded by hair on three sides – nasal, brows and ears.

"Thank you for a lovely evening," she said in a voice that she hoped sounded flat and without emotion.

She then walked to the anchor winch, and pressed a green button. She was actually quite surprised when an electric motor whirred into life, making the chain rattle through a hole in the deck. She got the impression McTavish was also surprised by her ability to make things happen.

Soon, the anchor clunked into place, and the motor stopped with a heavy 'click'.

"Oh," she said, quite pleased with her nautical ability. On reflection, she thought it more likely the yacht had been designed for idiots to drive – push a few levers, and you went wherever you needed to go. Strangely, she found this quite comforting, there being another way to shore without McTavish playing captain.

When McTavish spoke again, his voice was less confident than before, and not particularly coherent.

"Do you know what would be the most amazing thing in the whole world?" he asked.

Sara ignored him, and went to look in the wheelhouse. She turned on the ignition key, and somewhere an engine started. McTavish moved with sudden speed, turning off the engine and, at the same time, pushing himself against her side. He made no apology for this, but grabbed her shoulder, and turned her around until she was squeezed roughly in his arms.

"The most amazing thing in the world," he said, "would be to see you on the foredeck, dropping your gown, then walking towards me to say a proper 'hello' to Nessie."

With some effort, she managed to wriggle free, and escaped through the far door. McTavish left through his door, then ran around the front of the wheelhouse to face her.

"Please," he said, "I'll do anything you want. Now it's the end of the season, you can even stay in a guest room, it will be…forever, you are just so incredibly beautiful!"

Sara realised that if her vulnerable situation was to be decided by muscle strength alone, the outcome would be rape, after which the evidence, that is to say herself, could be disposed of over the side of the yacht. However, emotionally she seemed to be in the stronger position. McTavish would, no doubt, crawl about on all fours, if she asked. Perhaps, if she played to his vanity, she could outwit him mentally.

"Give me a few days to think about it," she said. "I could never do such a thing on an empty stomach. Breakfast at your hotel, I think?"

"I can cook you breakfast here," he croaked.

The boat was his territory, advantage to him, she thought. Then she looked at the edge of the deck, and realised it was where his kingdom ended, but throwing him overboard came down to physical strength, which took her back to images of rape. Then, looking directly at McTavish, she realised his mind was also working out a strategy, probably regarding a plan that involved a great deal of fantasy. Finally, he gave a satisfied nod.

"I understand you are giving me 'a chamber maid's consent'," he said. "This means it is in your interest to be nice to the person who looks after you."

He reached down, and put a finger on the tip of his penis, pushing it down a fraction, so the exposed tip was pointing directly towards her face.

"After the first time," he continued, "you will be so amazed by Nessie's performance that, in future, you will be begging him to keep on doing it!"

McTavish then bowed his head, though whether it was from shame, or the need to consult his biological absurdity, she had no idea. When he looked up, he had a serious look on his face.

"Sara," he said, "I need to ask you something."

"What?"

"Sara," he said.

"Keep it quick, and let's get out of here without any harm being done."

"Sara," he repeated.

"Change the record, will you...Oh!"

In the long silence that followed, McTavish took a step towards her, bringing Nessie dangerously close to her sheet.

"The animal charity does not exist," he said. "We all have things we need to keep secret."

Sara now found herself on the defensive.

"Like the way your cheques to the fishermen's fund keep disappearing from the box," she said, "together with the odd £20 note?"

"The fishermen are very happy with their ten grand," he

said, "and you've had free accommodation for eight weeks. So now we are to hold each other, then we are all happy. Once you get accustomed to Nessie's size, you will be begging him to come out and play all the time."

"And you would stoop to blackmail to achieve this?"

"Don't need to, you will be living free of charge in my hotel, and your son will be working in our kitchen. All sorted. Hunky dory, as you English like to say."

"Son? How did you know about that?"

"He told me, so I reckon you had your first shag at thirteen. You'd probably done half the boys in your school by the time you were fourteen. So no more 'Little Miss Innocent' act. Your time for little willies is over. Now, down on your knees to play with what a real man has to offer."

The shock of everything McTavish had said caused Sara's legs to give way. She sat on the edge of the wheelhouse step to consider how impossible her situation had become. Accuse McTavish of rape, and he would become the fine, upstanding councillor; she a woman whose visit to the town was characterised by fraud and general lies. McTavish then broke into her thoughts.

"It doesn't have to be like this," he said. "It does not worry me that you are a slut who abandoned her son. He's a good worker, so there is no reason why he should not keep his job in the kitchens. The important thing is that you now make friends with Nessie. What do you say we kiss and make up? That's Nessie talking, not me."

Sara realised she was now all alone, in the real hard world, one in which Nork had betrayed her to a pervert. She then remembered the other pervert she had met in the woods. She had survived that encounter because…Nork had rescued her.

Without his understanding of the world, it all seemed rather more difficult, unless all perverts were essentially the same. Then, the slut who had stolen her boyfriend came to mind, the stories mixing until she felt able to fully throw herself into the battle to survive.

"OK," she said, "I admit I fancy you, Nessie just frightened me a little – a lot – that is all, it's just so enormous."

McTavish made an uncontrolled thrust. From above came a great moan that she realised was exactly the same sound she had heard when being indiscreet with her bottom, what seemed like a lifetime ago. McTavish was once more under her power and control.

"At school…" she said.

"You've left school," said his voice from above.

"At college, one of the girls used to remove £5 notes with her teeth from any boy who would fold one across his thingy. She got surprisingly rich!"

"We do not part with money."

"In your case, I was thinking a newspaper would be more appropriate. There's one in the wheelhouse with a picture of handsome McTavish on it. Something to do with raising funds for charity. Back in a moment."

McTavish watched suspiciously as she went into the wheelhouse, relaxing only when she returned carrying a copy of his picture. She dropped the pages upon Nessie one at a time. Taking the bottom of the complete newspaper, she pulled him sideways to the clear deck, then turned him around until he was pointing in the required direction. McTavish could control himself no longer and began thrusting movements, while Sara ducked from side to side, like a boxer avoiding punches.

"If I'm going to remove these with my teeth," she said, "you'll have to stay still."

McTavish began to wail and shiver. She looked up to discover his eyes were fully closed with the hormonal surges of it all.

"I'm coming for you now," she said, blowing hard to lift the newspapers a fraction.

McTavish lost control of his breathing and began to snort erratically, while his uncontrolled thrusting eagerly awaited the exciting unpredictability of first contact...

The next thing he knew, something very heavy crashed into his back, sending him head first over the rail. Nessie tried to go underneath it, a reflex action making McTavish grab the rails with his hands to take some of the weight. This meant his unprotected forehead continued to arc around, until it crashed into the boat. He could not understand what was happening, but was fairly certain he was upside down in a world of drifting newspapers. For fear of losing consciousness, he quite forgot why he was holding the rail, and let go to nurse his head.

No erection, however solid a man might believe it to be, is capable of supporting the weight of his entire body. After being wrenched down towards his knees, it slid over the rail, allowing master and servant to remain united, albeit to free-fall into the icy waters of the loch. It seemed a long time before they found the surface, McTavish spluttering water from his mouth.

"Stupid cow!" he coughed as soon as he was able. "What did you want to do that for?"

Sara was so surprised by the spectacular result of her fast-moving shoulder-charge into a man's back, that she could do nothing but stare at the empty space, where, a few seconds before, he had been standing. Then, more sensibly, she ran around the boat looking for any possible way he might return. There was none; the ladder was up and at no place was the deck less than five feet above the water. She ran back to McTavish, half expecting him to fly back onboard, but he was still splashing about and calling her rude names. She watched him for a few minutes to see what he would do next, which strangely involved swimming to the side of the yacht, so he could claw at it helplessly. She responded by holding a half-empty champagne bottle over the side, then dropping it on his head. When he stopped swearing, she reminded him there were still five bottles onboard – all of them full – and possibly dropped from a much greater height. He swam away from the boat.

"Good," she shouted, "it seems we understand each other!"

In order to give herself time to think, she got the chair from the front of the boat, and returned it to the deck that overlooked McTavish. She then sat down to consider her new problem: let McTavish back onboard, and she might be killed; or leave him where he was, resulting in his almost certain death? Both of these outcomes seemed a little extreme. However, the important thing was that his bigger muscles were no longer a factor in the outcome of the situation. McTavish seemed to understand this, because his trembling voice was now politely asking to be let back onboard.

Sara thought this request too silly to be acknowledged. However, she had now worked out a compromise solution.

"I suppose I could always drop you the rowing boat," she said.

"Yes…anything!"

"And what have you to offer in return?"

McTavish looked up from the water, his teeth chattering too much to give a coherent reply.

"What you have to offer in return," she said, "is precisely nothing! Because, if I return to town to tell people you fell overboard while dancing naked on the deck, there would be few questions asked when your naked body turned up on some desolate shore. Me…well, I'm just the weak, feeble girl you plied with champagne, so was quite incapable of coming to your rescue. It seems my offer to lower the boat was overgenerous. Perhaps it is better to simply say goodbye now."

"No, please! I will do anything!"

"Then stay precisely where you are, and I'll winch down the rowing boat. The slightest splash in my direction, and the deal's off!"

She went to the boat, but it seemed most unsuitable. It had pumps, and all sorts of other stuff to stop it sinking. Oh well, it would have to do. After removing the oars, she winched it down, then used a boat hook to disconnect it from the cables. She then gave it a good push with the hook, to find herself quite impressed by how far it went, before it came to drift idly around in a circle. It was certainly further than McTavish could paddle by hanging his arms over the side, while under attack from an artillery of champagne bottles.

"All yours!" she shouted.

McTavish swam to the rescue boat where the trouble he had climbing over the side suggested he was in a pretty bad way. Out of the water, he might shiver intensely, but death was unlikely to be a problem now the sun had risen above the horizon.

"I'll be off then," she called, "hope you get on OK."

"But what about the oars?"

"Oars?" questioned Sara, with exaggerated stupidity. "Nobody said anything about oars. Anyway, the coastguard will find you a lot easier if you have to stay in one place. I'll telephone them as soon as I get back. If they pick you up in about four hours, would that be convenient?"

She tried to think of other things that might upset him, but could not.

Resigned to his fate, McTavish sat back shivering as the yacht engines started up. Quite suddenly, he saw a hopeful sign as Sara returned to the rail to look down on him.

"Hello," he called as feebly as he could, "ye not leaving me then?"

"In a minute, but I wondered if you could tell me where the brake is? I can't seem to find it." Thinking he might have missed the significance of this, she added, "I've found the thing to make it go faster, but I can't find the thing to make it stop."

With his last ounce of energy, McTavish managed a scream.

"It doesn't have a brake," he yelled, "you put it into reverse!"

Sara had vague memories of her father explaining the same thing, when she was aged about five. Now, she did her best to recreate the same giggle, but could tell McTavish did not understand the joys of early childhood chatter.

"Oh, you can't fool me, Mr McTavish," she added. "Daddy let me drive his car on the beach once, and I quite definitely remember him saying that you had to stand on something to make it stop. Reverse is what you do to make it go backwards."

By the expression on his face, it was clear he understood her completely.

"Perhaps," she said, "I could use the handbrake."

"Handbrake?" he whimpered. "It doesn't have a handbrake."

"Yes it does, that anchor thingy you were telling me about."

His voice rose an octave, but only in a quiet sort of way, like the top note of a piano.

"Anchor?" he squeaked. "You don't stop it by dropping the anchor."

She thought his new voice might be something to do with the cold, or possibly he did not like girls driving his boat, which seemed very old-fashioned. She tried to modify her voice to sound like the annoying girl from the cartoon of *Snow White* who, without seven male dwarfs, was completely helpless at anything not related to housework.

"But if it hasn't got a brake-pedal thingy," she said, "I thought I could just dangle in the anchor thingy in the water, sort of an emergency stop, if the water gets too shallow."

McTavish's response indicated that he failed to understand the basic laws of physics; dropping the anchor would so obviously stop the boat! She carefully explained that, in the old days, on approaching shallow water, someone would stand on the front bit of the boat, swinging a lead weight over the side.

"This," she added, "is where the phrase 'swinging the lead' came from, it being viewed as a doddle of a job."

Having brought the conversation to a satisfactory conclusion, she returned to the wheelhouse to study the controls. They seemed much the same as those on the family yacht, a vessel that her father frequently let her steer during their holidays off the African coast. This only ever happened when there was no land in sight, so deep down she knew it was only a game of pretend captain. As for parking the thing, her father seemed to believe that was a man thing.

Was the real world any harder than being a pretend captain? Probably, but fortunately this was not her yacht. Then her expression became serious, as she turned on the echo sounder.

"Oh," she said, astonished by how easy it all was. She hoped McTavish, as he sat naked in his little boat, would know the bottom of the loch was thirty-two metres below.

Having established the nature of the loch, she turned the ignition key, then waggled the fingers of her right hand towards the controls, to indicate she meant business. When all her muscles felt nice and flexible, she took hold of the left-hand stick and pushed it upwards until she heard a clunk. This indicated the automatic gearbox had connected to the left-hand propeller...she hoped. Slowly, the yacht began to move in a slight circle. After returning the stick to the middle, she went to the side to see what McTavish made of it all. He responded by screaming at her, to which she added a chorus, by running around the deck, erratically flapping her arms and yelling for help. When she could scream no more, she returned to the wheelhouse, and pushed both sticks upwards. The vessel behaved very much like the family yacht, the zigzag line only continuing briefly for the benefit of McTavish, who she hoped was watching her sail off into the sunrise, thinking about how good her Snow White impression had been.

"Base, McPherson," said a man's voice.

Sara jumped back in alarm, spinning around to find herself looking at a little box on the wall.

"Base receiving," said the box, "go ahead, McPherson."

"Good morning, Agnes," said the man, "go channel 24."

Then there was silence. *People of few words*, she thought, *but who, and where from?*

Looking around the loch, she noticed a small car ferry tied to a pier some way behind. It had been asleep when she passed, but now a lot of lights had come on. She held her course, considering whether a car ferry might be a more appropriate vessel to pick up McTavish. It would take him... somewhere. Anyway, she would still be at the hotel two hours before him. In any event, it seemed less complicated than telephoning the coastguard, who might arrange a rescue with unnecessary discretion.

She had seen her father use the ship-to-shore radio many times. It was not something she had ever done – too many ports, starboards and twenty-four-hour-clock talk for her liking. However, now she was a different person, who needed to sort things out for herself. She reached across to pick up the microphone, and pushed the button down.

"Hello," she said.

When there was no reply, she looked at the radio set. The dial was set to sixteen. Out of interest, she moved it to twenty-four. Immediately, the voices came back, the mysterious McPherson apparently being in the final, yet unsuccessful, stages of asking Agnes out on a date. Then a faint voice in the background could be heard.

"All cars loaded," it said.

"Time to go," said Agnes.

All cars, thought Sara, *that sounded positive.* Looking ahead, she realised the hotel landing stage was in sight. Being professional, she estimated her crashing time to be about twenty minutes. Added to this, she would need a further hour to get organised, plus fifteen minutes to reprimand Nork for telling McTavish she was his mother.

She gasped. McTavish must have thought she was over twenty. The cheek of it! Well, there was no way he was going to get away with that without there being consequences. She turned all her attention to the radio.

"Hello," she said.

Then, like a famous film heroine, she dramatically released the black button to await a reply. There was a short pause before a slightly confused, and possibly embarrassed, McPherson responded.

"Identify yourself," he said.

"Jane," she said. "Hello, Agnes," she added, because she sounded more friendly than the grumpy man.

Her instinct was right.

"Hello, Jane," responded Agnes, "he wants to know the name of your vessel."

"Haven't a clue. What I phoned to say is, can you see a rowing boat anywhere?"

After a few moments, the man came back.

"Starboard bow," he said, "yes, three miles to seaward."

"Have you got some binoculars?"

This time, a longer silence was broken by the man saying a rude word, for which Agnes chastised him.

Sara interrupted. "Does that mean the occupant of the boat is a naked man?" she asked.

Agnes made some further enquiries.

"Hello," interrupted Sara, "me again. I think he might need some help. I could not pick him up when I passed, because he was doing rude things to himself, and did not look safe.

Perhaps, if you have plenty of passengers on board, it might be possible to pacify him?"

"Hold the sailing," cut in Agnes, "I will be there in two minutes."

"Agnes," shouted Sara, "wait!"

"Yes," replied Agnes.

"I thought it might be good publicity for your ferry. I know Richard White from *The Herald* would give it a good splash, you know, 'Car ferry rescues naked man in rowing boat', that sort of thing. He keeps giving me his home telephone number. Try 35648."

"Got that," said Agnes. "Anything else?"

"You got a camera, in case Richard can't get there in time?"

"Yes."

"Then I can't think of anything else."

Sara turned off the radio. In her situation it was OK to make statements, but not to answer the questions that would almost certainly come once they got around to thinking who she might be. From now on, Jane did not exist, had never existed, except in the wild imaginings of a local community, who would no doubt spend many months speculating on where she came from…and where she had gone…

Nork also, for when they arrived in a new town, she would look after him better this time, at least after she had explained that delivering babies had nothing to do with arriving on a fencing panel!

NINE

Stephanie awoke in the middle of the night to find her thoughts disorientated by the sound of a gently hissing gas lamp. This, a deeply embedded memory from her childhood, took her back to a time when her mother and father were alive. Up to the age of four, the sound came to her as a comforting lullaby, helping her drift gently into a world of carefree dreams; then, on her fifth birthday, her father said she was now old enough to be trusted with matches, so could light the lamp as required. It was quite scary, sleeping in the dark, but she got used to it.

Then her mind leaped forwards, to remember she was now a grown-up, sleeping in the spare room of a mountain rescue cottage. The gas lamp had only been left on in case she needed to do any personal things in the night. This, presumably, being Jim's ultra-polite way of referring to using his facilities.

Realising Jim had correctly anticipated her needs, she wriggled out of the mountain rescue sleeping bag, then swung her legs down, to stand on the slate floor on which her single bed was resting. For a moment she looked down at Jim's shirt, falling to her knees, like an old-fashioned nightdress. How could he not own any pyjamas? Getting out of bed naked must be…

Thankfully, before the image could progress to anything dangerous, her mind transferred to a much safer memory, that of her father rowing across the loch, with a gas cylinder on the back seat of the boat. On reaching the jetty, he would swing it up with one arm, then carry it up the hill, as if it weighed nothing at all, whereas herself, aged four, could not even lift it off the ground!

Ever since these early years, she had considered electricity to be something of a bother. Gas lamps and log fires were much more friendly, and with a man like her father around to carry the heavy bottles, quite unnecessary in a domestic setting.

In a mood of quiet contentment, she used the gaslight to put on her boots, then made her way to the back door, where an oil lamp was hanging from a nail hammered into the frame. After lighting it, she stepped outside, then made her way along a path to the outbuilding, where a chemical toilet was housed. Here, she was rather impressed by Jim's hygiene regime, the walls being whitewashed and spotlessly clean. Even more impressive was the washing-up bowl on the shelf, which had both soap and a nail brush. Sadly no towel, the custom being to dry hands on your shirt, thereby not sharing anybody else's germs.

After her night-time visit to the outdoors, she returned to her sleeping bag and, once more at peace with her environment, fell fast asleep.

The next time she woke up, the sun was streaming

through the window. This caused a new set of emotions – those of knowing her life no longer bore any resemblance to what had gone before, not because she had spent the night in a strange bed, but because of the small boy sleeping on an airbed against the far wall. By default, she had become his guardian; no, more than that, for all practical purposes, she had become his mother!

Nork awoke to a softly spoken voice calling his name. He rolled over within the sleeping bag, and fell off the airbed with a thump. This made Stephanie, who was watching over him, laugh. She then handed him a mug of steaming liquid.

"Fresh-ground coffee," she said, "with plenty of frothy milk, well liked by all young men looking forward to another exciting day!"

Nork looked up at the smiling face, surrounded by a protective curtain of hair, that split the sunlight coming through a window into a million rainbows. He threw his hands across his mouth; he must not say 'mummy' because the last time he had used the word, it had made the woman ignore him.

"Coffee's on the bedside locker," said Stephanie. "I'm just making breakfast, so I'll let you get up in peace."

Then his new mother was gone, drifting gracefully away into the sunlight. He sat up and gazed about the room with whitewashed walls. After giving a nod of approval, he stood up, and quickly dressed. Then, walking into the main room, he saw a great hairy dog, resting inside a wicker basket. After looking up, the animal gave a long yawn.

"Is your name Sherpa?" asked Nork.

"Woof," said the dog.

"And my name is Nork," he said, "spelled without the 'e."

Sherpa stood up to have a good stretch. "Woof," he said, before trotting out of the open back door.

Nork followed, to find himself standing on a slate path, with rugged vegetation on both sides. Then, looking up, he saw a great display of mountains, their summits covered in snow. He had given up trying to divide what was sissy from what was not, but he still tried to avoid thinking about the word 'beautiful', if he remembered. What really mattered in a situation like this was going back to collect his bowl of porridge, then taking it into the wilderness to have a nice thoughtful breakfast.

Stephanie looked through the kitchen window to see Nork wandering into the wilderness. How like herself at that age, when she was free to wander, and get into all sorts of scrapes. Remembering her early-teenage years, she smiled. Soon, she too would be free to roam again, possibly teaching Nork to climb harder rock, or row a seagoing boat, beneath towering coastal cliffs.

Her thoughts of approaching freedom were then broken by the sound of Jim, shuffling about his room, presumably without pyjamas. To distract herself from such thoughts, she set about making him an egg sandwich, which she presented to him as soon as he walked into the main room.

"Sorry," she said, "I gave your porridge to Nork."

To distract him further from the theft, she handed him a mug of coffee. He seemed surprised by this, but not annoyed.

Jim, after forcing his gaze from the most wonderful woman in the whole world, looked out of the window, to see Nork wandering into the mountains.

"He's off again," he said, "on his own!"

"So?" said Stephanie.

"Well, we really need parental consent for what we are doing."

"No we don't," interrupted Stephanie.

"Oh, nothing complicated, I'll just call in to see his sister at the hotel. If she gives me their parents' telephone number, I'll ring them to ask for some sort of letter."

Stephanie was immediately on full alert. If the authorities got the slightest hint of the true situation, Nork would be sent to live in an orphanage. Of course, he would run away, but to where? And the people he came across next time might do all sorts of horrible things to him. Finally, she realised Jim's obsession for form-filling meant he could play no long-term role in her life. But for now, she just needed something really dramatic to stop him clumping in with his size-12 boots…

"Jane's not his sister," she said, "but his mother, who does not want people to know she got pregnant at the age of thirteen. I expect it happened when she was staying in a wigwam, at some pop festival or other. And, last night, she went out on McTavish's yacht, presumably to earn some money in return for sex. Can you now just accept that Jane needs to be in a home for prostitutes, while Nork needs to be with us?"

Using the word 'us' made her flinch. To put some distance between them, she added, "If you ever do anything to confuse this, I will hate you for the rest of my life."

She could not say why all the colour drained from Jim's face, only that it did.

"We need help," he gasped.

"No we don't," responded Stephanie firmly. "Today is just about having fun. You must accept that whatever happens is a woman's thing. Agreed."

Jim never talked about 'woman things', so responded with a nod.

"Good. Then eat your egg sandwich before it gets cold."

Nork returned from the wilderness to walk around the cottage and measure the outside with his feet. After many attempts, he decided it was sixty-two shoes by fifty-three shoes. By taking off a shoe, and using it to measure a window opening, he knew the walls to be five shoes thick. When everything was quiet, he would measure the inside and, by this simple device, make sure there were no spy passages. Such logical thoughts were then distracted by Jim walking out of the front door.

Nork hurriedly returned the shoe to his foot, then hobbled across, until his foot fell properly inside.

"I like the way your cottage is built," he said to disguise his guilt. "The way the stones are just put on top of each other is very clever. Did you build it yourself?"

"Ooh no," said Jim, thinking of wigwams. "This cottage is very old, some say 1600s."

Nork thought 1600 seemed unnecessarily old. He was certain people did not start living in buildings until – he knew so little of history – there were dinosaurs, and people living in caves...then now.

"What else happened in 1600?" he asked, so as to imagine it better.

"Don't know if it was that date exactly. In those days people just saw a bit of land they liked, and rummaged about for the stuff to build a house on it. Most people seem to think this cottage was built by a mine worker. Would you like me to buy you a book on local history?"

"Yes please. Do these mines go underneath all the mountains?"

"Long way, certainly."

"Under here?"

"Don't know, they haven't been worked for over a hundred years. Doubt if anybody really knows where they go."

"Do you think they go underneath the prison?"

"If you mean the hotel, then yes, more that sort of area. The whole settlement was founded on a rich seam of copper. The hotel used to be where the mine owner lived."

Tears began to well up in Nork's eyes. The child prison was simply built above an old mine tunnel. The man in the passage was merely a prison guard, not a ghost who could see through doors. Nork looked up to realise Jim was watching him curiously.

"Lot of questions," said Jim. "Any particular reason? You have clearly been a little way into the mines."

"Did you?" asked Nork, without committing himself.

"Of course, it was a lot easier then, before they put the bars across. When I was little, you could walk all the way to a great big chasm, at least the size of a cathedral."

Nork decided not to respond; it might be a trick question. Squeezing through the bars was probably illegal. Fortunately, Jim then looked at his watch, and mumbled something about being late for work. After hurrying to the Land Rover, he jumped inside, and headed down the track, until it was out of sight.

When Nork turned around, he discovered Stephanie watching him from the doorway. He thought she looked upset, so went across to tell her everything was wonderful. Her troubled look changed to a deliberate smile.

"I need to speak to you as a proper grown-up," she said.

He gave her a proper grown-up sort of nod.

"Thing is," she said, "Jim is insisting that we get parental consent, if we are to go on living here."

He laughed. "You can give it to me yourself," he said.

"No, I mean from who looks after you, officially."

"You look after me," he replied. "If you want, I'll sign a piece of paper to say so."

"Sadly the authorities need…Oh never mind about them, and perhaps if you continue working in the hotel, McTavish's council position will give you all the protection you need. This is your first option."

"Suppose," he said.

"Thing is…well, I need to get away from this madhouse… from the whole town, to start again…"

"No!" he cried.

"So, that leaves option two – that you come with me!"

"Yes, yes please!"

"But if you do, there's no going back. We will have to start again in some isolated village, probably on some remote Scottish island. I don't expect the locals will ask any questions. If they do, I shall tell them you are my nephew, who came up from England, after your parents went away."

"Nephew?" said Nork.

"Yes, that makes me your aunty, most definitely not your mother. Your accent marks you out as coming from a different country to me."

"Suppose," said Nork quietly, which sounded less serious than saying it loudly.

"And you are sure this is what you want?"

"Yes, Aunty," he said.

"But not yet," said Stephanie, "first we must plan our escape, which means it must remain very secret from everybody."

"Jim?"

"Absolutely from Jim, he would want to do it using forms… that do not exist. Anyway, the first part of the plan involves getting my Post Office savings book from my room at the hotel. All my pocket money, plus a few tips, have gone into this for the past five years, less what it cost me to buy a proper pair of boots and an anorak. I reckon there's enough money to keep us both alive for six months, while we get ourselves sorted."

"I can work," said Nork.

"As soon as we're sorted, young man, you'll be going to the local village school. That's part of the deal. I can earn enough money to keep us both alive until you are old enough to get a part-time job, maybe when you are thirteen. But more important than money is that what we have just agreed remains absolutely top secret from everybody else in the whole world."

Nork made a zipping motion across his mouth.

Stephanie nodded, and tried to put thoughts of going to prison for child-napping to the back of her mind.

*

Sara did a perfect docking in the main harbour, the bows rising up on something beneath the surface, grinding to a halt with a few feet to spare. The front bit of the yacht was at least two feet higher than it had been before, and the whole thing sat lopsided. It seemed quite secure, but she still threw a rope to the harbour wall before jumping across herself. She then wrapped the rope over a post, in case the tide came in. McTavish needed to see this, and think of her; the boat disappearing would have quite the wrong effect.

Calmly, she walked towards the hotel, thinking about how pleased Nork would be to hear they were leaving to start a new life, a long way from here. On reaching the lobby, she looked at the clock behind the reception desk. She reckoned McTavish's arrival was at least an hour away, but she still needed to move quickly. Meeting him in the corridor would probably result in her getting a punch on the nose.

On reaching the staff quarters, Sara entered her room to wake Nork, once more to go on the run. To do so on her own, from this remote location, was unthinkable. On seeing his empty bed, she turned to her own, to see two letters. She coped with '*Dear Mother*', but what followed about no longer being wanted left her full of remorse.

"Yes I am an awful mother," she sobbed.

Stephanie's note only increased the pain. Then, the '*Dear Mother*' in Nork's letter connected with something McTavish had said, while on the yacht. It had not fitted comfortably at the time but, given the circumstances, she had not pursued the issue.

"You have been at my hotel for eight weeks," he had said.

It was not possible that so much time had rushed by in the whirlwind of her life. Indeed, eight weeks was probably his rent calculation, but it could have been six. In truth, she had no idea how long she had been at the hotel, but it was simply too long not to have had a monthly period.

"I am an awful mother," she wailed again, this time appreciating the increased significance – of probably being pregnant.

She tore up the letters, hoping that the word 'mother' would go away, but it made no difference. Crazy insane, she fled up the steps, knowing only that McTavish was bearing down on her. What had seemed quite reasonable, when he was in the water, and vulnerable, now seemed highly dangerous. To meet him in the passage…on her own…without Nork – unthinkable. On reaching the lobby, she swerved into the Nork exit, then ran. Where did not matter, so long as it was away from the hotel.

TEN

10.45am:

Melanie thought she noticed a flash of blue scurrying across the hotel foyer. Looking up from her reception counter, she saw a set of overalls jumping up the stairs, three at a time. The name *M.V. McPherson* was glued to the back in white plastic letters.

Partly from a sense of duty but, more truthfully, curiosity, Melanie left her desk to see which employee of the car ferry was so eager to please one of the guests. The overalls tended to suggest he was somebody who worked on the vehicle deck – most probably McGregor, a man most famous for his brief encounter with the postmistress a year before. Melanie thought his most probable conquest was Mrs Pringle in room number 18. She looked the type but sadly, as a two-day visitor, she would provide little opportunity for any interesting gossip.

Having failed to identify the occupant of the fast-moving overalls, Melanie returned to the reception desk. From there she could see the stairs, so it was only a matter of time before her curiosity was satisfied.

10.55am:

Looking away from the stairs, Melanie saw Richard White from *The Daily Herald* walking towards her desk. As a regular visitor to the hotel, she knew him well enough to ignore the normal formal politeness, instead greeting him with a friendly smile.

"I wonder if you could throw any light on this?" he responded, placing a photograph on her desk.

Melanie looked at the photograph, without comprehension.

"Why am I looking at a picture of Mr McTavish," she asked, "…doing whatever he is doing?"

"Sitting naked in a rowing boat," responded Richard, "though I was rather hoping you could explain it to me."

He handed her some more photographs. The ones where he was climbing the ladder to the car ferry were so rude, she had to pretend not to look.

"I am lost for words," said Melanie, "though perhaps if I show them to the others, they might have some explanation."

"There were at least ten cameras onboard the ferry, they are hardly unique."

Mischievously, he gave her five prints, including two of the most explicit. Blushing intensely, Melanie slipped them into the top drawer of her desk.

Suddenly, McTavish came bursting across the foyer in a flash of blue. He growled at Richard, then lurched incoherently towards Melanie. She screamed, pushed her foot to the floor, and shot backwards on the wheeled chair. Pretending not to look at a photograph of a naked man was one thing, having his red face raging in your direction was another. The next moment he was by her side, pulling open the drawer where the spare keys were kept.

Melanie looked for an escape route, which was offered by Richard, who began taking photographs. McTavish raced towards him, then swung a fist that sent Richard sprawling across the floor. A lady guest, who had just walked down the stairs, screamed. McTavish imagined swinging a kick at the stupid cow, but confined his actions to a snort. The lady screamed again, then raced back towards the stairs. Having recovered his key, McTavish headed in the same direction. In desperation, the woman tried to defend herself with a fire extinguisher, but only succeeded in sending a great gush of foam towards the ceiling. McTavish ran through the spray, then onwards to the third floor, where he opened the door to his apartment.

On the ground floor, Melanie stopped shaking long enough to grab her coat and flee. Richard sat up, quite pleased to be involved in a story that was sufficiently important to include a journalist getting hit. Finally, he could run into the print room shouting "Hold the front page!", something he had always wanted to do, since leaving college three years before.

12.50pm:

Somebody who worked on the car ferry told his brother about the rescue, who told a barmaid, who mentioned it to Mrs Smith. This gossip chain of three was perfectly adequate to develop the story to the extent that it now included a full account of how McTavish had been seen worshipping his manhood as he sat naked in his rowing boat. In consideration of this, Mrs Smith, with two trusted friends, walked into the hotel to take tea, and generally nose around. On reception the telephone rang, but there was nobody on duty to answer it. After walking to the dining room, they were surprised to discover the cleaner had given up shampooing the carpet halfway through, and was now serving tea.

"Surreal ambiance," said Mrs Smith, while gazing at the teabag floating around her cup.

"Isn't that to do with three-legged penguins?" asked her friend.

Mrs Smith had seen a surrealist painting once. "No," she said, "this looks more like an elephant on stilts...that's about to fall over with an almighty crash!"

Eventually, her friend used the sugar tongs to remove the teabag and, after a few discreet sips, left to enquire after McTavish's health.

1.40pm:

Standing in the secret passageway, McTavish gazed into the staff room, to see four staff gathered around the first edition of *The Herald*. They were making the sort of speculations never before heard in the hotel. He wanted to bang the mirror with rage, but forced himself to remain silent.

Unable to bear it any longer, he closed the safety panel, then turned on his torch. Shining it along the corridor, he began to think the unthinkable – he needed a secret way of getting out of the hotel...possibly in a hurry.

The door at the far end of the corridor had been redundant for many years, the only authenticated use being in the late 1790s when his many-times great-grandfather had used it to escape some rebellion or other. There were lesser reports of smuggling to the loch, and one possible account of a dead body being taken along it, with a meat cleaver lodged in its head, but nothing was ever proved.

Feeling most vulnerable by his possible place in history, McTavish shuffled silently to the heavy door, just to reassure himself that, if people came calling in the middle of the night, he could flee without using a known exit, and thereby reach his yacht.

On reaching the door, he realised he was mistaken about there being a key hanging from the frame. In a moment of self-doubt, he thought it might all be a myth – nothing more than the ramblings of his grandfather, in the senility of his life. After trying the door to make sure it was safely locked, he returned to his private rooms, where his grandfather's box of ancient keys was kept. He would sort them out later; just at the moment, it seemed more important to find a bottle of whisky.

2.05pm:

Dressed self-consciously in his best suit, McTavish emerged from his apartment, quite convinced everybody would see right through his clothes to imagine his naked body. To defend himself by saying that manhood virtually vanishes in extreme cold, would make him sound ridiculous. Where the 'playing with himself' story had come from, he had no idea; he had merely been trying to hide the extreme shrinkage! He was certain the idiot from the car ferry could have found some overalls, before making him climb the ladder.

On reaching the kitchen, McTavish found Cook and a rather nervous assistant emptying cans of soup into a big cauldron. On the preparation table were many boxed ready meals from the village shop.

"Hello," he said, as politely as he could.

The nervous assistant turned away to stare at the wall. Cook looked at him, long and hard, to undress him with her eyes, then she shrugged her shoulders and sniffed.

"Most things are off," she said, "ignore the menu."

There was no longer any respect in her voice. There was simply a job to be done, and a wage packet to be collected at the end of the week.

McTavish looked about his once-busy kitchen. Two hours before dinner, he would have expected to find the chef, Cook, two assistants, and possibly a washer-upper. He wanted to shout out his rage, but knew that he couldn't.

"Just the two of you?" he said, trying to make it sound as if it were just another day.

"All the guests are gone," said Cook. "Heaven knows what's going to happen with the non-residents. There could be a crowd, or no one. We have enough dinners for thirty-six, if they're not too fussy. The two of us should cope with that."

McTavish was outraged by her insolence. "Get some more staff!" he snapped.

Cook squared her shoulders, and for the first time looked him straight in the eyes.

"I've got a boss who sits in a rowing boat playing with himself," she said calmly. "You get some more staff."

The nervous assistant gasped, then giggled. McTavish hovered, as he tried to come to terms with the new reality of his life. Clearly, shouting did not work, and he had left it too late to defend himself from the slander with some more creative explanation, regarding the shrinkage of his manhood. The only good thing about today was that the crazy girl and Nork had abandoned their room, so tomorrow he could begin some sort of comeback. He looked down at his feet.

"There are only two types of people in this world," he said, "those who leave, and those who get promoted."

"I'm good at home-cooking," replied Cook, "can't get the hang of all that fancy stuff the chef did. If you want foreign, I'm not the one you want to promote. How about sending Janet here to college?"

"Fine," said McTavish.

"Then we have a deal. Tell the accounts clerk that I'm acting chief cook for proper food, at £4.50 an hour."

"How much?" gasped McTavish.

"£4.50 an hour. I want to retire when Janet's trained."

She walked to the door. "Follow," she said. "I want to hear you tell the wages clerk, and about Janet going up to my old rate of £2.50 an hour. For that, if you vanish for any reason, we'll keep the kitchen running while you're away."

"£2.50," gasped McTavish, "that's £100 per week!"

"Very generous," replied Cook. "Hear that, Janet, you're being paid for your day at college."

Cook turned to look at McTavish. "Tell the wages clerk now," she said, "or you can work out how to make microwave ready meals for yourself."

Janet redirected her gaze into the soup, dreaming about all the things she could do with £100 a week. Tomorrow, she would buy Cook some of her favourite biscuits, to say thank you.

3.05pm:

McTavish only had a limited understanding of how the telephone switchboard worked, but all the temporary staff agencies were asking for a 50% premium, on the understanding he would accept whoever turned up. However, the hotel would only run at a marginal loss, until he could begin his comeback at the start of next season. Then, looking up from all the confusing switches, he saw men in suits approaching, all carrying a newspaper with the headline, 'Councillor McTavish Found Naked in Rowing Boat'. They dropped a copy on the reception desk.

"I take it you resign?" said the leader of the council.

McTavish could see no point in arguing. "Yes," he mumbled.

"Your application to develop a golf course behind Greenlands has accidentally fallen into the bin," said the council leader. "Do I make myself clear?"

McTavish nodded and, when he looked up, the men in suits had gone, but only to be replaced by men in uniform.

"Fire inspection," said the guy, who McTavish recognised to be the chief.

"Used fire extinguisher," said a voice in the background.

"Noted," said the chief. "Twenty-four hours to rectify, though if we find any of the others to be faulty, you do realise we have the power to suspend your operation?"

"Thank you," said McTavish, "I will sort it immediately."

The fire chief smiled sympathetically.

"Don't look so worried," he said, "it's got to be really severe for closure. Today we are just reviewing the premises. I see in 1968 you were going to investigate the addition of another stairway, and a guest evacuation plan."

"This is not routine," snapped McTavish.

"Ah, but now you are famous, it's most important that all our records are up to date. So, perhaps you would like to show us the new escape route, as we need to check the handrails and stuff."

An hour later, the fire crew returned to their truck. After all the doors were closed, the chief turned to Jim.

"It might have been a favour," he said, "but really it's me who should be thanking you. It's quite astonishing we accepted the original hotel application, with only one internal staircase."

"So, the two weeks to comply?" asked Jim.

"Nothing to do with favours," replied the chief, "we'd have been for the high jump if ever there was a fire. Even if he gets an outside escape built, I think we will still have to insist on another, to the back bedrooms. The things people got away with in the 1940s…lethal."

Jim gave a serious nod, but truthfully his mind was now focused entirely on Stephanie, and the evening they would spend together, both safe and warm in his friendly cottage.

ELEVEN

After washing up the tea things, Nork settled himself into an armchair, to read the books on local history that Jim had brought back from work. Soon he knew all about the mining operations of long ago, allowing him to understand his underground adventure without using any ghost theories whatsoever. They were simply holes in the ground – interesting, and, with a good supply of head torches, entirely safe.

Nork's other reason for keeping his head buried in a book was to show Stephanie how well he would attend to his studies after he started school. Also, by sitting quietly, he could secretly keep one ear directed towards the grown-up conversation between Jim and Stephanie as they sat either side of a wide table. Most of the things they talked about were not very interesting, but when the hotel was mentioned, Nork flapped his other ear.

"I can't believe," said Jim, "that they built such a large house with only one staircase."

"The domestic staff using the same stairway as the owners

must have been a bit awkward," said Stephanie. "An elderly confused uncle, coming out of a bedroom in his nightshirt, to meet a scullery maid going down to light the fire, did not fit well with the social conventions of the time."

To Nork the hotel no longer held any terrors. The spies were nothing more than a strange part of his growing up, which had now become history.

"They didn't," he mumbled, without looking up from his book.

"Didn't what?" asked Jim.

"Build the hotel with only one stairway," replied Nork.

Stephanie shook her head. "I've been pretty much everywhere," she said, "I think I would have come across another by now."

"Not the chimneys," said Nork, while still half concentrating on his book.

"That's true," said Stephanie, "but…" She looked at Jim. "You must know about chimneys," she said.

"Go straight to the chimney pots," responded Jim.

Nork had already discovered this, which was another good reason to cease his chimney exploring; it was just incredibly boring. However, the one in the 'Monopoly cupboard' was clearly a special, non-soot, sort of chimney, though all the ropes and things crashing about made it very complicated to explain. Besides, he had broken it, and did not want to get a reputation for such things. He decided to jump that bit.

"I should imagine they go to the bedrooms you were talking about," he said.

From the corner of one eye, Nork could see them watching him.

"Seems pretty certain," said Jim.

"I should know," replied Nork, "I've seen them."

He thought this quite a clever thing to say, because if he only saw them, it did not implicate him in the chimney demolition. Then he thought about the possibility of going back into the mines to show Stephanie what he had discovered. If he did not tell her about how terrified he had been on his previous visit, she would be really impressed, so like him even more.

"I'll show you if you want," he said.

"I'm never setting foot in that hotel again!" said Stephanie.

"Don't have to," he responded, "you can reach it through the mines."

He flipped through his book, then ran a finger down a page to find the word he wanted.

"Ventilation shaft," he said. "There's ladders and stuff that bring you up into the spy tunnel."

Stephanie gave a short laugh. "For a moment," she said, "I thought you were serious."

Nork looked up from his book, annoyed that she did not believe him.

"It's logical," said Jim. "There were all sorts of reasons for rich people to leave quickly, before Unification. If there was an old ventilation shaft, why not build a house on top of it?"

"But a spy tunnel?" said Stephanie.

"You know about the spies," said Nork, "you told me all about them."

"Yes, but they don't have their own special tunnel."

"How else are they going to watch us?"

Deciding Stephanie was a lost cause, Nork turned his attention to Jim.

"What's Unification?" he asked.

"When the house was built, England and Scotland were entirely separate countries," answered Jim, "mostly at war. Dundee had just been flattened by the English Navy, who took away all the treasure in great ships. I imagine escape tunnels were pretty much on the mind of anybody who had something worth stealing."

"Wow," said Nork as he imagined the two countries coming together for the first time. As the land masses crashed into each other, there would have been volcanoes hissing steam as the seabed rose up to build the mountains, over which they had later built the railways, along which he had recently travelled. "Wow," he said again.

Stephanie, who clearly understood none of this, interrupted his thoughts.

"If there is such a thing as a spy tunnel," she said, "how do the spies get into it?"

Nork put his head into his hands and gave an exasperated sigh. "Down the staircase of course," he said.

"Then what?"

"They watch us, it's what spies do, watch people."

"How?"

"All the mirrors are special. If you stand the other side, it's just glass. I don't understand that bit, but I know it hurts your nose when you walk into them."

Stephanie shook her head in mild amusement but, at the same time, felt goose bumps starting to form, due to Nork's ability to tell creative stories. And, the hotel did seem particularly well endowed with mirrors.

Jim looked more serious. "With regards to the stairs," he said, "we should be asking where, not if."

"Difficult to tell," said Nork. "Around the back and up the

middle, I guess. I only went as far as the second floor, but they carry on up. At the bottom, they come out behind the staff quarters."

"Then what?" asked Jim.

"At the end of the spy tunnel there's a big door into what looks like a cupboard, but secretly, it leads down to the mine."

Jim nodded, as if to say, 'Nork you are really grown up, and know all about exploring things'.

"As a matter of interest," asked Jim, "how do you know about two-way mirrors? I mean, what you were just talking about – a book, perhaps?"

Nork shook his head. "I only know that if I look from one side, I see myself. From the other, I don't know they're there, until I bump my nose."

"And people look through these?"

"I did not mean to."

"But others?"

"Of course, when the spy came down the stairs, I locked myself in the cupboard. I could watch through the keyhole – spying on spies, ha!"

Nork suddenly realised he had their full attention, which he liked. He put down his book and looked at them with an imaginary television around his head. He wondered what sort of things people in the television said; indeed, could they actually see out, or was it all connected to the funny mirrors where you could only watch one way? Perhaps the spies were simply people who did not have televisions to look at.

"In the old days," he said, "people used to light fires in ventilation shafts, to pull clean air through."

He thought this was the sort of thing people in televisions were expected to say.

"I think," he continued, "that was before they built the house on top." Stephanie was looking at him, and seemed a little pale.

"There's a big mirror fixed to the wall in my room," she said. "Please say you can't see through that."

"Not certain," replied Nork, "all the mirrors have panels behind them, and I never opened yours. You can see into our room though. It looks funny, watching from a wall's point of view."

"McTavish!" gasped Stephanie.

"Don't know," said Nork, "I never went upstairs, though I don't think anybody would want to spy on him. He's much too old to be running from anywhere…or whatever happens."

"I feel sick," said Stephanie.

Nork watched Stephanie run out of the room, followed by Jim. Nork did not like making people run away. When they came back, he would talk about something else.

Stephanie returned first. "There's a really big mirror in the bathroom," she said.

Nork nodded. "I bumped my nose on it," he said, "when I tried to walk through it."

As yet, nobody had expressed any sympathy for his nose, so he would keep on talking about it until they did. Sadly, Stephanie's only response was to sit down, staring at her feet. Then Jim came back.

"Can you draw me a map?" he asked.

Nork thought going down the mine with a fireman was not at all scary.

"I can show you," he said.

"Parental consent?" said Jim.

Stephanie looked up. "Forms, rules and regulations," she

snapped. "Can't you ever think about anything else, even at a time like this?"

"If Stephanie comes too," said Nork, "it would be legal, because she can give us consent as we walk along."

"She can't," said Jim.

"And why not?" demanded Stephanie. "Because I am a girl, I suppose."

She stood up, and stomped into the mountain rescue room, returning wearing overalls, several sizes too big.

"Me and Nork are going," she said, "so if you want to fill in any forms, he's with me." Then she put her hands on her hips. "Or do we go on our own?" she asked. "Your choice!"

Nork could not believe there was so much happiness in the world, and all of it seemed to be landing on his head. *Stephanie was with him.* She now had the power to give parental consent. Then he thought about the practical details.

"I only just fit through the entrance bars," he said. "We will have to use something to push them apart for a grown-up to get through."

Stephanie turned towards Jim. "We need a car jack," she said. "Can we borrow yours, or are you expecting us to walk all that way with a sledgehammer?"

Jim retreated from the argument by agreeing to everything Stephanie asked. Thus, half an hour later, Jim's Land Rover pulled up by the railway line that came down from the quarry. Nork was particularly excited to be wearing a helmet, with a lamp that could be focused on different beams, just like the grown-ups. At the entrance of the mine, Jim seemed determined to take charge of things, first turning to address his followers, then explaining this was nothing to do with work, they were just a group of potholers on a night out.

Nork thought it rather an odd thing to say, because he was the only one who knew the way, so would obviously need to stay in front. He set off, with Stephanie staying close behind. After finishing his speech, Jim turned around to discover he was alone. Being over six feet tall, he bent at the waist to look inside the tunnel. Deep within the mountain were two head torches. Jim walked into the tunnel until his helmet bounced along the roof with enough force to make him pause…not due to any pain, but because the bump had dislodged the beautiful memory of Stephanie struggling to gain sufficient height to kiss him on the jaw, on that wonderful evening when they had gone into the mountains together. She must only be a few inches over five feet tall, which, in this less romantic situation, gave her quite an advantage. Nork had an even greater advantage, allowing him to advance at a speed that kept the pressure on those who followed.

When Jim arrived at the bars, he discovered Nork had already wriggled through to the far side. Stephanie made her impatience known by tapping her fingers against the wall.

"Well, you have the jack," she said to Jim.

When, a little later, Nork led them into the big cavern, his followers took a moment to stand in wonder. While they talked about big cathedrals and stuff, Nork went to the end of the railway line, and lifted the stone slab, to recover the iron key. He then walked to the crack, down which he had descended two days earlier. Going up was always easier, especially as his little fingers knew the cracks into which they would fit. Indeed, he was halfway up, before he heard Jim cry out in alarm. But, he remembered Stephanie's rock climbing lesson of the week before, and knew the only thing that mattered was to stay focused, believing completely in his ability to reach the top. It worked, allowing him to sit on his ledge, and listen to Jim claiming that what he had just seen was impossible.

"If it is impossible," responded Stephanie, "how come we see a torch beam shining down, from halfway up the wall?"

More importantly, she knew that when she had taken Nork climbing, the hardest move he had managed was well within her abilities. Hence, she left Jim talking to himself, while she got involved in what proved to be quite an interesting climb. By the time she reached Nork, she had completely forgotten why they were here, this being the sort of stuff she had done many times, with her father. With the wild abandon of a teenager, she reached out to give Nork an enormous hug.

"Thank you," she said, "that was great fun!"

"It's where I have been coming to play," replied Nork modestly, just to emphasise how brave he was.

Jim stood alone at the bottom; it was impossible, no matter what Stephanie had said. Any fireman would use a ladder to ascend such a thing. Then he realised the only impossible thing was leaving the woman he loved in so much danger. He put a hand against the rock, but his bigger fingers only slipped off.

I love Stephanie, he thought. *Nothing else in the world matters.* It was thus he eventually arrived at the ledge, in a state of complete terror; but, as a fireman, he knew this was not an emotion he could talk about. Instead, he looked around to realise he had reached a tiny shelf, without any way to progress. Nork had brought them up a wrong turning. Jim realised that he should have been more insistent about the map. Then he frowned. Where was Nork? He had vanished into thin air. When expressing the impossibility of this to

Stephanie, she seemed unconcerned, merely telling him that he had gone 'that way'. She then crawled to a waterfall a few feet to her left, lay on her back, and wriggled into the tiny tunnel, from which the stream appeared.

Jim remained in a state of shock; now he really was stuck, doubting his ability to climb back down, or to advance. When he finally found the strength to move, the situation got a lot worse, because looking to where Stephanie had gone, he realised that really was impossible.

How long he stared into space, he could not say. Then the truth of the situation came to him – he could not let the fire brigade rescue him, nor could he let the only woman he had ever loved crawl towards her early death, alone. They would die together; that was all he could do now! Slowly, he turned to lie on his back, then pushed himself onwards, with the water washing into his ears.

As soon as Stephanie had enough headroom to turn around, while keeping her mouth above the water, she crawled quickly after Nork, to the first place she could rise to all fours.

"That was amazing," she gasped. "Certainly a grade two pothole, and absolutely the best fun I've had since the age of thirteen!"

She had now completely forgotten about McTavish, and only reluctantly turned her thoughts towards Jim.

"How slow is it possible to be?" she asked.

That question took about half an hour to answer, the time it took Jim to crawl into view.

"Lead on," said Stephanie to Nork, "let the fun continue!"

A little further up the tunnel, Stephanie found herself splashing her way through a quite ordinary river, as if she was thirteen again. On coming to a rusty iron-rung ladder, she followed Nork up to enter a quite ordinary cupboard. Nork put a key into the lock, and turned it.

Having the right key, thought Stephanie, *that's very organised for an eleven-year-old boy.*

Then he opened the door, and her thoughts immediately became overwhelmed by the rapid transition from potholing, to finding herself looking along an ordinary domestic corridor.

"Stairs," said Nork, pointing to the far end, "like I told you."

Stephanie followed Nork into the corridor, until he stopped, and opened one of the hatches.

In the next instant, Stephanie found herself, yet again, in a completely different world – one in which she was looking at Mark, the waiter, sitting on the toilet.

Then Jim staggered up behind her. A moment later, he also found himself in a different world – one in which he knew what it was to truly hate…McTavish had seen his Stephanie sitting on the toilet! With uncontrolled rage, he sent his steel-toe-capped boot crashing into the plywood beneath the glass mirror so aggressively, that it became an explosion of splinters, smashing to the toilet floor, in a shower of tiny pieces.

None of Mark's previous life experiences had prepared him for the correct procedure to follow when his toilet activities were interrupted by a man crashing through a wall. Confused, he leaped up with a scream, trousers still around his ankles. Before he could think about what to do next, the man had sprung across the floor, and pulled the door with such force, that its feeble bolt flew across the room. Mark responded with a dazed blink, which was all the time it took for the man to disappear into the passage.

Before Mark's heart rate had stabilised, he saw Stephanie walking into the room, sideways, like a crab, so as to present him with her back.

"I promise I'm not looking," she said as she too walked into the passage.

Nork was not yet old enough to understand why grown-ups thought going to the toilet was embarrassing.

"Hello," he said, unabashed, to Mark.

He then went into the passage, and followed Stephanie into the staff room, where he set about making the coffee.

Mark decided that pulling up his trousers, without first using toilet paper, was too disgusting to even think about. However, he had only just started this essential hygiene routine, when Stephanie returned with Cook. She was no longer looking sidewise, instead grabbing spectator number four's arm, to pull her across the room. Then they both disappeared into the hole, where not two minutes before, a mirror had been. At that, Mark gave in and, after pulling up his trousers, went to follow the ladies.

Nork made the coffee, his brow furrowed to show Stephanie how serious he always took grown-up activities. If she was watching him through the mirror, it would be like he was inside a television.

After a few minutes, Jim came back down the stairs to tell Stephanie he had sorted everything, but on reaching the staff room, he only found Nork stirring three mugs of coffee.

"It's OK," said Jim, "I've telephoned the police. They'll be here in fifteen minutes. You did really well!"

Jim then returned to the bathroom, the only thought on

his mind being that of using his fists to batter McTavish's face to a pulp. Here he waited until his aggressive desires had reduced to a manageable fantasy. He then advanced to the passageway, and walked to stand beside the woman he loved.

"It's OK," he said, "I have telephoned the police. They will be here in fifteen…no, I guess ten minutes now."

"You've done what?" screamed Stephanie.

"The police. I expect McTavish will be waking up in a prison cell tomorrow."

Stephanie's father had only ever taught her how to be kind and gentle. Hate was not an emotion she had ever learned, but Jim was pushing her to the absolute boundary. How could any man be so evil as to get a whole police force chasing one small boy?

"You…you!" she breathed, partly to register her disbelief about what he had just told her.

Jim realised Stephanie was lost for words, except for repeating 'you'. He understood that now was the time to take her in his arms, and tell her everything would be OK.

"Me…me," he responded, his voice little more than a whisper. "You are safe now," he added.

He went to take her in his strong arms, but they only closed around thin air, and when he looked around, Stephanie was nowhere to be seen.

Stephanie raced to her old room, where she grabbed her document case from the bedside locker, then pulled the blankets from her bed, shoving them into an empty pillowcase. She then raced up the stairs to the foyer, where she discovered the reception desk to be abandoned. Then came a great cacophony of police sirens, getting louder, suggesting they were all heading in her direction.

Jim must have waited before confessing what he had done, presumably so the police would have time to capture Nork, and drag him away to an orphanage. Well, she would show him!

Swerving from the main exit, she followed the 'Nork route', to reach the outside of the building undetected. Here she stood, lost to the dark night, trying to think rationally about what Nork would do.

He would know that any running away overland could be followed by Sherpa. He would have to break the scent, which meant crossing the loch. She could only hope that he had the good sense to take her wide-beam boat, which was almost impossible to capsize.

In the few seconds it took her to consider this, the front of the hotel became a chaos of screeching tyres and blue flashing lights. This was followed by the sound of many boots tramping across the pavement, making her think they might be racing to see who could get to McTavish first.

No, McTavish was only his historical name. He was now universally known as 'the pervert', who liked to sit naked in a rowing boat, while playing with himself. Whichever constable clipped the handcuffs on him first was certain to get his picture on the front page of *The Herald*.

After the hotel frontage had gone quiet, Stephanie emerged from the darkness to walk innocently along a well-lit pavement. Only when a hundred yards down the high street, did she risk drawing attention to herself, by breaking into a trot. Soon, she stepped into a shadow provided by an abandoned harbour warehouse, it being most important not to alarm Nork by making a sudden appearance. For, however stable her boat might be, it would not stop him falling over the side if he jumped up in a panic.

Gazing from the darkness, she saw the loch's rippling surface glistening beneath a starlit sky. A little way out, she could make out the splash of an oar, tending to suggest the other had already been lost. This was confirmed after her eyes became accustomed to the dark, for she could see a boat going around in various disorganised circles.

Stephanie found her mind travelling back to a time when, aged about five, she had struggled with the same boat. Her father had come across the unexpected incident, and immediately swum across to take grown-up control of the situation. On reaching the side of the boat, he had shown no anger towards her experiment of taking the family transport without telling him. Just love. She could still remember his face now as he looked up from the water, smiling, without a cross word being uttered.

And now, as Stephanie stood on the harbour, she understood the world as her father saw it. The hate that Jim had sent her way had passed her by, without making any serious contact. All that mattered now was the need to protect a child, in this case Nork, all alone, in a big rowing boat, possessing only one oar.

Stephanie knew the shale bank guarding the seaward entrance to the harbour meant Nork was still in relatively shallow water, larger vessels being forced to moor against the old commercial dock. Walking quietly, she made her way along a projecting harbour wall until level with the shallow water. Here, she dropped her pillowcase luggage on the timber planks, then sat on the edge, before easing herself over the side, which was of no concern since her clothes were already wet after their potholing expedition. As expected, the descent was very much like entering the shallow end of a typical swimming pool – a few cold tingles, followed by her feet touching the bottom at the same time as the water came up to her waist. However, unlike a swimming pool entry, she then collected her luggage, and began wading out with it held above her head. This only left the problem of how to announce her arrival without causing Nork to leap from the rowing boat, and make a swimming escape into the darkness.

By the time she was within thirty feet of the rowing boat, the water had risen towards her shoulders, but was this close enough to rescue Nork, if her announcement caused him to end up over the side?

"Hello," she said quietly, "it's me, Stephanie."

The darkness made it very difficult for her to see his response, other than a general leaping up and wobbling about while standing. In so doing, he let go of the second oar.

Stephanie repeated her name three times, then carried on wading towards him. After throwing her luggage into the boat, she gathered up the oar, then went off to find the other. Eventually, she returned with both and, after throwing these onboard, pulled herself up over the stern, allowing the bow to rise without any capsizing movement.

"Not quite the organised escape I expected," she said, casually, "but it will do!"

TWELVE

Jim's desire to punch McTavish on the nose was so great, he decided his only safe option was to remain in the basement until the temptation was taken away in handcuffs. Then, shortly after hearing the muffled sound of police sirens drifting down the steps, he looked up to see a sergeant standing in the doorway.

"My men are having a race to see who can clip the handcuffs on McTavish first," said the sergeant. "It's just a game we play sometimes, against those pompous individuals we do not like. But, if what you say is true, I prefer to use this…"

The sergeant tapped the side of his hat with his truncheon, then walked into the spy tunnel. Jim thought it odd that his hat had any use beyond telling criminals that he was too important to wear a normal helmet.

After the sergeant had been in the tunnel for a couple of minutes, he heard the sound of footsteps leaping down the stairs. After hitting stone slabs at the bottom, they stopped.

"Going somewhere?" asked the sergeant.

Jim walked away; the desire to punch McTavish on the nose had not yet abated. Then, thinking about how McTavish had watched his Stephanie taking a bath, he hoped the criminal would resist arrest, thereby giving the sergeant an excuse to use his truncheon.

After the sergeant had triumphantly marched his captive up the steps, Jim decided it was now safe for his Stephanie to emerge from her hiding place, so he could take her home to his cottage, where she would be safe…forever!

"You…you…" she had breathed, before getting all nervous, and running away to hide, so overwhelmed by her new emotions, that she did not know how else to react. How Nork fitted into the plan, he was not certain, but once he had thought of a better way of explaining the legal difficulties surrounding parental consent, he would take the boy across the mountains, as promised.

On reaching the reception area, Jim remembered his Land Rover was still at the quarry. There was no way he could expect Stephanie to walk all the way to his cottage after what she had just endured. He hurried upstairs to find a policeman, whom he hoped would give him a lift to collect his vehicle. This agreed, they both went about the building shouting to Stephanie that everything was safe now. After searching every room, Jim reached the only rational conclusion – that Stephanie had found the experience so traumatic, she had decided to walk home and get Nork safely tucked up in bed.

After being taken to his Land Rover, Jim drove quickly back to town, slowing down only when he reached the cart track. Soon he would see his exhausted house guests staggering up the track; but in the event, he merely found himself amazed that Stephanie and Nork had managed the five-mile walk to his cottage in maybe one hour. For this to be achieved, they must have fled the hotel in terror.

On reaching his cottage, he quietly opened the door, then walked across to light the gas lamp. Realising the door of the guest room was open, he went across to close it, until some basic instinct made him peep inside, just to say goodnight.

The bed was empty. Nork's airbed on the floor, unoccupied. Stephanie had clearly got confused, and headed to his room.

How long he stared into his deserted bedroom, he could not say. He only knew that by the time he had finished searching the cottage and garden, it was 2.15 in the morning. So where were they?

Panicking now, he could only think of two places that Stephanie might consider to be an overnight resting place. The hotel was one, but that had been eliminated. His cottage was the other. Then, he remembered some of the things Stephanie had told him over the past day or so. For reasons he could not understand, she had said that if the police were involved, Nork would find it necessary to run away. Yes, everything Stephanie had said fitted in with the conclusion that Nork had run, and she had gone after him, to try to save him.

Without wasting any more time, he called for Sherpa, then threw the mountain rescue rucksack across his back. Once outside, he walked a little way down the main track, where he gave Sherpa Nork's sleeping bag to smell. The dog walked around in circles for a little while, then stood still, in the doggy equivalent of shrugging his shoulders.

Jim knew this meant Nork had never walked up the main track to his cottage. For some reason, he had fled the hotel, then followed his dream of crossing the mountains. Stephanie would know this, and had given chase. Pleased by his logical thinking, he walked directly to the track that went into the base of the glen, and once again, gave Sherpa the sleeping bag to smell. This time there was no hesitation; he was off!

Of course, Jim knew they were not only following his new scent, but the weaker ones made on his first attempt to cross the mountains. However, that was not important, because if Nork deviated to a new trail, Sherpa was certain to stop, and say, 'woof'. Though in all probability, he would catch them before even arriving at the rescue shelter.

After about two miles, just short of the shelter, Sherpa stopped to give the air a good sniff. "Woof," he said.

"Well done," said Jim. "Find."

Not that Sherpa needed any new instructions; he was off, racing perhaps twenty yards from the path, where he looked down and said a much quieter 'woof', the sort that meant he had found a body.

Jim bowed his head in horror; Sherpa had followed a well-worn animal track, the sort city dwellers often mistook for a public footpath. Jim knew this one petered out beneath a steep gully. Mountain Rescue frequently attended to accident victims near the bottom. But this time, deep down, Jim knew he was responsible for the tragedy that he would soon witness.

*

Sara's brain knew only one thing: it was surrounded by a black void, a space without form or structure. Accepting this, her body made a decision to shut down the blood supply to its surface, its challenge now simply to keep the internal organs supplied with sufficient warmth to stay alive until the next heartbeat.

Somewhere within the black void, her brain became vaguely aware of a dog trying to attract attention to her pathetic existence. Then came a voice, asking if she was OK. There was no enthusiasm to respond; she did not want to die, nor did she want to live, both required too much effort. So, she kept her face pressed into the heather. Let the world do with her as it will; all her decisions had turned out to be bad, it was time for others to take over; they could not get it more wrong. A hand came to her cheek, then felt about her neck.

"Go away," she mumbled.

"That solves the problem of a pulse," said a controlled voice, "but you are very cold. Have you been shivering?"

Complicated questions were too difficult to answer, or at least she had no inclination to do so. The last thing she remembered was being lost, and feeling relieved when a twisted ankle had brought her face crashing into the heather so she did not have to walk any more. Now she thought about it, she might have shivered once, but nightmare and reality were too intertwined to tell them apart. Inside her head, a voice kept telling her she was a useless mother; less coherent were images of being pregnant. If she pretended to be unconscious, she would not need to answer any more questions.

Then she heard the voice talking about helicopters. At the same time, something happened to her big toe. With her last ounce of energy, she curled into a little ball, to make all the unpleasantness go away. Then her parents came to mind; she decided the only important thing left for her to do with her life was to not let them find out how it had ended.

"My name is Jane," she whispered in a faint voice. Then came the blackness for which she had so longed…

*

Having established the girl still had sensation in her toes, Jim removed the sleeping bag from his rucksack, and began to roll it up her legs.

"A party dress," he mumbled to himself as he lifted her shoulders, to get her fully inside. "And sandals," he added.

She was truly unconscious now, so there was no further need for him to be polite.

Knowing the helicopter was on its way, he saw no point in trying to warm the sleeping bag from the outside. This was a case for hospitalisation, so he looked around for a suitable landing site. After finding the nearest patch of level ground, he returned to the girl. Placing a hand on her face, he was unable to distinguish between the temperature of her skin and the cold night air. Her breathing was hardly noticeable; she would not have survived prolonged stretchering to non-specialist facilities. There could be no doubt that the helicopter was about to save her life. As to her recovery, it would be slow and painful. They might take pity on her, but in all probability she would end up getting a lecture, as well. In this part of the world, you got told off for not wearing a good anorak and solid boots; sandals and a party dress may, or may not, leave them speechless.

Suddenly, it occurred to him, this might be Nork's mother. She looked the type to go to strange festivals, and call her son after some obscure pop band. He shone the torch on her face; it appeared white and lifeless, the sort those not accustomed to coming across hypothermia victims would take for dead.

Then his medical interest subsided, and he studied her skin for any signs of disguise. For the first time, he was seeing her close up, as she really was, without makeup or false distraction. It was the face of a teenager, he was certain of it. She was not Nork's mother, nor did it seem reasonable that they had common parents. He had seen Nork sleeping peacefully in his cottage, but gazing upon the girl, he could see no similarity. Nork had a great mop of tangled black hair; this girl was completely ginger. He wished she would open her eyes to see what colour they were. Nork's were deep blue; if the girl's were any different, it would seem unlikely they were even brother and sister. Most probably they were cousins, on holiday, each set of parents believing the other was checking up on them. One set of parents could be quite ordinary, calling their daughter Jane, the others following some New Age cult, calling their son Nork. A Nork, he seemed to remember, was Icelandic for a twist of rope. Perhaps he had been born with a twisted knot of hair?

He wondered how he was going to explain all this to Stephanie. She would not like finding out that she had been so wrong about the 'mother' thing. Even worse, she had adapted her life to take account of the falsehood.

"Nork should stay with us," she had said, "his mother should go to a home for prostitutes!"

He had only really focused on the word 'us', which he had liked; the rest had seemed completely irrelevant…until now. This girl not being Nork's mother rather changed things. She did not look like a prostitute, and the odd time he had seen her around the town, she gave the impression of being rather innocent and unaccustomed to the ways of the world.

Then he heard the distant sound of a helicopter, and his mind turned to saving the girl's life.

It only took a few seconds for the helicopter to break the

horizon. It then flew across the loch, holding its height, so as to fly midway into the glen. Jim hurried to the landing place and waved his torch, until he thought the crew were close enough to see him, when he flashed it six times. They rose slightly, then took a direct line towards him. Soon, their powerful spotlight took over, and they landed where he had previously stood.

The pilot did not bother to stop the rotor; instead two crew jumped down and, after a brief acknowledgement, proceeded to lift the sleeping bag onto a stretcher. Three minutes later they were curving back into the sky. In fifteen minutes, Jane would be in hospital, where they would remove all but her underwear, and lower her into a lukewarm bath. When they opened the sleeping bag to find her wearing a party dress and sandals, they would be confused, but improvise. Jane would know nothing of this until the controlled warming returned her to consciousness, with a few hazy images. To her, it would seem a very strange world, and sadly, a painful one, as the blood returned to her frozen extremities.

Sherpa liked seeing the helicopters. It meant the search was over, and he could go home for a nice munch of his favourite biscuits. He was, therefore, rather surprised, and quite cross, when 'his man' continued walking into the mountains. However, it was an easy scent to follow, so he decided to put up with it, without whining.

On reaching the rescue shelter, Jim looked inside, half expecting to see Nork and Stephanie huddled in the corner. However, he now accepted that he had little understanding of the situation, so was not unduly surprised to find it uninhabited.

Then the other half of his brain came to life to see things

from a different perspective. Nork had heard the helicopter, then fled faster than Stephanie could catch him. Why Nork had done this remained a mystery; possibly it was something complicated, relating to Jane not being his mother. Realising this, Jim walked directly away from the shelter for a hundred paces, then circled around it. Sherpa sniffed the ground ahead, but made no response, until they returned to the path along which they had arrived, when he gave a long whine.

"I don't understand either," said Jim, talking to the dog. "The facts are, Nork is not inside the circle, nor has he crossed the boundary. The only possible conclusion is that he had not run this way."

Sherpa looked at him in a way that said, 'I could have told you that ages ago.'

Then Jim found himself even more confused. Where was Stephanie?

Slowly, he found some sort of answer. His Stephanie was the most wonderful, gentle person in the whole world... except for the time she had told him, "Jane should go and live in a home for prostitutes." That had been spoken with a vindictive voice. So, if necessary, she would do nasty things to protect the boy, to prevent him from coming into contact with the authorities. Like he had done, by telephoning the police. Both Nork and Stephanie were on the run from himself! In that moment, he made a life-changing decision. When he found Stephanie, he would...

What he would actually do was impossible to predict, because whenever he saw her, his brain went all peculiar. But, sometime during their next conversation, he would promise that she and Nork could stay in his cottage, without any form-filling or speaking to the authorities. He would even take Nork across the mountains without parental consent. He still did not understand why everything was so complicated, but at least now he had a plan. The key to finding out the mysteries of the situation surely lay in speaking to Jane. She might not be Nork's mother, but in some way, they were still connected.

By the time Jim returned to his cottage, he realised that before he was safe to drive, he would need sleep. However, this would be better, because by going to the hospital this afternoon, Jane's recovery would have advanced to the stage where she was in bed, and he could talk to her, hopefully in a private recovery room. She would know what to do, or at the very least, give him some clues as to where Nork and Stephanie might be hiding.

THIRTEEN

Mostly, Jane was pretending to be ill; it made her amnesia easier to falsify. Anyway, things still ached, just not to the extent where she needed to be lying on her back, staring at the ceiling, apparently unable to understand basic questions.

The police had been twice now. She thought their first visit was mainly out of concern, and possibly to find out who she was, besides the go-cart girl. Their second visit, after midday, was more worrying, since they kept asking her questions about Nork. On their next visit, they would probably arrest her for child-napping, but only in their dreams. While she could convince the nurses that she needed to be in hospital, her miraculous recovery would catch them unaware. Once she was out of the window, she could then become anything she needed to be. To the police, she would just be a girl, called Jane, who had mysteriously appeared...then disappeared with the same level of efficiency.

McTavish worried her less now. Only from a position of authority did he hold any power over her. Also, the nice nurse had told her about his recovery from the rowing boat, which fitted in well with the discovery of the mirrors in the hotel. Sadly, her pretend amnesia meant she could not ask the nurse about the details, only say, "Who's McTavish?", which probably cut short the good bits about his arrest!

The Nork situation was more serious. She was glad he had escaped, but without his witness, she might be in all sorts of trouble, once the authorities discovered they were not related. At the very least, she would be on a child-napping charge, but there might also be darker speculations resulting from their domestic arrangements. Sharing a bedroom with an eleven-year-old boy had all sorts of horrible possibilities. Once the gossip chain got going, fiction very quickly became fact. Her greatest fear was that her parents would find out. For them, it was better if she quietly rotted away in prison, without making a fuss.

She had learned many things from Nork, but doubted if she could keep up his perfect belief in a world where nothing had happened before a set date. Indeed, for her, it seemed impossible to talk without occasionally referring back to an earlier time, unless she went to the other extreme, and acquired full amnesia.

But what if, as she was being led to the court in handcuffs, a television crew stuck a camera under her nose? Remaining silent would be of no help; her parents would see her picture on the screen, and die of embarrassment. Her only course of action was to disappear, and pretend this weird phase of her life had never happened.

"You've got a visitor," said a voice.

"I'm not in."

"Ah, but this is the man who saved your life!"

"What does he want, a medal?" With complete horror, she

realised the man had already entered the room. "I'm sorry," she added quickly, "that was so rude. I merely meant, you should not have bothered."

With exaggerated illness, she rolled into the foetal position, and cupped her hands around her face. She could not bear to look at him. He had seen all her indignities, maybe even been there when her sheet had been removed to reveal her miserable body, made podgy in the McTavish restaurant, then ravaged by exhaustion.

"I'm just a silly girl in sandals," she mumbled, "I've been told already, so no more…no more anything. You should have walked on by, and saved all this fuss."

She felt somebody sit on the edge of her bed.

"That's fine, nurse," said a deep voice, "I may stay for some time."

Uh! Like she had no say in the matter. She would simply refuse to talk to him. Then she heard the nurse leaving, which she thought must be against some regulation. This was a solitary room to which her bed had been wheeled for the interview with the police. It was not fair to leave her virtually naked, with a man she could never remember meeting.

"I wasn't particularly looking for you," said the man, "and you had no sign on your back saying, 'please leave me to die.'"

She remained silent. This was just the 'nice' policeman they sent to get a quick confession. Most probably, he had never saved her life at all.

"We were trying to find Nork," continued the voice.

He was a policeman! That's why the nurse had left them together in the room.

"Why do people keep talking about Nork?" she asked.

"Because he was your room-mate."

He did not use the word 'brother', and perhaps the statement was even an implied threat.

"I don't remember," she said.

"So, what do you remember?"

"Here."

There was a long silence before the man spoke again. "The police told me that you were pretending to have amnesia," he said, "but they have no idea why."

"Banged my head, I suppose."

"No, you were lying in the heather."

She felt the bedclothes lift, then, incomprehensibly, the man pinched her toe.

"Do you remember that?" he asked.

"What, people pinching my toe?"

"Yes, in the mountains, you were still conscious then."

She had forgotten it, but thought she might remember it now. Also, the man's voice sounded familiar, but it was all very confused. Her last clear memory was twisting her ankle, and according to the man, bouncing her head on the heather. His questions were too awkward, so she returned to silence, hoping he would go away through boredom.

"I've got nothing to do this evening, either," said the man. "Suppose I better get a comfy chair to settle myself down. Don't worry, I'll still be here when you wake up."

"That's harassment," she mumbled.

"Very probably. I don't suppose anyone's brought you any grapes? I'm quite hungry."

"I'll scream!"

"Then what?"

"The nurse will come and throw you out."

"Then what?"

"I'll get some rest."

"Then what?"

"Oh, shut up, you're worse than Nork."

"Really? How very interesting!"

Jane put her fingers in her mouth. She then sensed him getting up from the bed and moving about, but it was difficult to tell where. When he spoke again, he was so close his breath warmed her face.

"Oh well," he said, "if you're going to scream anyway, I may as well get thrown out for something that does not make you look silly."

Next thing she knew, his lips touched the back of her hand. She tried to retreat, staring at him in astonishment.

"I…" she began, before her voice failed. He was gazing into her eyes so intensely it made her shiver. "I…" she repeated. "Help."

"Much better than a scream," he said, "for then the nurse would come, and I would end up having to climb back through the window, when there is so much talking to be done."

"You kissed me," she gasped, "that's surely not legal interrogation?"

"Ah, rules, yes, Stephanie warned me about those, they keep getting in the way of things."

Then, astonishingly, without a further word being spoken, he rose from his knees, and left. She watched him walk out of the door, then pushed herself up to get a better view into the passage. It crossed her mind that he was not a policeman, as she had first thought, but some weirdo, who had coincidentally saved her life. Desperately, she wanted to know what had happened in the mountains, because whatever it was, it appeared to make him fancy her. Sadly, twenty-four hours were genuinely lost from her memory. It annoyed her that, with seventeen years to choose from, fate had chosen that little bit.

Eventually, the man returned carrying a comfy chair and, sitting down, made himself comfortable by her bedside.

"Nork is not your brother," he said. "Now I have established that fact, perhaps I should tell you something about myself. My name is Jim, and for a brief while, Nork planned to stay in my cottage, with Stephanie, until I messed things up."

"Who's Stephanie?"

"I believe she spoke to you at the hotel."

"I wouldn't know."

"But you told her Nork was your son."

"No I didn't. I wonder what made her think that."

"Perhaps Nork told her. Maybe he found it embarrassing having a sister, when you are in no way alike, except that you have clearly caught his pretend amnesia. The problem you have, is that a twelve-year-old boy can normally get away with only talking about the previous twenty-four hours. There is something of an assumption that an older teenager has a definite history. Anyway, I thought you might be cousins. Any warmer?"

When Jane remained silent, Jim began to relate his own story, starting with Stephanie's arrival at his cottage, and her request to borrow Sherpa. After he had finished, Jane squiggled her nose.

"I see," she said, "and you think I might be able to explain things?"

He nodded.

"Well, you saved my life, and for that I owe you something. But nothing I say must be repeated to the authorities. It would cause Nork all sorts of problems."

Again, he nodded. When Jane remained silent, he looked up.

"I'm listening," he said.

"This situation is too serious to be agreed with a vague nod," she said. "Until you understand this, I have nothing to say."

It took Sara a great deal of effort to lean across, and recover the standard-issue Bible from the bedside locker. She passed it to Jim.

"I might have neglected Nork before," she said, "which is something I will regret for the rest of my life, but I will not betray him now."

Jim found himself quite bewildered. It seemed that Nork had persuaded two ladies that they needed to defend him, for the rest of their lives. How? Slowly, his mind recalled Stephanie's words: "If you ever betray Nork," she had said, "I will hate you for the rest of my life." And what had he done? Telephoned the police!

But what this girl wanted was even more committing. For him, to swear on the Bible, meant he could never tell the authorities anything, and who could foretell what the future held? Then he nodded to himself. His future was with Stephanie. Somehow, the hurdle Jane had placed before him would have to be jumped. After taking the Bible in his shaking hand, he made the oath Jane wanted.

"OK," she said, "the first thing you need to understand is that Nork knows everything there is to know about running away. He will know that on land, Sherpa will be able to follow his scent, so his first priority will be to break this trail before you can catch him."

"I mean him no harm."

"Without knowing his past life, we can have no idea what might cause him harm. All we can do is respect his wish, that the authorities never capture him. Quite apart from the morals of the situation, I truly believe he would risk his life to avoid being captured."

"OK, sorry, but how can he break the scent?"

"That is obvious. His only way to leave the town is across the loch."

"Not possible, it is much too wide, and quite able to kill those who enter its cold water."

Sara managed a smile. "The first time I met Nork," she said, "was about two months ago. He was drifting in from the sea, clinging to a fencing panel, firmly believing he had crossed an ocean. Certainly he had been out there for a complete tide and, to lose his bearings, he must have been out of sight of land for much of it. The notion that he would drown, trying to cross a big lake, is the most ridiculous thing I have ever heard. OK, so you call it a loch, to make it sound more serious. I still say it is a big lake. Nork is certain to omit the word 'big'. To him, it is just a bit of water, across which his scent will be lost."

Inexplicably, and without premeditation, she used her last ounce of strength to lean across and kiss him on the cheek.

"Thank you for saving my life," she said, "I might be able to make something of it yet. Now go, and if you do catch up with Nork, give him my regards. Tell him I am sorry that I wasn't interested in playing Monopoly or climbing trees."

Suddenly, she reached across and grabbed his arm.

"Remember," she said, looking directly into his eyes, "if anybody asks, I've got amnesia. The last person to annoy me was McTavish, and you know what happened to him!"

She lay back down, feeling strangely better about life. She needed to recover her wits; pretending to be ill would now require a lot more effort.

*

Jim left the hospital feeling totally confused about life. Clearly it was not possible for a small boy to cross the loch; Jane had got that so wrong! Also, she had made him swear on the Bible that he would never get the authorities involved, presumably including any rescue that he might need to make. And, if Nork had gone into the loch, did searching for his dead body still require complete secrecy?

By the time Jim had driven back to his cottage, he realised the situation was even more serious than he had first thought. What he needed to do was walk a great circle beyond the town's boundaries, with Sherpa sniffing the ground. But there were many sections of rough territory where Sherpa could not go. Anyway, such a search would need the complete mountain rescue team, branching out to cover maybe fifty possible escape routes. But using the mountain rescue team was the same as informing the authorities; certainly the police would get involved. Jane had made him swear an oath on a Bible that was impossible to keep!

It was late afternoon before Jim narrowed his options down to one single course of action. Take Sherpa for a quick sniff along the loch's shores, and when he found nothing, go to tell Jane. She would then have to release him from the oath, for only then was there any hope of saving Nork's life as he lay helpless in some gully or other, with a distraught Stephanie by his side, holding his hand, falsely telling him everything would be OK.

After recovering the pillowcases from the beds on which Stephanie and Nork had slept, Jim whistled to Sherpa, to indicate another rescue mission was about to begin. Sherpa responded with a look of disbelief, but followed his man to the Land Rover anyway, albeit walking slowly, to register his strong disapproval about all the rescues he was now expected to do.

On reaching the harbour, Sherpa was given a sleeping bag to smell. He gave it a good sniff, then vaguely looked windward, before walking a zigzag line in roughly the same direction. Eventually, he picked up something more definite, and walked to a projecting harbour wall which provided a breakwater for the smaller boats, moored close to shore. The scent was strong now, until near the end, where it vanished. Here, Sherpa looked over the side, said 'woof' twice, and sat down. As far as finding people went, this had been an easy assignment.

Jim understood Sherpa sufficiently well to distinguish between a 'definite woof' and a 'maybe woof'. Thus, he gazed across the cold, icy waters of the bay, then outwards towards the loch. In that moment, he realised Nork was dead, and that he was responsible. But Stephanie would have been trying to follow him, with plans of a rescue. Shaking with fear, Jim returned to the Land Rover, where he gave Sherpa Stephanie's pillowcase to smell.

Sherpa liked this scent much better; it belonged to a lady who gave him brown-covered biscuits. Indeed, it meant the smell had a special place in his memory. Happily, he set off, and quickly returned to the harbour wall, along which he trotted until the scent disappeared. Then he turned to look across the water, and gave a long whine. Where had the brown-covered biscuits gone?

Again, Jim stared across the water. The double scent confirmed everything beyond doubt. Nork had thrown himself off the harbour wall, and Stephanie had tried to rescue him, which explained her disappearance from the world of the living. Clearly, this was a job for the police, but equally, his oath meant he could never speak of it.

Jim sat on the harbour wall to think about what had happened, but firemen were not allowed to cry, so he quickly moved his mind to what he needed to do next. Eventually, he managed to convince himself that a harbour master was not really a member of the authorities. Without any particular plan, he walked towards his hut, to have a general talk about things. Then, as is the way of such conversations, Jim slowly included some details about Stephanie going missing, to which the harbour master laughed.

Yet again, Jim had an almost overwhelming desire to punch somebody on the nose.

"I assume this is Stephanie from the hotel?" said the harbour master, after his amusement had died down.

Jim nodded.

"But she is the best oarswoman I know," responded the harbour master. "I reckon she made her first solo crossing of the loch when she was six! By the age of ten, she could handle a seagoing boat in a force five. I often got calls on the radio from some concerned fishing boat that had passed her. Apparently, she would just shout back to the crew that she was fine. The idea that she has come to any harm on the loch is the most ridiculous thing I have ever heard. You mention a boy… With Stephanie to look after him, he will be fine."

Then, the harbour master came from behind his desk, and walked to the harbour wall.

"Her boat's not here," he said. "I expect she and the boy are having tremendous fun out there, somewhere or other!"

As Jim drove home, a great flood of tiredness began to wash over him. On reaching his armchair, he sat down, and remembered nothing more until he was awaken by a great banging noise. Turning his head to the mantelshelf, the clock told him it was nine o'clock, presumably the following morning. The banging noise was coming from his front door.

Without much enthusiasm, he shuffled to the door, to discover two policemen standing the other side.

"You look awful," said the sergeant.

Jim remembered the Bible, so instinctively decided not to respond to the statement until his mind had left its sleepy phase.

"Coffee?" he said.

Without waiting for an answer, he walked to the gas ring and sorted out three mugs. He heard the police walk in; Stephanie was quite right, they did have great clomping boots. Nork would have heard them a hundred yards away, and have been out of the back door long before they arrived. She was right about everything; in order to have saved the boy, he should have listened to her actual words, and not just the general poetic nature of her voice. Suddenly, it occurred to him that she knew Jane was not Nork's mother. She had said that just to shut him up, for if that was what she truly believed, she could not have taken Nork without parental consent.

When the coffee was made, Jim took the three scalding mugs to the table where, only two days before, he had sat opposite Stephanie, to gaze into her eyes. Now, he was staring at two policemen.

"We've come about the boy," said the sergeant.

"The boy," said Jim vaguely. "Do you mean the one who discovered the old mine workings? I thought you said his exploring things was OK."

"After the expedition, he was seen quite well and healthy, so of course it was fine. Oh, I so enjoyed putting the handcuffs on McTavish. He really looked down on us, you know. Never have the words 'you're nicked' sounded so sweet to my ears."

The constable, standing behind, coughed an interruption.

"Of course," continued the sergeant, "the problem with the boy is that he does not appear to come from anywhere. Nobody from John o' Groats to here has heard of the go-cart push. He just sort of appeared, and now he has disappeared, to mess up our missing person's record. The girl's amnesia, which we suspect to be an act, is not helping either. It seems she also just appeared, so we were hoping that you might know something."

"Can't help, sorry. They just walked into town, got no idea from where."

"Nothing they might have said in casual conversation? A surname would be good. There's no record of a Nork anywhere in the country, while there are Janes all over the place."

"They were just known as Jane and the boy. Perhaps Nork is foreign, sounds vaguely Scandinavian."

"We thought of that, but what everybody picks up on is the girl's very posh English accent. It probably means her parents expected her to join the aristocracy, which is fine, except for the fact her dress was a Marks & Spencer sheet. This makes her a strange, middle-class sort of person. From the point of view of our investigation, the sandals are a complete nightmare!"

"So this is an investigation then?"

"If Jane would explain things, possibly not. Her silence is causing us to consider that some crime may have been committed. How old do you reckon the boy was?"

"Eleven."

"You seem very certain."

"He told me."

"Let us say he did not tell you. What would you give as his maximum age range?"

"No younger than ten, no older than twelve."

"Young twelve, or old twelve?"

"I have no reason to believe he is not eleven."

"That's more or less what everybody at the hotel thinks. Too young, probably?"

"For what?"

"Between ourselves, the most common reason for a girl of Jane's age to run away is sexual, though this can take many forms. The hospital ran a test for the benefit of her own health, and she is indeed pregnant. Her appearance in our isolated town is therefore very easy to explain, but the boy? Brother gets sister pregnant is a good reason to go on the run, but nobody will put his age at thirteen, and most query twelve."

Jim realised he had been right not to tell them of his earlier theories; it would lead to all sorts of complications.

"No," he said assertively, "you can rule that one out. Stephanie mentioned how strange it was that Nork still believed himself to be delivered by…non-biological means. In respect of sex, he was a child of the Fifties – men wear trousers, girls dresses, and that is the end of the matter."

"Ah, yes, Stephanie. I believe she made friends with Nork at the hotel. And now she has also disappeared!"

Jim listened to the police talking about weird uncles, and children going on the run to avoid child abuse. Slowly, he came to understand this was the case, but the children had resolved the situation by their own actions. It was not for him to interfere. Instead, what he needed to do was to visit Jane in hospital again, and talk to her honestly about things. And this time, he would listen to what the girl was saying, because only then would he have any chance of finding Stephanie… and Nork…if they were still alive.

After returning to the hospital, Jim quickly made his way to the side room where Jane was staying. On finding her bed unoccupied, he went back to speak to the nice nurse, whom he had seen on his previous visit.

"Gone," she replied, in answer to his enquiry.

"What do you mean, gone?" he demanded.

"How many types of 'gone' are there? In this particular case, Matron did her round at six this morning, and found her bed empty. She was officially pronounced 'gone' at 6.30. The police weren't very happy about it; now they have two missing people, who never existed."

*

Sara was perched on a narrow bench made from a single tree trunk, cut down the middle, then opened out like a book, using cruel splinters for words. Either end of the so-called bench was poked into opposing, rough stone walls. No effort had been made to pretend it was possible to lean back, or slouch sideways. Presumably, it saved them nailing up a sign saying, '*Bus stop – not to be used as a residence*'.

Eventually, she looked down to the rough concrete floor. *So this is what it's like to be homeless*, she thought, *owning nothing but a hospital sheet and a pair of sandals...*

She frowned; her current situation was pretty much the same as it had been when spending the night in the quarry hut – cold, hungry, and with her current level of possessions. Yet she had not considered herself to be homeless then. Something else must have changed...

After some thought, she realised the difference was Nork. If he was here now, it would not be so bad. This bus shelter represented homelessness because she was completely on her own, destined to die of starvation, without anyone being particularly worried.

When her shivering came to resemble an epileptic fit, she continued her walk, hoping the exercise would reduce the pain within her icy-cold legs. After a hundred yards or so, she noticed a small church on the opposite side of the lane. Outside, a large crowd of well-dressed worshippers had gathered. To prove they had not seen her hobbling departure from the bus shelter, they all turned to look at the church, presumably waiting for the doors to open.

A little way beyond the church, the lane was edged by a dry-stone wall, perhaps three feet high. On the other side of this, a solitary cow looked up, a great clump of stinging nettles sticking out from either side of its mouth. It seemed so interested in the flip-flopping noise made by her sandals, that it stopped munching to regard her thoughtfully. She decided this was a proper cow, 'dressed correctly in black and white', with a cute little fringed hairdo on the top of its head. Indeed, she had an overwhelming desire to feed it some grass on the flat of her hand. Pulling up a couple of handfuls from the verge, she nervously held it towards the animal. The cow, equally nervous, looked at the offering, trying to work out if it was safe.

Remembering the way Nork had made friends with a load of shaggy beasts made her smile. After the death-defying encounter was over, Nork had casually asked if she knew how to tell one end of a cow from the other.

Expecting he was going to say something rude about udders, or men-cows, she had pretended not to hear. "One end goes moo, the other poo," he had answered. Smiling at the joke now represented rather a long delay.

Now, she thought, *what a horrible place to be. Why can't it be two months ago, when I was first walking into town, with happy, cheerful Nork by my side? Then, on reaching the high street, I would take my life in a completely different direction – to a haberdashery shop, to buy the biggest box of safety pins they had…*

But before her thoughts of a golden age with Nork could progress, she was distracted by a conventional cow carefully using its enormous tongue to lift the grass from her hand. "Nice cow," she said.

Talking to a cow! How lonely was that? But it had such big, sad eyes, and wanted to be her friend…unlike anyone else. Then, more importantly, she realised if a police car happened to come along the lane, her days of freedom would be over. What she needed now was not a friend, but a place to hide from the hostile, daylight world.

Looking along the dry-stone wall, she saw that about

half a mile up the lane the open grassland gave way to dense woodland. She hobbled towards it, until coming to a gate, which she opened to reach a narrow footpath, the overhanging branches making a pleasingly dark tunnel.

Feeling relatively safe, she now realised that no matter how bad the problem might be, there was always something you could do; after which her mind went around in circles, until deciding that in her particular circumstance, there really wasn't. The only remaining purpose of her life was to organise things so that her parents would be spared the embarrassment of finding out how it had ended, not particularly in this wood, but soon, when starvation took full control of her body. Then she remembered all the pigging-out she had done at the hotel. This had built up so much fat reserve, that her death would come from the cold, for, when she had arrived in Scotland, it had been early Summer, and now it was mid Autumn.

Using the last of her energy, she staggered deeper into the woods. Then she began to crawl. It suited her mood, and allowed her ankle to take a break from the pain of hobbling. On reaching a stream, she bent her head to suck the water. Then she rolled over to await the darkness, when she could return to the outside, and put some telegraph poles between herself and the hospital.

*

At the hospital, Jim hovered about the car park, fully aware that his official enquiries had led him nowhere. Then he had a strange idea: what about doing things unofficially? Uncertain of his approach, he returned to the building to find the nurse he had left ten minutes earlier.

"You return so soon," she said, "a regular visitor, indeed."

"I expect the sheet from her bed was missing?" he asked.

"What? Oh yes, strange but true!"

"She's from England. They do a lot of strange things down there, it seems a sheet is all she needs. How about the sandals?"

"Gone. The police weren't very happy about that either. They seem to think they should be used in evidence."

"On the contrary, evidence is the last thing they need. At the moment they have absolutely nothing – no people, no bodies, no nothing. And now the sandals have disappeared, there are no loose ends for them to tie up. I feel a wise constable would simply forget the strange events had ever happened. Perhaps you might mention it to the constable, if he comes back. In the meantime, I wonder if I could possibly beg the pillowcase from her bed?"

"Weird. Is this official?"

"No, is that a problem?"

"Just need to know. If anyone asks, I'll say I've not seen you."

The nurse kindly went off to get the pillowcase. Jim was amazed by all the things that happened unofficially; he was sure there should be a stock-control form that needed to be filled in for pillowcases.

When the nurse returned, she was holding a pillow.

"Sorry," she said, "the pillowcase has gone to the laundry. Will this do? It's from her bed."

Jim looked at her in astonishment, to discover she was looking directly into his eyes.

"Remember," she said, standing a little closer, "if I ever have a fire at home, you owe me a favour…also a pillow. Just so you don't forget, I've written my home telephone number on a card."

She slipped the card into his jacket pocket.

Weird, thought Jim. However, probably no more weird than walking out of the building carrying a pillow.

On reaching his Land Rover, Jim offered the pillow to Sherpa. Being an intelligent animal, he lifted his head so that his man could slide it onto the seat. Then he stared at his man, unable to believe that he was walking away, carrying the pillow, and expecting him to follow. Sherpa wondered if he should learn to growl, not all the time, just when he was expected to find people every day.

After walking halfway around the building, Sherpa's nose became overwhelmed by a great trail of pillow scent. He set off at a trot, feeling slightly better about things, given that the scent was freshly made, and therefore, most probably, quite short.

Jim looked at the nearby window, then followed Sherpa to a pedestrian exit that led to a housing estate at the rear of the grounds.

"Praise the Lord," he said. It would have been a lot more complicated if Jane had headed to the main entrance, with the busy street beyond.

*

In her previous life, Sara had pretended not to see homeless people as they sat on the pavement, begging for money. It was not something she had ever talked about, since her friends all understood such things 'never really happened'.

However, once or twice, she had wondered how they

could just sit on the pavement and ask for money. Their very first time seemed an impossible barrier to cross. Only now was she beginning to understand how it worked: when the hunger became unbearable, she would sit on the pavement and ask, hoping for silver, but gratefully accepting copper. Not here, near the town, where the police would pick her up, but away, where she would be an anonymous, unknown girl in some distant doorway.

Her first positive thought came after a few hours, when she realised that everybody around here knew her as Jane, the girl in a designer dress. It was her trademark. How often they looked at her face was uncertain; to most men it was probably just a vague blob, above her precarious-looking gown. If she obtained some proper clothes, her fame would be gone. Hair dye, makeup and dark glasses would complete her disappearance. How to achieve this remained a mystery. Maybe she could steal some clothes from a washing line, but shoplifting cosmetics? She was too 'wanted by the police' for other things to risk it. Getting a job, or drawing 'dole' was likewise out of the question. So her destiny appeared to be sitting on the pavement, collecting small change, unless...

She shuddered. Could she really let a man 'do it' for £20, and solve all her problems in one go? She had only had sex once, and that she could not remember! The next man she had seen naked was McTavish. Yurk, for £20 it would be somebody like him...or worse. No, sitting on the pavement it would have to be and, with her head bent down, people could not look into her eyes, so it was not so bad as being hungry.

Suddenly, a great crashing noise came through the bushes. She rolled tightly into a ball, until whatever it was had passed her by.

"Go away!" she whispered, at what turned out to be dog, who then lay down beside her. The dog gave a tired sort of bark, then used her shoulder as a pillow for its own chin. Sara thought the animal was being much too familiar for a first acquaintance.

"Shoo," she said, "cats over there, hundreds of cats."

There was more rustling now, and she screwed up her face at the unwelcome invasion of her privacy.

"Go away!" she said, at whatever was standing behind her.

"You don't seem to be as good at escaping as Nork," said a voice.

She untangled herself from the dog, and very slowly sat up.

"Oh, it's you," she said. "I rather imagined dogs could not follow a scent along pavements."

"For a busy street, that is true, but a quiet housing estate is a different matter. Also, sitting down in a bus shelter helped. Anyway, you seem in better condition this time. You did well to pick dense woodland and a stream. Clearly a pupil of the great, legendary Nork!"

Embarrassed by her awful condition, she looked at her feet, then pulled the sheet across her quagmired legs. She tried to remove the straggles of hair from her face, hiding them behind her back so he would not see the muddy tangle it had now become.

"What do you want?" she asked. "Will the police find me?"

"I need your help to find Nork and Stephanie," he replied. "As to whether the police will find you, I have no idea. They could if they wanted, I suppose, but I doubt if they will bother to launch a massive woman hunt."

"So, you're really not the police then?"

"No, but why are you so desperate to avoid them? You hardly look like a criminal."

"They're chasing me. I believe the word child-napping might be used."

"Intriguing. Nork did not give the impression of being kidnapped."

"McTavish said…"

"McTavish is not police, even though he is spending a lot of time with them at the moment. More a visitor, really."

"He knows Nork is not my brother."

"The police did mention something about it, but not about kidnapping, more to do with children running away together."

Sara immediately tried to adopt an indignant posture. "I am not a child," she said.

"Maybe not, but there is only six years between you. A bumbling High Court judge would hardly be able to tell the difference."

"I refuse to be called even a maybe-not child," she insisted. Shyly she swivelled away as Jim sat beside her. "Say it," she mumbled.

Jim remained silent for a few moments and, when he spoke again, it was certainly in the tone of a grown-up talking to a child.

"If you were a man…" he began.

"I am not one of those either!"

"No, but if you were, bringing a girl-child to a shared hotel room may well see you joining McTavish in prison. A woman is less certain because running away with a boy-child might be seen as maternal instinct, albeit misguided. Your age is your friend. The best thing you could be at the moment is fifteen."

She spun around to confront him. "I am most definitely not fifteen," she retorted.

"Shame, then the police would simply take you back to your parents."

She cut him short with a scream. "I am seventeen!" she said.

"Still, hardly an age where you are likely to kidnap a child, and the boy seemed very pleased to tag along. Besides, a hotel is hardly the same as taking him hostage in the hills."

"So why did the police keep coming to see me at the hospital then?"

"Mainly because you remain silent. Clearly you have things to hide, but I can't imagine they are very serious. Tell them, and I expect they'll go away."

"But McTavish said…"

"McTavish said a lot of things, mainly to get you into bed, I suspect."

"He didn't!"

"Very pleased to hear it, though perhaps, later, you would like to tell me how he came to be sitting naked in a rowing boat. But for now, I think, we had better get you somewhere warm."

Without warning, she felt herself being lifted into the air.

"Put me down this instant," she demanded, "or I will bite your ear!"

"Your knee prints tend to suggest you have been crawling," he said. "You may not be so bad as the last time, but that ankle needs rest."

"Not the hospital!"

"Sort of gathered that, perhaps my cottage, if you have no particular objection?"

"I'm not having you carry me through the streets."

"I have parked the Land Rover by a pedestrian gate to the woods."

"So, by your definition, this is kidnapping?"

"No, it's an unexpected solution to an unimagined situation. Perhaps you could put your arms around my neck, as at the moment, I appear to be carrying a dead body."

It's adult-napping, she thought. Then she remembered being pregnant, so thought it might be classed as 'unmarried-mother-napping'. Though whatever it was called, it was not how she wished it to be. Still, it was better than lying in a ditch! Just at the moment, sitting at a kitchen table, eating beans on toast seemed like Heaven. If he thought her a child, he must feed her. And beans were probably what she would be given.

As she bounced along, her isolated thoughts became all jumbled up. She began to feel sorry for him. Why was he wasting his time on her pathetic existence? If she was a nice person, she would tell him to leave her by another stream, allowing him to walk away. Then she found her mind returning to food, but the man probably thought her so fat she had no need of it. Realising that his arms must feel like the worn-out springs of her bathroom scales, she put her own arms around his neck to share the load. It would be a shame if his abiding memory of her was that she made his arms ache.

FOURTEEN

Sara's first night inside the rescue man's cottage was dominated by an overwhelming desire to sleep. How long this lasted, she could not say, nor did it matter; the important thing was that she had not woken up in a muddy ditch. Slowly, her confused early-morning thoughts came to realise something even more amazing: there was no immediate need to start crawling anywhere.

Eventually, her aching muscles found just enough energy to sit up and organise the pillows at the top of her bed into a soft, gentle incline. After resting her back into this, she took her first proper look around the room, which seemed to be about ten-feet square, the rough stone walls painted with whitewash. The only furniture was her bed and a hard wooden chair that acted as a minimal bedside locker. An airbed resting on the slate floor against the opposite wall, she did not consider to be an item of furniture.

Vaguely, she remembered the rescue-man saying something about this being the room where those who got themselves into difficulty in the mountains would occasionally spend the night. When he had told her this, she had become more relaxed about being taken back to his cottage. Not that he had given her any reason to fear him, but she now realised men in general were impossible to understand, and therefore unpredictable. Indeed, how else could she account for McTavish's extraordinary belief that she might let him 'do it' if he kept on asking; or, indeed, the equally ridiculous idea of her first and only boyfriend giving all his pocket money to Janet for a half-hour lesson behind the picture house, just because she had told him to be patient?

After staring at the stone walls for a few minutes, she decided the whitewash represented a level of cleanliness that she rather liked. Slowly, it made her feel better about her life; not only was her room bright and cheerful, but the lack of clutter made it seem very hygienic.

Now, properly awake, she tried to remember the rescue-man's name. Jim, that was it. This pleased her, for if he intended to throw her out of his cottage immediately, he would have been more formal, and called himself rescue-man number five or something.

After a few minutes of watching the early-morning sunlight streaming through the only window, her thoughts were distracted by a knock on the door. She pulled the bedclothes up to her chin.

"It's your cottage," she called.

The rescue-man walked in and dropped a pair of boots on the chair beside her bed.

"I don't understand girl clothes," he said, "but feet are all the same. If you want that ankle of yours to get better, it will need support, so don't even think about wearing sandals for at least another week." He then presented her with a massive pair of thick socks. "Unless you want blisters," he added, "you will need these as well."

Sara looked at the offerings. He seemed to know how to cater for a girl's rescue needs, but doubted if Marilyn Monroe would be very impressed by his idea of footwear.

"Thank you," she said, not knowing the man well enough to be less formal, and having no idea of the etiquette involved when receiving such gifts.

"Breakfast will be ready in five minutes," he said.

Sara remembered how the bathroom scales at the hotel had been really horrible to her towards the end of her stay. What awful things this man had seen already, she had no idea, but her sheet was often unpredictable, and her first rescue was surely the most undignified moment of her life. Hopefully the helicopter crew were too professional to make jokes about not being able to take off, but they had probably thought it.

"I'm not hungry," she said.

He appeared to ignore her, instead placing the back of his hand gently on her cheek, turning her head to gaze directly into her eyes.

"You're not diabetic?" he asked.

"No," she sighed.

Then she realised his actions were in complete contradiction to his words, or perhaps he was leading up to taking her pulse in a medical-romantic sort of way. Then he would sit on the bed, and ask why her heart was starting to race. She breathed out weakly, and completely, to make herself thinner, and in need of support. Then she held out her wrist, to keep him moving in the right direction, but he seemed totally unaware he was under attack.

"You look well enough," he said, "though possibly a little dehydrated, and some sugar in your porridge would not go amiss."

Yesterday, while sitting in his Land Rover, he had provided her with pie and chips. Then, on reaching his cottage, he had tormented her with a great bowl of rice pudding.

"I pigged out yesterday," she said.

"That was to stop you passing out. I expect there's still a build-up of lactic acid to get rid of. Legs stiff?"

Yesterday, she had only been able to move like a robot, but today, at least while settled in bed, things merely ached. Being carried to the rescue vehicle had been nice and, on reflection, necessary. For some strange reason, she was now desperately hungry.

"I'm fine," she said, "honestly."

"Porridge is a good way of taking in water," he replied, "and with plenty of sugar, it will bring your glucose level back up."

She was going to say, 'no way,' but stopped herself just in time.

"When I am hungry, I will eat," she said firmly.

He looked at her even more intensely, indeed, sternly.

"I should really have taken you to the hospital," he said. "If your condition had been a fraction worse, I would have had no choice. I presumed you did not want me to call a doctor. The only reason the police haven't been to see you is because it would not cross their minds that I might snatch you from under their noses. The last thing I need right now is to be found with a starving girl in my cottage."

"I am not..."

He waved her objection aside. "There is rarely any great

drama with exhaustion," he said. "More often the victim just faints and can't be bothered to get back up. If I say you need food, you need food."

Then, without warning, he stomped out of the room.

Sara suddenly felt quite miserable, and rolled over to face the wall. The rescue-man seemed genuinely cross, and all because she did not want to become a fat pig. It was too awful, Jim looking at her body and seeing only a mass of wobbling fat.

"Coming ready or not," said a voice as the door got kicked open. Nervously, she turned away from the wall to see him holding a large bowl, surrounded by a tea towel. He held this above her bed, which pretty much forced her to take it. Then he stepped back but, on reaching the door, he turned around.

"I don't like arguments," he said, "I don't understand them. Let us come to an arrangement where you eat properly, then we shall not need to argue again."

"Or be silly," she said.

Without hesitation, he told her such a thing was impossible. She smiled. Before, he had merely been saying what the mountain rescue people expected him to say, when finding people in the hills, who had not undergone years of SAS training. When he did not have time to think about the rescue manual, his inner-self did not consider her silly at all. She watched him turn from the doorway, then take two steps to look out of the window.

"In Winter," he said, "you can look out from here, and see…nothing. That is because when the wind blows from the mountains, it is quite possible to step from a snowdrift, directly onto the roof. Up here, to be silly is to be dead!"

"Oh," she said, realising that he was only talking about

people in general, while giving no particular consideration to her own circumstances. "Is it silly to ask how you get out of your cottage when the snow is over the roof?" she asked.

"It's nothing a good shovel won't solve. There are cross-country skis near the back door. Town's about thirty minutes away downhill, two hours back. The glen rarely loses road access for more than a couple of weeks. Like I said, living here it's not possible to be silly, only dead."

"You are still cross with me?"

He paused. "I am sorry," he said, "I simply do not understand the ways of you city girls. I presume you do things differently down south. Let us not argue any more."

She nodded, but mainly because her mouth was full of porridge. Realising she liked the sound of his voice, she swallowed quickly.

"You don't like cities?" she asked.

"Fort William is quite nice in short measure. Traffic's a nightmare though."

Sara was fighting with the need to consume more porridge. "Glasgow?" she asked, keeping her conversation to one word.

"Amazingly big. You can see it from the hills above Loch Lomond. Don't think I would ever want to go inside though. You can get everything you need from Fort William, so why bother?"

She got the impression Fort William was pretty important around these parts. If he ever took her clothes shopping, she must remember to exclaim how amazing it all was. Oh, and complain about the traffic. She resolved to look it up on a map, to see where it was, and therefore avoid saying anything silly about it. Realising Jim was leaving, she called after him.

"Please stay," she said, "or I could join you in the living room, if you have a few safety pins, for my…dress?"

"Fine," he replied, "back in a moment."

He returned with a first aid case and dropped it on the bed.

"Plenty of pins in there," he said, "for your…party dress."

After finishing all the porridge, Sara swung her legs from the bed, to put on the socks. She struggled with the boots, since they were the sort people wore to climb Mount Everest. However, once standing, she found herself able to clump around, without suffering any pain. She then stuck a few safety pins into her sheet, and clomped into the main living area, with a volume of noise an elephant might make as it walked from one part of its zoo enclosure to another. In any event, it was enough to make Jim aware of her entry, because he immediately got up and…

Sara could do nothing but stare in astonishment as he kneeled before her, proving beyond doubt that men were prone to doing things that were impossible to predict – in this case, possibly dangerous things, as he felt about her boots. What would he do next, and how could she sensibly react to a hand wandering up her legs?

"These are my old boots," he said, "from when I was a teenager. I outgrew them before they wore out. I knew they would come in useful one day."

He then went on to describe how to take the laces around the back, so as to get extra support for the ankles. But she found it impossible to concentrate on his words; the tingles shooting up her legs were too electrifying.

Sadly, without developing his boot fetish further, he stood up and went to a huge cast-iron thing, set against the wall. He opened one of its doors, to reveal it was on fire. After taking four logs from a nearby basket, he threw them inside, and re-closed the door. He then walked to the big table in the middle of the room, picked up a tray of bread dough, and put it into a different compartment, closing the door with a solid 'clunk'.

Sara decided the huge cast-iron thing was called a 'steam engine', because that is what it looked like, probably dating from the Victorian era, when everything was powered by burning stuff.

"Take it out in forty-five minutes," said Jim. He then pointed towards the back door of the cottage. "There's plenty of butter in the store," he added.

Sara did not think this made any sense, but did not feel sufficiently confident to ask him to explain, for fear it would make her appear silly. Instead, she watched him put on his boots, even larger than her own.

"You were quite right about Stephanie and Nork," he said. "The harbour master reckons they'll be on the loch somewhere, camping overnight, on the bank, I expect. Fire Chief said I could use the rescue launch to have a look around. I don't suppose you have any idea where they might be?"

Sara sat on a hard wooden chair, then bowed her head towards the table. Partly, she was overwhelmed by guilt; if he found them, it would mean she would be evicted to make room for those he considered more important. She so desperately wanted him to fail. Then she felt even more guilty; he had saved her life – twice. How could she be so cruel to wish him misfortune? In the few seconds she had to decide, she came to one very important decision – that she would never tell him a lie, whatever the consequences might be for herself.

She explained about never telling him a lie, then added the fact that Nork considered a safe distance from the police to be 5,400 telegraph poles. "Got no idea what that is in nautical miles," she concluded, "but certainly, far beyond the local loch."

Jim spun towards her, his face full of anger.

"They went out on a rowing boat?" he shouted. "My Stephanie would never do anything so dangerous as go beyond..."

Then he remembered what the harbour master had said about the fishing boat captains radioing him about a lone girl rower they had just passed, while in the middle of a force-five gale.

"You are worse than the harbour master," he said.

Then he whistled to the dog, and stomped out of the front door. Sara remained seated at the table, shaking slightly.

"I shall never tell you a lie," she said quietly, "no matter what the consequences for myself..."

After the sounds of the Land Rover had faded away, she looked around the room in which she had been abandoned, and was now trapped, on account of her having 'nothing to wear'.

She tried to force an ironic smile. Before, having 'nothing to wear' meant her existing wardrobe was slightly out of date. Now, having 'nothing to wear' meant only having a sheet, so that going outside for any length of time, in Autumn, would make her appear silly, and therefore, dead, possibly buried beneath a snowdrift until the Spring, when those who found her would gasp at the hospital stamp on her sheet.

"It does not even have a designer label!" they would exclaim, horrified by the thought of it.

But she must not allow herself to drift into daydreams about future events that were impossible to predict. The important thing was to concentrate on surviving just one more day, which was best achieved by assessing her current surroundings.

Looking about the room, she realised the walls were so thick that the leaded windows appeared to be set into tunnels. She strongly suspected the leadwork holding the small glass panels in place was genuine seventeenth century, as opposed to a modern, double-glazed imitation. Since these windows were set into opposing walls, she reasoned the room must run the entire length of the cottage, making it a general living space, with no differentiation between kitchen and other activities. This allowed for a massive table, made from thick oak planks, to stand at its centre. She thought such a table would have been designed to seat an old-fashioned Victorian family, with a dozen or so children. The room had nothing in the way of sofas or armchairs in which one could slouch, presumably because there was no 'boiled-cabbage machine' to make slouching necessary.

Nork, she thought, *what have you done to my brain?* But, however hard she tried, she could not think of a television as being anything other than a device for dulling the brain, thereby controlling the population, who would otherwise be demanding useful things to do.

"The hoarding masses will not be rioting today," she could imagine the Prime Minister saying, 'because they are all glued to their 'boiled-cabbage machines." It amused her that Nork had even got the Prime Minister using the phrase.

So, for Sara, the question now became: *How do I fill my days without a 'boiled-cabbage machine' to look at?*

Well, she had partly answered this already. Without 'a box' to look at, the mind automatically floated away into a world of daydreams, in which you made up your own stories. Possibly, such thinking would help her plan a life that did not contain so many mistakes; though, in her case, it would be more to do with trying to correct the mistakes she had already made.

On leaving her daydream, she looked around the cottage to realise there was nothing in the room that required electricity, nor were there any electrical sockets or light bulbs. This, of course, she knew to be impossible. For one thing, Jim had mentioned butter, and you could not possibly have that without a refrigerator, and what about a vacuum cleaner?

Gazing at the floor, she realised it was made entirely of slate slabs, the uneven surface worn down by many centuries of tramping boots. Jim had actually invented how not to have a vacuum cleaner: don't bother with carpets, just buy a mop and bucket to clean with just soap and water.

Sara remained staring at the floor until the smell of baking bread made her look towards the 'steam engine'. It seemed too dangerous to approach, but eventually the thought of the bread catching fire gave her the courage to open a door, and peep inside. To her astonishment, the loaf was nicely risen, with a perfect crust. Taking this out and placing it on the table made her feel better about life. She got up and went across to where Jim had pointed the butter might be found. But there was nothing to indicate where it might be. Well, at least the butter only being imaginary meant the loaf became a zero-calorie food, since eating it dry was too horrible to contemplate.

Suddenly, an even less desirable thought came to her. Last

night, for the first time since the age of three, she had used a chamber pot which had been left under her bed. But now, a more complicated biological need was starting to make its presence felt. Where was the bathroom? That was easy to answer, there being a tin bath hanging from a nail near the back door.

OK, she thought, *where is the smallest room in the house, which, given the tin bath, could be really small?* She opened the door to the right of the room where she had slept, to gaze at a load of mountain rescue equipment, including stretchers and three enormous first aid boxes. On the floor were three sacks. Further investigation revealed these contained potatoes, porridge oats and flour, presumably survival food for the times when the snow came over the roof.

After leaving the mountain rescue room, she went to a door on the left of the room in which she had slept. Opening this, she found herself gazing into a normal-sized room, containing a single bed, side locker and wardrobe. This was clearly Jim's bedroom. Turning around, she looked about the main living space, realising there were no doors she had not opened.

"Curiouser and curiouser," she said, remembering her *Alice In Wonderland* book. Using this as a reference book, she realised there must be another 'secret' door somewhere, because otherwise…OK, Alice did not have biological needs! But the principle was the same; there must be another secret door somewhere, possibly disguised to make it look like a back door by using planks of rough-sawn timber, held together with heavy-duty nails. But, given there were no more doors left to open, it had to lead to the smallest room.

After opening the disguised door, she found herself staring at a path of well-trodden earth. Looking up, she saw this wandered into the mountains, until becoming lost within the general wilderness of things, all of which rather implied she had actually opened a back door. Then, even more curious, she realised there was no fence to differentiate her immediate surroundings from the general wilderness, which made the idea of a back garden a purely imaginary concept. Then her attention was drawn to a little shed to the side of the path, perhaps thirty yards from the cottage. Feeling ever more like Alice – lost in a surreal world of wonderland thoughts – she walked towards it. Hey, these boots were not bad! Very sensible, unlike what she was otherwise doing, walking towards a shed while wearing a sheet.

On reaching the shed, she looked inside to stare incomprehensibly at what she had discovered. Basically – very basically – this cottage demanded its residents adopt a way of life that had not changed for 1,000 years!

After using the 'facilities', including a Victorian water bowl to wash her hands, she looked around for a towel, which appeared not to exist. She shrugged her shoulders, then casually dried her hands on her sheet.

On leaving the 'hut', she took a few moments to take her first good look around. There was not another house to be seen anywhere, just wilderness, and mountains.

"Up here," she said to herself, "to be silly is to be dead."

*

It was late evening before Sara heard the sound of a vehicle pulling up outside the cottage. She felt a little frightened. Would Jim still be cross with her? How could she survive without the shelter he was providing?

Jim walked through the door, followed by Sherpa, who headed straight for his basket. In order to do something that could not possibly cause any offence, Sara squatted beside the animal to stroke its head. From the corner of one eye, she watched Jim walk towards the back door, where he got down on one knee...again! But this time, rather than pursuing his boot fetish, he took a screwdriver from a hook on the wall, and prised up a small flagstone. Reaching down to a hole below, he recovered some butter and a bottle of milk.

OK, thought Sara, *this man has invented how not to have a refrigerator*, which rather completed his invention of not having electricity.

Jim went across to the table. On seeing a full loaf, he looked at her, possibly slightly annoyed.

"The deal is," he said, "that for as long as you stay here, you are to eat properly, which I can see you have not done!"

He cut the bread, and spread a great slab of butter across the first slice, which he passed to her. Next, he went to a grinding machine, and began turning the side handle. The smell of coffee entered the room. At that moment, Sara thought the taste of fresh-ground coffee, with bread and butter, seemed like absolute Heaven. Also, it appeared to be the only condition of her residence – that she indulge in such things!

Half an hour later, she was sitting at the big table, opposite Jim. She decided to apologise for not eating properly. In response, he turned to look at her, his face giving the appearance of being worn out and tired.

"No," he said, "it is I who should apologise to you. The harbour master did some radio work for me. A fishing boat captain has recently seen a girl rowing a boat, northwards, about…oh, it does not matter where. Thing is, there was a boy sitting on the back seat. So, next weekend I shall be away in the Land Rover, because I will find them. I must, I cannot live without Stephanie."

Sara lowered her head to hide her guilt. Her own happiness depended on him not finding Nork and Stephanie, because now she had come to realise that her attraction to Jim was not because he had saved her life – twice – or because he was her only source of shelter, but because…

But she could not admit to being in love, because he would consider that to be silly.

*

After living in Jim's cottage for three days, Sara realised the 'steam engine' was not likely to explode if she used it to boil a kettle of water. Also, she found using the hand-grinding machine to prepare her morning coffee quite relaxing, and the end result far better than anything she had drunk at her parents' house. They only bought their coffee beans already ground, albeit from a very upmarket shop, but it still lacked a certain something, necessary to start the day.

On realising all of this, she sat down at the table to have a good think, not about the amazing mug of coffee, but about her parents' house…because that's what it was now – the place where her parents lived. Her own home was here, in Jim's cottage, where everything was slowly starting to seem rather normal. Then, without thinking, she went to lift the corner flagstone to get the butter for her morning sandwich. Uh! Even the idea of living without a refrigerator now seemed possible.

As she ate her bread and butter, her mind wandered into daydreams, as it often did nowadays.

If I had a magic wand, she thought, *what would I want?*

The first item was easy: she wanted a romantic relationship with Jim, but that was impossible. When he found out she was pregnant, he was certain to throw her out before the dirty nappies arrived. This, she thought, justified all her tears that followed.

The second item was slightly less impossible: she wanted Jim to take her into all the beautiful scenery that she could see outside the window. In this environment, she decided, you did not go 'hiking' as her parents would understand it; rather you tramped places in big clumpy boots like the ones she was wearing. These now seemed entirely normal. Then, remembering her sheet, she realised this was also impossible. Even going outdoors to visit the facilities at the end of the garden made the first symptoms of hypothermia send her body into uncontrollable shivers.

As her 'magic wand' worked through all the ways she might want to fill a typical day, she realised her failure to think of anything that was possible had nothing to do with her home. It was all because of the way she had arrived, her general vulnerability, being pregnant, and the need to rely entirely on Jim to keep her alive. Then, finally, in the late afternoon, she thought of something she wanted that might actually be possible. She wanted Jim to call her Sara, to hear his voice as she nuzzled her face against his chest...

No, not the last bit, because that fell under the heading of 'impossible', but to hear him say 'Sara'...That would confirm the 'Jane', who foolishly paraded about the hotel, wearing a sheet, no longer existed.

That evening, Jim came home from work and announced he was taking five days' holiday to go to find Stephanie. He then dumped five cans of evaporated milk on the table, and went into the mountain rescue room. He returned carrying a large rucksack, together with a tent.

"Make yourself at home," he said as he walked back out of the door.

She raced to the window to see him turning the Land Rover around, with Sherpa gazing back, looking equally horrified. Then, a few minutes later, they were gone.

Of all the things she had wanted, five tins of evaporated milk had never crossed her mind. But these, it seemed, were all Jim thought she needed to make her life complete. Then came an even more horrific thought: five days searching coastal towns and villages was serious. He might return with Stephanie and Nork, making her eviction inevitable.

*

On the fifth day, Jim returned…alone. He sat at the kitchen table, head buried in his hands. Sara did not interrupt his thoughts, but made him coffee, together with a meal of boiled potatoes and freshly baked bread. It was her third attempt at making a loaf, but she would not talk about the disasters that came before…

Eventually, Jim told of his adventures, that ultimately ended when Sherpa refused to leave the vehicle. He had managed to get one confirmed sighting of a girl and boy in a rowing boat, sixty miles to the north, so at least this narrowed down his search area for his next attempt to locate them. Then he looked up to study Sara.

"And as for you," he said, "I have decided to accept no more silliness, so I've booked another day off work. Tomorrow I'm taking you to buy some sensible clothes. Not here, it would cause too many problems – unless you want to get the police involved – so we are going to Fort William."

"Wait, clothes shopping?"

"No more nonsense with your silly English fashion," he interrupted. "Here, we don't even think about using the word 'cold' until the thermometer drops to -15. In that dress, you will be dead by the end of November."

Sara could not bring herself to tell him how she had spent much of the previous five days in bed, shivering, trying to keep warm, until she lit the 'steam engine' to make herself an evening meal.

"I've got no money," she said quietly.

He shrugged. "There are more important things than money," he replied. "I have enough saved to look after Stephanie and Nork…when I find them. But, just at the moment, you need proper clothes. It is a condition of remaining here that I do not come home one night to find you dead from cold. We are leaving at six tomorrow morning."

He then picked up his coffee mug and stomped to his bedroom, to shut himself inside. Bravely, Sara made up a plate of potatoes, with a chunk of butter. She then went to tap on the closed door.

"You need to eat properly," she called, "I'm bringing your food in now."

She walked into his room and placed the food on his bedside locker.

"While I am looking after you," she said, "it is a condition that you eat properly. I made rice pudding earlier. I shall bring that to you five minutes from now!"

Oh well, she thought as she stomped back towards the door, *if I am going to get thrown out, it might as well be for everything*. She turned to face him.

"My name," she said defiantly, "is Sara."

There, that should give him something to think about besides 'Stephanie this, Stephanie that…' Stephanie who needs to duck under doorways to avoid dislodging her halo!

*

That night, Sara lay in bed, daydreaming about Fort William – its high street all magically lit with rainbows, the shops with sparkly windows, all selling clothes. She decided to get a red dress, with thin shoulder straps, but not expensive…or silly. She would have to stand in her bare feet to get the right effect and, perhaps, if her ankle was better, she could give him a little twirl to raise the hem. She frowned, unable to imagine Jim buying ladies' underwear, or herself, having the cheek to ask for the cash to sneak away on her own. And it was not just clothes she needed, there were so many things required before her crazy sheet-wearing days of Summer could come to an end, to become sensible for Winter. And how was she going to finance her really personal monthly needs?

The daydream shattered. In three months, she would have an enormous bump, and he would know she was eating for two. Invading Jim's life could never be anything more than a temporary solution to avoid being homeless. Keeping her sheet suddenly seemed like a good idea, since it would double as a maternity dress to hide her expanding tummy. He might not even realise she was pregnant until January, and surely he would never kick her out into hundred-foot snowdrifts, or strap a pair of skis to her boots and push her towards town, safe in the knowledge that her duck-like figure would never be able to waddle back up the hill.

The following morning, Sara left her room to discover Jim pouring a huge bowl of porridge, which he slid in her direction. Like she was going to eat all that! It would create quite the wrong effect as she stood before him in her little red dress. However, the first quarter of it would be fine, after which she could pretend to have indigestion. Jim, meanwhile, went to check a thermometer on the outside wall. He returned, shaking his head.

"Five degrees," he said. "That porridge will keep you warm on the inside, but that party dress will end up being a shroud for your frozen body."

He went into the mountain rescue room, and returned with a mummy-style sleeping bag, the sort with a hood to stop your ears getting frostbite. In response to her objection to becoming a mummy, he explained that his Land Rover came from an age when travel rugs were commonly placed over the legs of lady passengers to keep them warm. She responded that all cars must have heaters because such essential equipment was surely part of the MOT test! But, apparently, his vehicle had some sort of exemption. Thus, she revised her opinion on how much porridge would be required to make a late-Autumn journey, somewhere near the Arctic Circle!

All things considered, it was not how she had expected her amazing clothes-shopping trip to begin, ultimately wriggling into a mummy-style sleeping bag, with just her face peeping out of the hood. Her next discovery was that the old Land Rover did not, in the modern sense of the word, have a suspension system. Jolting along the track, it turned her tummy into a food mixer full of porridge. If Jim had mentioned this unfortunate combination of circumstances earlier, she would have sacrificed all her pride and left the cottage carrying an armful of pillows to sit on.

As their Arctic journey progressed, Sara found herself quite impressed by Jim's sensible driving, which never went above forty miles an hour. Also, tucked inside the sleeping bag, she was quite warm. The fact that her mummification totally lacked sex appeal was irrelevant; soon she would be wearing a red dress, which would make Jim exclaim, "Wow, that looks totally amazing!"

On reaching Fort William, Sara's first impression was of a gentle town, so much so, that she completely forgot to exclaim, "All this traffic, it is a nightmare!" Anyway, she had a much greater problem to deal with: in a short while, she would publicly need to wriggle out of her sleeping bag to walk into a clothes shop, wearing what the assistant, given all her years of training, would immediately recognise as a sheet!

Eventually, Jim turned into a small car park. After getting out of the vehicle, Sara wriggled from her sleeping bag to immediately be surrounded by a bitterly cold wind. Quickly, she pulled on her boots, then nervously looked along the pavement, to find it bustling with pedestrians. Ahead lay one very embarrassing walk…

However, rather than setting off along the street, Jim walked through the first doorway he came to. She followed him inside to find warmth, which led to a nice happy feeling. Then, looking around more generally, she became confused by seeing a lot of outdoor equipment. Without really understanding why he had brought her to this place, she followed him to a far corner, that had…well, the sort of things somebody accustomed to climbing in the Himalayas might recognise as clothes.

Jim greeted the shop assistant as if he knew him personally. He then explained that 'the lady' needed a full outfit, something to survive the Winter living in his cottage. The assistant raised both eyebrows, but Jim appeared not to notice.

Ten minutes later, Sara stood in the changing room, to realise the assistant, presumably with Jim's knowledge, had played a horrible practical joke. Not that there was anything wrong with the clothes – for a man, going into the backwoods to cut down trees!

The shirt was a great thick weave of tartan. The top of her legs were covered by baggy knee-length breeches, with buttons at the front, which she supposed went quite well with her pre-existing man boots, and thick socks.

Well, she thought, *Jim deserves a good laugh, then, after he has seen just how horrible the shop assistant has been, we can go to a proper clothes shop together…even if it is 500 yards further down a busy street.* However, just to reduce the comedic effect of her clothes, she pulled a great woolly jumper over her head to take on the figure of a hairy yeti.

After she had clomped from the changing rooms, Jim looked at her for a moment, then turned to the shop assistant to give him a lot of £10 notes. Sara was pleased Jim had bought something for himself, because it would make her feel less guilty when he later paid for a proper dress. Strangely though, Jim said goodbye to the evil shop assistant, and headed for the door. Then the horrible shop assistant handed her a bag.

"Your…err…" he said. "They'll…err…yes!"

Sara looked inside the bag to discover what might be

three pairs of double-cotton knickers, or, more reasonably, something to do with surviving the Winter in Antarctica. She laughed a little, before realising he was serious.

However, she was now one step beyond survival mode, allowing her mind to consider hygiene issues. She returned to the changing rooms to inspect what, in Victorian times, might have been thought the height of industrial-style underwear. Then, after giving a cough of embarrassment, she hauled up the necessary fortifications to her modesty.

On returning to the street, Jim immediately started walking, which pretty much forced her to follow. Surprisingly, none of the pedestrians stopped to stare, possibly because they thought her to be a real lumberjack, which made her quite cross. After a few hundred yards, Jim stopped by the doorway of a small shop.

"Err..." he said.

Sara scratched her head, trying to work out what all this talk of 'err' might mean. Whatever it was, Jim handed her a £20 note.

"Get what you need," he said awkwardly.

Sara looked through the adjacent doorway, and realised it was the sort of place to sell ladies' underwear. She wanted to laugh, then tease him, by saying 'brassiere', but decided against it, because he was obviously a clothes-shopping virgin, whose clumsy ways needed to be treated gently.

Five minutes later, Sara came out of the shop, with the support she needed, plus some more pants, discreetly hidden beneath some handkerchiefs, in a carrier bag. Jim responded with a friendly nod.

"Right," he said, "now you are wearing proper clothes, I can take you to the cafe for dinner."

She knew Jim called lunch 'dinner', but that was not the issue. The issue was, that his clothes shopping did not conform to anything a lady would understand, though she had to admit, she did feel very warm…and ready for chopping down trees!

After a nightmare walk along the street, Sara followed Jim into a large cafe. He went directly to the counter, while she headed to the darkest corner of the room. She had been in this situation before, with Nork…

"Oh, please don't let this become another entertainment for the guests," she mumbled, sadly louder than she had intended, because it made one of the diners look in her direction, which she thought a bad omen.

Jim returned with two pint-sized mugs of coffee. He then presented her with a menu.

"I'm having pie and chips," he said. "You have whatever you want."

All the money he was spending on her! Embarrassed, she shrugged her shoulders.

"I'll have the same as you," she said.

After he had gone to order their food, she looked around the cafe. Nobody was laughing at her. In fact, this close to the Arctic Circle, she almost seemed to blend in with the other customers. OK, she was at the extreme end of ultra-warm, which, she supposed, was the complete opposite to being ultra-silly.

After the meal was over, Jim looked at her. "Happy?" he asked.

Strangely, she was not unhappy, more confused. She managed to respond with a nod.

"Now you're organised with sensible clothes," he said,

"your next task is to contact the police. If you tell them your story, as you told it to me, I can't imagine they will give you any problems. To me, it seems, it was more a case of Nork kidnapping you."

"I don't want the police," she said, "they'll contact my parents."

"We will have to talk about that later, but not until you are ready."

"I'll never be ready to face them."

"You will. At the moment my cottage is your refuge, but you can never go outside. Only after you have satisfied the local police that you are not a kidnapper of children, will you be free to walk to town. Otherwise, the four walls of my cottage will become your prison. OK, I understand you don't want to tell your parents you are pregnant, but…"

It was lucky for Jim that she did not have a mouthful of coffee; the shock of his statement would have sent quite a spray in his direction. Instead, she just stared at him for what seemed like an eternity.

"You know I'm having a baby?" she eventually gasped.

"That's what normally happens when you are pregnant. Now finish your coffee and, since you are wearing sensible clothes and boots, we'll go for a nice little walk up the glen."

She blinked, scratched her head, then turned away on her chair. If she had seen his face for a moment longer, she would have been unable to stop herself running around the table, throwing her arms about his neck, and saying all the things she had dreamed about.

But he only wanted to hear that from Stephanie!

After a gentle hike along a most pleasant lane, Sara looked around the impressive glen, then upwards to the high mountains, their tops covered with snow, yet she felt completely warm and comfortable. She wriggled her toes in her boots, which gave her a rather nice feeling. Then, she thought about their return journey, when she would be a proper passenger in the Land Rover, driven by a friend as opposed to being a mummy, bundled up in a sleeping bag, like a parcel that needed to be taken places. When she got home, she could then sit by a nice warm 'steam engine', with the gas lights gently hissing, while drinking the most perfect cup of coffee in the whole world. And now the clothing problem had been resolved, she would be free to go places in the near-future – after working out how to convince the police she was not a fugitive from justice. It seemed to her that Jim was right about everything…except where Stephanie was concerned.

As their walk into the glen continued, Sara began to feel so comfortable in her new clothes, that she had a sudden desire to climb the highest peak she could see, until Jim told her it was Ben Nevis, which at this time of year, would need crampons and a walker's ice axe. Her response was to smile in a way that did not imply commitment, but as the walk continued she began to nod as she conducted negotiations inside her head.

The deal is, she thought, *I climb Ben Nevis with you, but not before you sort out a better bathroom for me.* After all, it would not be proper to return home, all cold and exhausted, to sit in a tin bath. She concluded the deal by imagining a handshake, changing the nature of her smile to something more natural, because it meant Jim was now officially her best friend, who had just agreed to buy her a proper bathroom – albeit without realising it!

Having sorted out the practical details of their relationship, Sara came to realise how comfortable it felt to be walking beside her best friend. She then wondered if she could tell him things about her childhood, of which she had never spoken to anyone.

"Earlier," she began, "in the cafe, you ended a sentence with the word 'but', or more correctly, I interrupted you. Anyway, I think you were going to say that my parents would come to accept my condition, because that's what parents always do."

"They might throw a complete tantrum for a couple of days," he said, "but eventually, yes, they will stop screaming hysterically, to say how much they love you."

"My parents never do displays of emotion," she interrupted. "They don't need to. Thing is, I was brought up by a nurse, then sent away to boarding school when I was seven, so it was not necessary for them to get involved in my life. For them to disown me now is an easy matter, no different from the time they packed me away to boarding school. And they still have three 'recognised' children to impress their friends – two with high-flying jobs in London, the other a diplomat in Hong Kong. I am their only disappointment, and not necessary to make up their number of socially acceptable offspring, so going back to see them would be rather pointless."

"You could write to them," he replied. "They might like to know you are still alive?"

"Doubt that," she said, "but in a letter, yes, at least then I need only tell them the things they want to hear – living in a lovely cottage, with a great and supportive friend, that sort of thing."

"And when your parents know the situation," said Jim, "I'll

have a quiet word with the local police, just to get you legal. Though you look so different in your new clothes, I doubt if anybody would recognise you as the Jane who always wore a party dress. OK, you might need a balaclava, but in Winter, unless you have a passion for cold ears, you will probably want to wear one of these anyway."

"What, more clothes shopping!" she joked. But sadly, he did not laugh at her joke. "Sorry," she added quickly, "that was presumptuous."

She swiftly moved on to tell him more about her life. All this happy talk continued until they returned to Fort William where, for some unknown reason, Jim went back into the outdoor shop. He emerged holding a balaclava.

"If you are going to tell your parents that you have a strong, supportive friend," he said, "then you can also tell them that he refuses to let you walk around with cold ears!"

She smiled. If her letter included the word 'he', she would have to quadruple the size of the cottage, and put a dividing wall down the middle. But she was sure she was up to the task, because at school her creative-writing ability had always won great praise from the English mistress.

FIFTEEN

Doris – Sara's mother – was five days away from her fiftieth birthday, an event that she knew would bring the swirling beast of time raging through her body, to announce that her life had reached the halfway point...if she was very lucky! Occasionally she was able to view the forthcoming catastrophe less dramatically, understanding that the second half of her life would be spent sitting in an armchair, wondering when her carer would arrive with her bedtime mug of cocoa.

Peter – Sara's father – understood this because he had faced the same traumatic experience three years earlier. He therefore decided to distract his wife from the cruel march of time by booking a flight to Spain, where they had a yacht permanently moored on the Mediterranean coast.

Two days later, Doris and Peter were sitting comfortably on deck loungers to watch the Rock of Gibraltar approaching off the starboard bow. On this occasion, they only had two crew: a cook and a qualified freelance captain who, for reasons of social convention, was always referred to as the first officer. The plan for this evening was that on leaving the

Mediterranean, the first officer would turn left – as Doris preferred to call it – and begin a voyage down the coast of Morocco…

Yet something was wrong. They had seen this lump of rock a hundred times before, and it no longer made them gaze up in wonder. As for sailing down the African coast… twenty years ago, it had been an amazing experience, but now it just involved looking at more ocean, and visiting the same old ports to drink coffee. Yet neither of them could find the courage to use the words 'boring' or 'mundane', but in reality, that is what it had become.

But, emotionally, it was far more complicated than just being boring. In those early years, their four children had been onboard, making interesting comments and generally learning about life. Then, after docking, they would rush off to explore places. Now, without their children, what was the point of doing the same old thing, over and over again? Certainly it was not the sort of activity Doris needed to distract her from her impending old age.

Thinking of this, Peter left his lounger to have a quiet word with the first officer in the wheelhouse. On his return, he moved his lounger closer to Doris, then reached out to take her hand. Turning, he saw her eyes gazing blankly at the Rock now passing them by on the starboard side. Probably she was thinking, *that rock is even older than me.*

"When we get to the Atlantic," said Peter, "we are turning north, then going all the way to Scotland…to visit Sara!"

They had not seen their daughter since the awful experience of…the thing they had never talked about. After receiving her letter, four months later, they had written a socially correct letter in reply. This expressed satisfaction that she had an apartment on a big country estate. More importantly, they had explained that given the circumstances, it would be better for her to remain in Scotland. According to their convention, they expressed affection by enclosing a cheque for £5,000, so she could get anything special she might need. After that, letters passed back and forth every three months or so, but they had never visited her, since all their holidays involved going south.

Doris looked at Peter. "Doesn't that involve going across that awfully rough sea?" she asked.

"Bay of Biscay," said Peter, "yes, but the first officer has done it before, though we'll have to head to Portsmouth first, to get the charts we need to follow the Scottish coast."

There, thought Peter, satisfied with her surprised expression, *let's see if you're still thinking about your fiftieth birthday now!*

*

A week later, their yacht made 'slow ahead' into a Scottish loch, with Peter watching the echo sounder. Doris had no interest in things that kept going 'bleep', so looked around to gaze at all the beautiful mountains. Then her mind turned to Sara, as she tried to image the vast estate where she now lived.

Eventually, Peter saw a picturesque hillside town off the port bow. Had he been cruising the Italian coast, he would have thought it the sort of place holidaymakers never wanted to leave. Here, so close to the Arctic Circle, with Winter icebergs drifting in from the ocean...Well, come September, all the holiday homes would be abandoned, while the locals became nothing more than great fur coats hurrying along the streets, desperate to find shelter before frostbite took away their ears…no, surely all the men wore kilts, so they had more important things to worry about!

"Oh look," said Doris, "a town over to the left."

Peter let the shallow observation pass without comment. However, the first officer gave a shudder; the term 'left' rather emphasised the vague nature of where he was expected to go; he was not familiar with Scottish lochs, and knew one accident could lose him his commercial licence.

After a few moments, Peter picked up the radio mic to call the harbour master, requesting a pilot to guide them into port. The harbour master responded by saying there was no need; instead, he would observe them with binoculars, and use a signal flag to point where they had to go.

This made the first officer even more nervous, but thankfully Peter took control of the wheel and, following the direction indicated by the signal flag, made slow ahead towards the harbour. It was a bit unorthodox, but it seemed to work OK, because after ten minutes the first officer was able to throw ropes ashore.

After securing the mooring lines, the harbour master looked along the length of their yacht, then raised his eyebrows to signal he was impressed. The respectful formalities completed, Peter felt able to step onto the quay to greet the master with a handshake. In response, the master said he knew it was safe for their vessel, because it was roughly the same size as McTavish's yacht – the vessel that had once used the mooring for taking on fuel and water.

"Went bankrupt six months ago," he added, with a dismissive sniff. "His yacht was seized by creditors, so this length of wall is yours for as long as you wish." The master then looked a bit embarrassed. "Though I'm afraid," he added, "I will have to charge you £10 a day."

Peter knew that to be about a fifth of what he would expect to pay for an overnight mooring at an upmarket port near London. Was the man trying to offer him charity? He gave the master £100, because anything less would be too embarrassing.

"I've paid for ten nights," Peter told Doris later, "because I rather like the look of this town, and I have no idea how much talking you'll want to do with Sara, but you must remember to communicate how much you disapprove of her previous behaviour."

Doris nodded. She then explained that her clothes were completely unsuited to a place so near the Arctic Circle.

"So, before seeing Sara," she said, "I must acquire a Scottish wardrobe. If her house friend turns out to be the Laird, it is important to be dressed correctly."

Later that afternoon, Peter accompanied his wife into the high street – until she stepped inside the most expensive clothes shop available. From past experience, he knew that she would not emerge for at least an hour, so he walked back down the hill to take a closer look at a large three-storey building he had noticed on the way up. It was all boarded up, but a sign above the entrance indicated it had once been a hotel. He calculated that if the attic had been used for staff accommodation, it would have around thirty guest rooms. In London, assuming the run-down nature of the place was superficial, he could reasonably value the building at £3 million. But here? Being generally curious about the value of things, he looked at the estate agent's 'For Sale' board in the adjacent car park. After checking his watch, he realised he still had forty-five minutes to waste before Doris was likely to emerge from the clothes shop, with more parcels than she could sensibly carry by herself.

Casually, Peter walked up the street to the estate agent's office. Here, the man behind the desk told him that the hotel owner, ex-Councillor McTavish, had gone bankrupt and was now in prison. Peter had only been in the town for an hour or so, yet this was the second time he had heard McTavish's name. Clearly the man had once been important around these parts, and his departure had left a power vacuum that needed to be filled – like Peter had just occupied the harbour wall where McTavish had once serviced his, most likely, slightly smaller yacht.

"... Hence," the estate agent was saying, "the hotel is an absolute bargain..."

Peter only needed to waste forty-five minutes, which was insufficient to let the agent follow the social conventions normally observed when speaking to a customer. He turned to leave.

"Just £300,000!" shouted the agent.

Peter carried on walking out of the door.

"Maybe £250,000?" the agent added desperately.

Peter thought this price seemed to follow the same principle as the harbour mooring. No, the hotel was only about 10% of London prices. But he was only wasting time, until his wife emerged from the clothes shop.

On leaving the estate agents, some instinct made Peter return to the abandoned hotel, then walk around the car park. He estimated it could easily take sixty cars. That was a serious amount of land! Then he glanced at his watch, which made him hurry to the clothes shop. The important thing now was to tell Doris that she looked absolutely amazing – in whatever it was she was wearing.

The following day, Peter went to the harbour master to show him the address on Sara's letter. The master responded by saying he could get the necessary taxi down here in half an hour.

Such service, thought Peter. He gave the master £20 and told him to organise it, and not to bother with the change.

Half an hour later, Peter was surprised to see a Land Rover taxi waiting by the harbour office. He had imagined that for £20 he would get a proper car, not – as he looked at the number plate – a five-year-old Land Rover. Oh well, it would have to do.

A little way from town, the taxi turned off a narrow lane to make its way up an old cart track. It could only be a shortcut, which Peter thought quite unreasonable for £20, especially after the bouncing and swaying got so bad, they ended up having to cling to the seats in fear of their lives. Then, quite inexplicably, the driver stopped the vehicle, and got out to open Peter's door, before going around the other side to hold the door open for the lady. Peter raced to protect his wife from the taxi driver who had, quite frankly, taken advantage of their £20.

"Thank you kindly," said the driver, doffing an imaginary cap.

Then he reversed the Land Rover onto a bit of scrappy ground, turned around, and slowly bounced back down the track.

Peter and Doris looked at the rough ground on which they had been abandoned. After taking a few moments to recover from their terrifying ordeal, they looked around to see a vast landscape of rugged mountains. Failing to locate a country house where Sara might live, their gaze settled on a low building of rough stone. It appeared to occupy a bit of wasteland, that is to say, it was not surrounded by a fence, or even a hedge, it was just a hovel, sitting in the mountains, without any boundaries suggesting land ownership.

Doris and Peter again looked around to see where the nearest proper house of any description might be. But there really was absolutely nothing apart from wilderness.

"I expect the taxi driver does not like the English," said Doris, using her voice that she reserved for talking to lower-class peasants. "This is clearly some sort of prank," she added. "He probably does it to all those who speak correctly."

Peter agreed. Then he noticed a curl of smoke twisting from the hovel's single chimney. Also, a few yards to its left, a battered-up Land Rover parked on a bit of waste ground. These two observations gave him a clear, if highly undesirable, plan of escape. Whoever lived in the hovel might give them a ride back to town. Indeed, it was probably all a confidence trick organised by the man who had claimed to be a taxi driver.

Finally, Peter decided the time had come for him to take manly control of the situation. He advanced to the hovel's front door, and gave it a tap. Then, fearing a great, hairy tramp might suddenly appear, whisky bottle in hand, he sensibly stepped back. When there was no response, he suggested to Doris that they try around the back. Cautiously, they followed the outer wall of the hovel until…

The scene that greeted them was so incomprehensible, they could do nothing but stare in complete shock. Peter automatically put a protective arm around Doris, to keep her upright, as she went into a semi-faint.

What they were looking at was their daughter…digging

up potatoes! She was wearing knee-length trousers, with braces, and possibly a lumberjack shirt. Her feet were lost inside a pair of boots, like those worn by men employed to dig holes in the road.

*

Sara was very proud of her vegetable garden. She had created it from the wilderness – one of the many activities that had taken over her life, now she did not have a 'boiled-cabbage machine' to stare at. And she had helped Jim build a fence around it, with a gate that squeaked slightly on its hinges. It told her that she was now entering her own private space, though in truth, the security was only there because of the deer, who had no understanding of property rights when it came to juicy runner beans.

When her basket was full of potatoes, she stood up, and turned. She stopped dead in her tracks, simply to stare…

When writing to her parents, she had always been very careful to tell them things in a way they would like to hear – a house in the country, set in many acres of land, that sort of thing. So, what should she do now?

After a few seconds to think about the unexpected situation, she realised it was her own life that was entirely sensible, while the city folks, from down south, were all highly eccentric. It seemed like a plan, that is to say, to act normally, and let others change their attitudes towards a more sensible way of life. She walked towards the cottage.

"Supper will be ready in half an hour," she said, as calmly as possible. "I'll just put the kettle on for coffee."

Not that she felt that calm; for one thing, she had never

mentioned anything in her letters about having a baby, who, in fifteen minutes or so, would be waking up for his feed. Well, her parents came from a generation who thought unmarried mothers brought so much shame on the family name, they should be disowned and sent away to live with distant, lower-class relatives.

After washing the potatoes, Sara put them on the 'steam engine' to boil, together with the kettle. As she set to work, hand-grinding the coffee beans, she could feel her parents watching her back.

Let them; she had been in their situation once, watching Jim going about, doing normal things. Of course, her baptism into his way of doing things did not include the discovery of a fifteen-month-old toddler, settled into a cot by the side of her own single bed!

Slowly, Doris and Peter realised that Sara was suffering a complete nervous breakdown. Almost certainly drugs were involved, but they would be tolerant and, once they had rescued her from this life of poverty, they would employ a top psychologist to help her get better.

"It's OK," said Peter eventually, "we are here now. Our yacht is moored in the harbour, and you can stay with us tonight. Tomorrow we can buy you some proper clothes."

Sara let them ramble on as she applied herself to the task of making coffee.

"Excuse me," she said as she kneeled down by their legs to lift up the flagstone to recover the milk.

"No refrigerator!" gasped her mother. "You poor, poor thing."

Sara shrugged. "We don't have electricity," she said, "so a fridge would be pointless."

Then Doris caught sight of the tin bath hanging from a hook on the back wall. At that, she did pass out.

Sara went into her room to get a pillow for her mother's head, at the same time glancing at her soon-to-be-awake baby…ah, there was another problem. On his birth certificate, Sara had recorded his name as Nork, because it would make him stand out in a crowd. Also, she rather liked the idea of it being Icelandic for a twist of rope. He had a more ordinary middle name that he could use later on, if he so wished, but for the time being, it was irrelevant. Nork was just Nork, the baby she loved more than anything else in the whole world. Jim came a close second, but that was irrelevant too, since he still worshipped Stephanie, and frequently spent his days off searching the coastal settlements, trying to find her.

Sara had recently completed an advanced first aid course – another of the many activities that derived from not having a 'boiled-cabbage machine' to distract her. It meant she was now a useful member of the mountain rescue team, who was quite able to sort out basic medical issues. Hence, on leaving her bedroom, she confidently pulled her prostrate mother into the recovery position, made slightly more comfortable by putting a pillow under her head. Sara then went to the 'steam engine' to pour three pint mugs of coffee. After placing the mugs on the table, she gestured for her father to sit down, but he responded by kneeling beside Doris to hold her hand. Sara again looked at the clock.

OK, she thought, *we can't have my mother passing out twice. May as well get it all over and done with in one go!*

"I'm just going to pick some sprouts," she said. "Father, while I'm away, I want you to look into my bedroom, from where I just got the pillow."

She then picked up a basket and returned to her vegetable patch. It took a few minutes for her father to appear in the back doorway, where he remained, at a safe distance, staring at her with utter disgust.

"Do I assume the thing you have just asked me to look at is your illegitimate child?" he asked.

Though she had half expected it, the question made Sara feel rather cross.

"He is the most loved baby in the whole world!" she responded defiantly.

"Well, I hope the father is going to make an honest woman of you!" he shouted, his voice serious and aggressive.

She had been intending to tell Peter that Jim was not the father, but something made her unable to speak the necessary words. Her main desire in life, she realised, was for Jim to actually be the father, and she could not bear to say anything to the contrary. So, she silently returned to the task of picking the sprouts. When she turned around again, her father had gone.

Quietly, she returned to the cottage, to peep out of the front window. On seeing her parents walking away, she shook her head in disbelief at how silly their shoes were. There was no way they would make it back to town without getting a twisted ankle. She raced after them.

"To be silly is to be dead," she shouted, pointing to their ridiculous footwear. "Give me a couple of minutes, and I'll give you a lift back to town in the Land Rover," she added.

'The Land Rover Jim bought me,' she wanted to add, 'and in which he taught me to drive. Kind, gentle Jim...'

But her parents ignored her, pretending she did not exist. Well, at least it was now official. Resignedly, she went back into the cottage to feed Nork.

Meanwhile, Jim was driving back from work, when he saw a middle-aged couple hobbling down the track towards him. He shook his head in disbelief; they were wearing the silliest footwear he had ever seen beyond the town's cafe area. Bringing his Land Rover to a halt, he got out to give them a lecture, stopping himself just in time, as he recognised them from the photograph of Sara's parents that had arrived with their last Christmas card.

"Hello," he said, "I'm Sara's friend. Jump in, we live in a cottage at the end of the track."

"You...you..." stammered Peter. "How dare you get our daughter pregnant...and...and...brainwash her into staying...to dig up potatoes!"

Jim was going to explain that he was not the father, but some instinct kept his mouth closed. Probably because he quite liked looking after Nork, and did not want to deny Peter's assumption. The outcome of his silence was that he watched the couple hobble around the Land Rover to continue their journey towards the town.

"It's three miles to the first telephone box," he called after them. "As a member of the mountain rescue team, I cannot let you go that far in such ridiculous footwear."

But they pretended not to hear. After giving a heavy sigh, Jim got back into the Land Rover and turned it around. As he approached Sara's parents, they stepped aside to let him pass. A mile further down the track, he came to a cottage similar to his own, this being his nearest neighbour. He parked around the side of the building, and went to tap on the front door. When a man in his mid-forties answered, Jim explained what was required, then went inside to take a cup of tea with the wife. The man went to their back yard to prepare some transport…by harnessing their pony and trap.

"Sara's parents," Jim explained to the wife, "they are from England."

She gave an understanding nod, then set about making the two cups of tea. About twenty minutes later, she went to look out of the front window, until a pony came trotting back down the lane, a middle-aged couple bouncing about in the cart behind. They looked distinctly unhappy, but at least they would return to town with reasonably intact ankles.

By now, Doris had somehow completely forgotten about the traumatic milestone of her fiftieth birthday!

*

After the pony and trap had rattled into the distance, Jim's mind turned to his recent conversation with Sara's parents. Something about it troubled him, so instead of returning home, he went for a walk up a nearby mountain. On reaching the summit, he turned around to slowly cast his gaze across the world he knew…and understood. Or at least that used to be the case. Now his cottage looked different. How? From this height, it looked like a tiny model building that revealed no details, beyond the fact it had walls and a roof.

Eventually, Jim adopted his extreme-thinking position, that of sitting on a boulder, elbows on knees, chin cupped in hands. This made him realise why he had been troubled on leaving his neighbours' cottage. It all came down to his instinctive reaction not to correct Sara's parents concerning their assumption that he was the father of their grandson. Slowly, he came to understand that over the preceding months he had acted as Nork's father... OK, not fully, when it came to changing nappies etcetera, but for the other stuff, in a more general, caring sort of way. This brought him face to face with the big question: did he actually want Nork to be his son?

That question, he decided, was too big. He tried to break it down into smaller chunks. In the years to come, would he be happy to take him into the mountains, or pick him up from school? There were so many possibilities, all made unpredictable by Sara, who might, without warning, find another place to live...with another man.

He had become rather accustomed to going home and finding a nice warm cottage, possibly with Sara baking bread, or taking a rice pudding from the cooking range. He also liked all the fresh food that came from the bit of mountain she had claimed for a garden. In fact, for the first time, he now realised he would hate going home to an empty, cold cottage, as it had been before she had arrived...to totally disrupt his life! The cottage, he realised, looked different because he knew Sara and Nork were inside.

Why had his eyes become full of water that escaped to run down his cheeks? Deciding it was all too embarrassing to think about, he got up and walked back to his Land Rover, not knowing what to do about this strange situation. He only knew that after his brief conversation with Sara's parents, something had changed.

*

After dismounting from the pony and trap, Peter and Doris took a dignified walk across the harbour towards the safe sanctuary of their yacht. Here, they hurried down the stairs, where they told Cook to prepare something lavish for dinner at 8pm. Then they hurried to their individual cabins, to take a shower in the en-suite bathrooms. Dressed in clean robes, they emerged to sit on their beds, both traumatised by the distressing circumstances they had recently endured.

At 7.45, they dressed for dinner, to enter the dining room at precisely 8.00. Now, surrounded by civilisation, they finally relaxed, indulging in small talk and conversation of no particular consequence, as expected of their high social grouping. Order restored, they automatically smiled and nodded at each other's observations…but inside their heads, their tormented thoughts swirled around in a world of their own.

That night, Peter lay in bed and considered how best to deal with Sara's nervous breakdown. Obviously, she could never return to England, but perhaps he could buy her a proper house up here, and set up a trust fund, so her daily living expenses could be met. His only condition would be that she took psychiatric help to free her from the abusive relationship in which she had become trapped. If that did not work, he would give the scoundrel-man £5,000 to disappear, somewhere unknown.

Having resolved this problem, Peter's mind drifted towards the hotel, or more precisely, an empty building, whose dusty outer walls disguised a huge amount of potential profit. Also, buying it meant he could avoid purchasing a house for Sara, because she could have a flat on the top floor. This would allow the hotel staff to watch over her, to prevent any relapses into her nervous breakdown.

At just gone midnight, he got out of bed, to work on a budget, which assumed the hotel had forty bedrooms, with an occupancy rate of 60%. With a good manager, the figures looked very positive. Indeed, it was an extremely sensible and economic way to proceed. Back home, he could then refer to the awkward complications associated with Sara as the 'Scottish situation'.

After gazing blankly at the hotel budget for a few minutes, he became aware of noises coming from the cabin next door. Doris could not sleep either, but now he had a solution. For the first time in many months, he went to tap on Doris's door. After giving a discreet cough, he entered. She was sitting on the bed, trying to disguise the fact she was almost in tears. He sat beside her to put a comforting arm around her shoulders. She went all stiff, causing him to withdraw it and place his hands on his lap. He decided not to tell her about the hotel idea, for it was still only an accountancy calculation. However, concentrating on a nice house, he explained his solution to the 'Scottish situation', which Doris understood. The fact that she no longer had a daughter meant they could carry on with their lives, except…except what?

Something was niggling at Doris's brain.

Obviously it was occasionally necessary to do unpleasant things to make babies, but intercourse now, at the age of fifty? Without thinking, she put her arms around Peter. 'Take me away from this place,' they seemed to say.

Peter understood, because he too wanted to escape the harsh reality of the 'Scottish situation'…

So, the following morning, for the first time in five years, they were 'sharing a bed'.

After breakfast, Peter went for a long, brooding walk around the town. There was no evidence of crime or vandalism. He walked a hundred yards along the high street looking for litter, which he knew to be a good indicator of how the citizens behaved after the pubs closed. He failed to locate a single sweet wrapper. Indeed, if the town was not so close to the Arctic Circle, he might rather like to live here… or at least take a permanent mooring at the harbour, were it not for the icebergs drifting in from the wild Atlantic!

Presently, he remembered the draft budget he had prepared for the hotel had included two men to guard the door, and generally repel those of evil intent. Yet, what he was observing suggested they would not be necessary. The revised expenses forecast left him no choice but to visit the estate agent's, and to ask to look inside the empty building. Most likely, it only required a splash of paint to add a couple of million to its value.

Peter knew a lot about buildings, and how to find their weak points. But after looking around all the rooms, he could find nothing to detract from its strong, basic structure. Yet the man from the estate agents, who followed him around, looked really nervous. Why? The only thing Peter could find wrong with the building was the scandal – the fact the previous owner had gone to prison prior to his bankruptcy. This was not like making a discovery of dry rot or woodworm.

Peter turned to the estate agent, and gave him a power stare which made the humble man step backwards.

"So," said Peter, "sold as seen. That means there is something that you are not telling me."

"No, no," replied the agent, "the building is completely solid, and I have not yet shown you the stable block around the back."

"To distract me from whatever you are trying to hide" said Peter. He stared at the agent without blinking. "So what is it that you are not telling me?" he asked.

"Err..." said the agent reluctantly, "there's a bit of a problem in the basement."

Peter maintained his 'power stare'. The agent took another step backwards. But inside his head, Peter was confused. He had measured the walls to find them three feet thick, added to which the old plaster had no cracks, so there was obviously no movement in the foundations. He was sure the basement was fine, but, of course, he was not going to tell the agent that!

"Foundations," Peter said, "the problems they cause often gives a building negative value, especially if it's 400 years old, with a preservation order."

"It's not that exactly..." stammered the agent.

Peter saw the agent take an involuntary, nervous glance towards the dusty reception desk. Without waiting for an explanation, Peter went to a door behind the desk, then plodded down the stone steps beyond.

"I don't like going down there," called the agent, who made no effort to follow.

Peter never scratched his head, it being a sign of weak, indecisive thinking. But, what he discovered in one part of the basement, certainly put his controlled, powerful body language to the test. In one of the rooms, a dozen or so men and women were all lounging about as if they owned the place. Just coming to the boil on a camping stove was a saucepan of baked beans. The rest of the room was complete chaos, made more smelly by a scattering of wetsuits, climbing gear and cast-off clothes. In fact, it looked rather like a jumble sale at a Scouts' hut! Also, he noticed an unusual amount of torches and potholing magazines. Then, the biggest man stood up to face him.

"Like we told the other fella," he said to Peter, "we have a total right to be in this basement."

"Absolutely," replied Peter; it was very much in his interests to have squatters on site; it would mean that whoever was dealing with the McTavish bankruptcy just wanted to get rid of the place. This perhaps explained the revised asking price from the agent. And in his experience, squatters rarely stood their ground when facing a strategic military approach, combined with a few £10 notes, casually waving about in search of a back pocket.

"Follow me," said the man.

Peter decided the man was the dominant male, who could become a key ally in any price negotiation that might arise with the land agents. Hence he asked for his name.

"That is no concern of yours," said the man, "but call me 'Crowbar' if it makes you feel better."

It made Peter feel much better, for it had just taken another great chunk of money off the hotel valuation!

Peter followed Crowbar along the corridor until he stopped to shine a touch down a large hole in the ground.

"That's the Nork potholing route," he said. "Leads to a chamber, from which miles of passages shoot off in all directions."

Slowly all aggression faded from Crowbar's voice, as he gave a poetic description about crossing an underground lake on an airbed. It was a very long poem, spoken in a gentle whisper when the epic nature of the darkness demanded it.

"But all you need to know," said Crowbar, eventually, "is that where we are now standing is part of an escape route established by the mine owner two centuries ago, and unless you get an Act of Parliament to reverse it, I have as much right to be here as yourself. You might also like to consider that serious potholing frequently requires the use of crowbars to prise apart steel bars, which horrible little men like yourself put across entrances to stop us having fun. So, go away and, like we told the other horrible little man who came nosing around, take that stupid estate agent with you! I assume he is waiting upstairs, wetting his pants again?"

Despite all his experience, Peter had never come across an estate agent who had actually wet himself during negotiations. How on Earth could he value the hotel now? Then, unusually, he found his mind floating back in time, to his university years...

He had been potholing on three occasions. Nothing serious, or more important than going to Wimbledon to watch the tennis, but it had been fun, in a studenty sort of way. And now, the hotel he was proposing to buy appeared to be sitting on top of a major potholing system. A weaker man might consider this a problem, but all Peter saw was a lot of potholers sitting in a basement cafe, buying coffee and wanting food, for even such weird people had money to spend.

*

Peter followed Crowbar back to the room of assorted potholers, none of whom seemed to have any interest in going anywhere soon...except down the hole. Peter put a £20 note on a table.

"Take me down," he said, "after lending me a boiler suit, that is."

Crowbar shook his head. "The Nork route's a grade two," he said. "Starts off on a natural underground river. Novices tend to die rather quickly from panic attacks on those!"

Peter added another £20 note. The man seemed to flinch, but the money went untouched.

"If we go in from the bottom end," the man said, "I'll take you through some easy stuff…and let you borrow a boiler suit."

Peter added a third £20 note.

"OK," said Crowbar, "but if you have a panic attack and die, it's nothing to do with me." Then he took the £60.

Peter was happy. He had managed to put a financial value on what the estate agent considered to be a problem. But Peter understood what he was looking at might just turn out to be a 'gold mine'.

Three hours later, Peter emerged from the cave to stand in dazzling sunshine – a man reborn, with all the vigour of a twenty-something, ready to take on the world. For him, there would be no more boring cruising about the Mediterranean. He needed a challenge. Equally important, he decided the hotel escape tunnel had once been used by Bonnie Prince Charlie…whenever that was. He would have to work out the details later; the important thing was that all the rich American tourists would absolutely love a close encounter with such an essential part of Scottish history, and then return Stateside to tell their folks back home all about it.

As for the potholers? Well, they could have a cheap cafe in the basement, that could also be reached through a side entrance that came down from the car park. It would become a hotel catering for rich and poor alike… Or, possibly, the insanely rich and just the insane!

*

Peter never kept any secrets from his wife but, on returning to the yacht, his step faltered. This was big! Oh well, better to get his confession over and done with. On entering the dining area, he announced his presence with a cough.

"I've just made an offer on that hotel in the high street," he said, "and they are certain to accept. So, I'll need to stay here another month, until I can get a local manager."

He expected Doris to be surprised, but she looked up, her eyes full of tears.

"Call that a confession?" she said. "I've just been to see our first grandchild and her scoundrel boyfriend. He made me a cup of coffee, using that hand-grinder thing. Tomorrow, Sara and I are taking 'the little one' for a ride in the pony and trap, that our…Err…just adores!"

"A ride with Err?" questioned Peter, very surprised with her news.

"For the time being," she responded, "I will call him 'Err', because his real name is just too difficult to deal with."

And that night, once again, they 'shared a bed' – an activity that would then continue for many years ahead.

SIXTEEN

Jim stood nervously before Peter, to call him Sir as he formally requested Sara's hand in marriage. Given his troubled history regarding parental consent, Jim rather expected the reply to include the word 'no'.

"Well," responded Peter, "from what Doris tells me, that dream has occupied our daughter's mind for the past two years, so I see no problem with your proposal, except…"

He paused to make a deliberate cough, thereby communicating the embarrassment he felt about discussing whatever was coming next.

"…What I find difficult to deal with," he continued, "is the gift she wants for a wedding present."

Until a few seconds ago, Jim had been terrified that his proposal would cause objections, but now they were discussing wedding presents?

"What she wants," continued Peter, "is a hole knocking through the wall in the mountain rescue room, then an en-suite bathroom added to the side of your cottage. It has to be done this way, otherwise the door to the new facilities would open directly onto the kitchen area, which is against building regulations. But it doesn't stop there. In order to get a lorry up your track to empty the septic tank, we will need a bulldozer to make it less of an obstacle course. Then there is the problem of heating all the water required for a bath. With bottled gas, you will be replacing the cylinder every week. However, if a septic-tank lorry can get through, then so can a gas tanker to fill up a bulk tank. Sara's like that, works everything out. I've even got the drawings of how the bathroom should look. Now, do you still want to marry my daughter, given all the changes it will bring into your life?"

Jim felt his mind going around in confused circles. Sara had been thinking about this for two years and, for all that time, he had been going on and on…about Stephanie. He quickly said, "Yes, fine," then turned away, and left the room, before his future father-in-law could see the tears of regret running down his face because of the two wasted years.

Peter shook his head in despair. His daughter wanted a septic-tank lorry to arrive at her cottage, once a month, as a wedding present. Luckily, he had moved to a small Scottish town where his old city friends could not jeer at him. But Sara had been quite firm on the matter: she would have Jim, Nork, and a bathroom; there was nothing else in her perfect life that she needed.

*

After relocating to Scotland, Peter quickly acquired a reputation among the locals for being slightly odd, a view supported by Doris, who failed to understand his desire to do things like…

Well, last Winter, Peter had joined Jim and Sara as they tramped up Ben Nevis, to join the normal New Year's Eve party on the summit. Apparently, all the proper Scottish climbers did it. Doris failed to see how any statement that dealt with a lot of mad people crowding onto the summit of Ben Nevis, in the middle of Winter, could include the word 'normal'.

"It's quite a flat summit," Peter had explained, after he returned home. "Sara and Jim built me a really mice igloo to sleep in, before sorting themselves out. When they came to visit me in the morning, they brought me a really lovely mug of coffee..."

Doris failed to understand how such a statement could include the words 'nice' and 'lovely', but since such activities had given Peter the muscular body of a fit twenty-year-old, complete with a flat tummy, she was not going to make a fuss about it...because the consequences were rather delightful!

Given her husband's unusual ideas, Doris was surprised when he went away to naval college, to study for his yacht master's certificate, like normal people who happened to own a yacht. He even started to say 'nautical mile', which, apparently, was a bit longer than a proper mile.

"A naughty mile," she had responded, "because it's like that extra helping of fudge cake you secretly nibble at the end of a dinner party!"

This remark had made him very cross. "In the Mediterranean," he had said, "you can be silly, but, off the Scottish coast, to be silly is to be dead!"

How this statement could be reconciled with his other activities, she had no idea, but that was not important. The main thing was, she could sit on the front deck of their yacht without fearing they might crash into something. This allowed her to relax as she watched the seabirds using the upward draughts created by the towering coastal cliffs to swirl around in great circles.

It was thus, one afternoon, while feeling totally safe on the foredeck of their yacht, that she spotted a Northern Fulmar circling around the vessel. Thinking quickly, she rushed to the wheelhouse, where she removed Peter's sardine lunch from a plate left on a little shelf near the doorway. She held this up for the bird to see, then threw it over the side. In the next instant, the graceful bird swooped down and, fish in beak, flew towards the cliffs, presumably to eat its dinner in peace.

"The Northern Fulmar often scavenges from vessels," called Doris, "though mostly from fishing boats, so we were very lucky to see one from our yacht."

Peter could not understand how the loss of his lunch could be described as 'lucky'. But his wife had started to do many odd things since moving to Scotland, yet he still loved her, all the same.

After the excitement caused by the bird, Doris swung her binoculars along the horizon, until she located a small rowing boat bobbing up and down on the swell. The two occupants appeared to be children. Surely they were in big trouble; for one thing their boat seemed to be on a collision course with their yacht. However, before she could alert Peter to the fact, the rowing boat took an obvious turn towards the cliffs. Peter responded by blowing the horn – twice – which confirmed to the other boat that he had been to naval college to study boating stuff.

Doris went into the wheelhouse and handed Peter the binoculars. She then pointed towards the rowing boat.

"What do you reckon to that?" she asked.

"Starboard to starboard passing," he said. "I know it's unusual, but in a situation like this, it's correct for the smaller boat to take the shallow water. Anyway, the two blasts of the horn confirmed that arrangement."

Doris gave a heavy sigh. "No," she said, "go outside and take a proper look."

Doris liked steering the yacht, so long as Peter did all the boring stuff with charts. This left Peter free to go outside and study the rowing boat through binoculars. He was surprised to see the girl on the back seat was not far beyond her teenage years, and the rower was definitely a boy, but he sure knew how to row!

"Most unusual," he called from the deck, "a small boat out here is almost always handled by some salty old sea-dog."

On returning to the wheelhouse, he spoke more quietly, reflecting the serious nature of the situation.

"The complete image of freedom," he said. "Freedom to live, and freedom to die…which, in this case, is destined to happen quite soon, because around the next headland the current is four knots against them. In that wide-beam boat, they will never make it. We'll have to turn around and offer them a tow."

"If we are doing that," interrupted Doris, "I'll pop downstairs to make up a picnic box. We can pass it across to them on a boat hook."

*

In the rowing boat, Stephanie turned her attention from the yacht, to look at the next headland.

"In a little while," she said to Nork, "we've got a four-knot current against us. Also, close to the rocks, there's a tidal rip with unpredictable consequences, so take us half a mile out to sea, then I'll take over because my arms are fresh."

"Yes, Aunty," replied Nork. This meant he accepted that in the rowing boat, she was the boss.

A little later, Stephanie was pulling hard on the oars to get around the headland, and making just enough headway to see, from the changing angle of the cliff face, they were making some sort of slow progress. Then Nork looked behind, to see how far they had come.

"That yacht's coming back," he said. "Reckon they are on a collision course with our stern."

"Given the current," said Stephanie, "we are now a vessel 'restricted in her ability to manoeuvre', so have the right of way. My only concern is pulling these oars."

"Yes, Aunty," said Nork.

They had just escaped the worst of the current, when the approaching yacht pulled level, barely twenty yards away. Then they saw a lady on the deck, holding up a box and pointing to it. Slowly the yacht closed the gap, until the lady put the box onto a boat hook and held it over the side, so that Nork could recover it.

"Thought you might have needed a tow," shouted a man, from the wheelhouse, "but it seems not. Anyway, hope you enjoy the picnic."

Then the yacht drifted away, until well clear, when it used its powerful engines to surge ahead.

Nork looked in the box that was now on his lap. "Four cans of Coke," he said, "plus sandwiches, and a whole fruit loaf, with a full packet of butter."

"What nice people," said Stephanie. "I'll pull into the bay, there's a shingle beach and some woods beyond. We can camp there for the night, once we've pigged out on that!"

Skilfully, she took a little pressure off the portside oar, and headed for the calmer waters of the bay.

*

Doris was doing her most favourite thing in the whole world – sitting before the 'steam engine', as Sara called it, with her feet all warm and comfortable in thick socks. Nork was sitting on her lap, learning to read a picture book. To her left, Peter and Jim were engrossed in a game of chess. Sara was drawing basic pencil lines on a canvas, ready for her next oil painting, which the tourist gift shop in town was always eager to buy. Not that she could paint portraits, or anything complicated, but she seemed to have a gift for snow-covered mountains.

In the background, the gentle hiss of a gas lamp gave the room a warm and cosy feeling, befitting the happy family unit they had now become.

"Today," said Doris, half talking to Nork, "we saw the most extraordinary thing from our yacht – a young girl and boy in a rowing boat, miles out at sea."

Peter was too excited by a possible 'knight to a6' move, to correct her, both for using ordinary 'miles', and the plural, when the rowing boat was less than one nautical mile from the cliffs. Sara, however, suddenly dropped her pencil, and turned around.

"A boy and a girl?" she asked casually. "Is that normal?"

"Looked as if they were in training for the Olympics," said Doris, "so it was probably normal for them."

Sara looked at Jim, but he was merely shaking his head.

"I completely failed to see the knight to a6 move," he said. "Reckon you've got mate in three."

"Reckon I have," said Peter. "Come on, Sara, your turn…"

*

Stephanie was sitting cross-legged in the small tent, to watch Nork as he huddled over a little camping stove, waiting for the water to boil. There was just enough powder to make two final mugs of drinking chocolate. After tonight, future bedtimes would be humble occasions, but it was nothing Nork had not endured before.

Stephanie knew Nork was worried about returning to the town from where Jim had tried to hand him over to the police. But now, if he wanted to take his 'A' levels, he could no longer live as a fugitive. Also, she was fed up begging for scraps of work, often walking five miles to do a bit of housework for a grumpy old man, who lived halfway up a mountain. Now, their otherwise generally fun time – dominated by climbing and rowing – needed to give way to the practical need of finding a 'proper job'.

Returning to the town where McTavish had his hotel, had not been Stephanie's first choice. However, her mind had recently recalled a vague recollection of her late father once saying something about owning the cottage where they lived. She had no idea if her memory was correct, but if it was, land ownership seemed like a good way to start their new life.

"Are you still worried about Jim?" asked Stephanie.

Nork responded with a nervous nod.

"But now you have some legal paperwork and are about to

start your 'A' levels. If he tried to hand you over to the police again, they would laugh at him. Besides which, I would punch him on the nose. Anyway, I don't suppose he will remember us, and he certainly won't recognise you. At your age, five years represents an awful lot of change."

"Suppose," said Nork.

Stephanie knew he was not totally convinced. They would certainly need to have a plan B that could be activated quickly, if things got complicated.

*

Twenty miles away, Sara snuggled up to Jim in bed.

"Did you really not hear what Doris was saying about the boy and girl in the rowing boat, all at sea?" she asked.

Gently, he stroked her hair.

"What silly things I might have thought important five years ago," he whispered, "are now my greatest regret. All that matters now is that the woman I married is feeling totally secure in my love. All else, except for Nork, is irrelevant… that is the Nork sleeping next door, rather than the one we both assume to be the Nork in the rowing boat," he reassured her.

*

Two days later, Stephanie was gazing at the now-derelict cottage, where she had spent her early years.

"I never got to say goodbye to my father," she said to Nork. "You see, I was out exploring the bog, when it got too dark to return safely. Nothing unusual about that, I often stayed out all night, but this time was special, because I had finally found a way to reach the hard ground on the far side. I got home the following morning, all excited to tell my father about what I had achieved, but he had already left for work, in the skiff, for the last time. And now, here I am, ten years later, or thereabouts, looking at where we used to live. But please follow me, I don't want to do this on my own."

Nork followed her through the doorway. Half the roof had collapsed, meaning they had to duck. The furniture was essentially firewood. It was like Stephanie had told him: this place had no value, because nowadays people wanted road access to their property.

But their situation was not ordinary. Stephanie had already told him that, if they somehow managed to buy a skiff, he could get to school in forty-five minutes. And yes, she had a slight worry that Social Services might poke their noses in about it. But surely they could not hide away until Nork was eighteen, unemployed, and with just five 'O' levels to his name, obtained through homeschooling, followed by a major commute to the examination centre.

On entering a back room of the cottage, Stephanie pulled away the remains of a sideboard, then lifted a slate from the floor, to recover a steel box.

"Things like this don't seem important when you are thirteen," she said, "and not important now, if we choose to walk away."

She removed a bundle of papers from the box, and peered at them. After a little while, she looked at Nork.

"Well, that's sorted," she said, "my parents purchased a hundred-year lease on the cottage in 1952. It seems that I also own the land fifty feet from the outer wall, on all sides. So the question is, do you want to help me get this place into shape, or…I don't know…something else, I guess?"

"I want whatever you want," said Nork.

"And I want what you want," responded Stephanie, "which gets us nowhere at all!"

Stephanie was still in a sombre mood when they reached the cliff face where, five years earlier, Nork had undertaken his first climbs. But this time was so different, because he barely glanced at the easy stuff, walking directly to the far end of the cliff. To the untrained eye, this looked like a blank, overhanging slab, but an experienced climber would see a few ripples, and perhaps dream about having the finger strength to make a one-finger pull-up on a barely-visible pebble hold. Anyway, standing below this, Nork threw off his rucksack and began to pull out the climbing gear.

"It's not possible," said Stephanie, "even my father thought so. He often came to look at it and imagine himself as a spider, with eight hands that would stick to anything!"

"Then, in honour of your father," he responded, "I name this soon-to-be-climbed route, Sticky Fingers!"

"Yes, Nephew," said Stephanie, confirming that when it came to climbing, he was the boss.

Half an hour later, Nork was pulling himself onto a grassy strip of flat land beyond the top of the cliff.

"Safe," he called.

For such a hard climb, Stephanie would normally confine her activity to the ropework, keeping her feet firmly on the ground. But this was different; she could feel the spirit of her father watching her, made proud by seeing the boy she had cared for, now having grown into a fine young man. Then her father's voice drifted into her mind. "You can do it," he said calmly – a phrase she had heard many times as he had encouraged her up some new climb or other. Then, the rope to her harness went tight.

"Climb when you're ready," came a voice from above.

"Yes, Father," she murmured.

For the next five minutes, all she thought about was her father. Sometimes he was watching her, at other times he was keeping the rope tight, to make her feel safe. And so it was that she came to collapse on the grass beside Nork. Tears were running down her cheeks. Gazing skywards, she was finally saying goodbye to her father.

She felt Nork rest his face against her shoulder. He knew what she was thinking, because they understood each other completely. Then she sat up to look around the glen she had come to love...but Nork must freely agree to staying here.

"Right," she said, "now we are grown up, we have to consider grown-up things. All I own in the world is a derelict cottage, a rowing boat, a lot of climbing gear...and, temporarily, £45. If I do not find work quickly, we are in danger of going hungry again. We can go across to the town or, if you want, we can return to the wilderness, and somehow scratch a living. But then, what will become of us in five years' time when we are even more grown up?"

"We have a cottage," said Nork, "transport, all the climbing gear we need, and enough money..."

"Not really, we will have to get you a school uniform, for one thing."

"We have enough money," said Nork. "Though tomorrow, I think we should go across the loch, to see whatever is to be seen. The only condition I make, is that if Jim tries to hand me over to the police, you punch him on the nose while I run, then meet you at the harbour…like we did before."

Stephanie smiled. "Running away with you led to the most rewarding five years of my life," she said. "Jim did me a great favour by being a horrible person. And yes, if the need arises, I will punch him on the nose!"

*

Helen, a receptionist at the town's Bonnie Prince Charlie Hotel, prided herself on being a very sensible teenager, who liked all accessible sports. This was helped by the fact that when she was thirteen, her parents had put her into the 'right sort of tennis club', where she was able to meet the 'right sort of people'. Back home, down south, she now had a mantelshelf scattered with trophies, including those for rowing, swimming, and lacrosse. This was her first Summer job, the hotel owners being old family friends of her parents. While these owners knew she had only just completed her 'O' levels, and was going back to school in September to start her 'A' levels, the rest of the staff did not. Hence, when working on the reception desk, her mind was fully dedicated to the task of pretending to be eighteen. Then, one morning, she looked up from her very sensible typing, at fifty words a minute, to see a double-dream sugar-lump of a boy walking towards her. Her instant reaction of breathing, 'ooooh,' had not been intended, it just sort of happened.

Moments, hours, months passed by…as is the case in lovely dreams!

His piercing blue eyes made her tremble. His broad chest seemed to be bursting out of his shirt – a sleeveless one that revealed two enormously powerful arms. She forced herself to look down at her typewriter.

"Yes," she said, "can I help you? Or have I already said that bit?"

"No," said a slightly older lady standing next to him, "your first word was a sort of 'ooooh.'"

Shyly, Nork took a step backwards, to hide behind his aunty. Equally shyly, Helen looked down at her lap.

"We were just passing," said Stephanie, "and noticed the name of the hotel has changed. We seem to remember it was called McTavish's?"

"New owners," said Helen. "As to the name, this is the building from where Bonnie Prince Charlie escaped. There's a tunnel from the basement. We do guided tours, then you get onboard a rowing boat to cross the lake…I mean loch. I'm all confused now!"

Bravely, Nork looked over his aunty's shoulder to give Helen a boyish grin.

"So Bonnie Prince Charlie escaped underground, waving an oil lantern about?" he asked.

"Not exactly, that bit's for American tourists, but the boat's a real replica, made of proper wood. However, it's only licensed to carry twelve, so you have to book in the middle of Summer."

The boy nodded. "With real wooden oars?" he enquired.

"Yes, real wood…oh, you are making fun of me, aren't you?"

"Not in the slightest," responded Nork, "though perhaps I am making fun of the American tourists. How do they enjoy the tunnel?"

"Mostly they turn back, but it's still something to tell their folks back home. Anyway, we can take them to the other end of the tunnel in our minibus, so they still get to cross the loch in a rowing boat."

"Oh," said Stephanie, "that sounds much too horrible and dangerous!"

The boy laughed in a most delightful way.

"And the tunnel," he said, "that sounds very frightening."

"I've done it," said Helen proudly. "With a proper guide it's rather fun, so long as your waist size is less than thirty-two inches." Then she looked furtively around the foyer. "In truth," she said, "it's called the 'Nork route'. It's a famous grade two pothole."

Stephanie stepped around to the back of the reception desk.

"Youth is so wasted on the young," she said, "it's time I took control of this situation."

She quickly studied the girl, then turned to look at Nork.

"Sensible shoes for running about," she said, "short nails for rock climbing, and sensible hairstyle that can be quickly washed after potholing."

She offered the girl a handshake.

"I've got a rowing boat in the harbour," she continued, "perhaps you would like to join us, after your shift? We can go across the loch to do some rock climbing, given all your sporting sensibilities."

The girl ran from behind the reception desk. "Don't go away," she called, "if anybody asks, I'll be back in five minutes."

Stephanie thought her very punctual because, five minutes later, she returned with a middle-aged lady, who examined them with a kind smile.

"I can see what you mean about him being a double-dream sugar lump," she said.

The girl gave a frustrated scream, then turned to face the wall.

"Thing is," continued the lady, "we're acting as Helen's guardians, so cannot let her go climbing without first asking her parents. But I've got a feeling we've met before. You were in a rowing boat, two days ago?"

"Yes," said Nork, "and thank you very much for the picnic."

The lady liked polite children, so gave a nod of approval. "Wait here," she said, "I'll be back in five minutes."

"Seems a friendly place to work," said Stephanie, "though unusually dedicated to the idea of being back in five minutes."

"It's my Aunt Doris," said Helen, as if talking to the wall, "and yes, it is very friendly."

Five minutes later, Doris returned with a waiter from the 'posh' restaurant. After the new arrival had made himself comfortable behind the reception desk, Doris asked them to follow her to the car park. On reaching the rear of the building, she pointed upwards.

"Peter, my husband," she said, "had this climbing wall erected last year, just to give the potholers something to do when…well, I don't really understand what they do, besides getting wet and soggy, but it seems to keep them out of mischief. Anyway, after your health and safety introduction, I'm sure you could use the wall, without getting parental consent, so long as I remain here to stop you doing anything dangerous."

Doris then went into the old garage, that now had a sign above the door saying, 'Bunkhouse'. Nork had seen these before, but had never stayed in one, because for Stephanie, even £2 a night was more than they could sensibly afford. Anyway, bunkhouses tended to be crammed with sweaty bodies, when their tent was much nicer.

Doris returned with a man who announced himself to be

a climbing instructor. He then rambled on about the safety procedures, while Nork looked along the wall to study a single, great overhang. Sometimes he would simply nod at what the instructor was saying.

"Right," said the instructor eventually, "you will need to start on routes that have all their holds identified with yellow paint. If you work really hard, you should be able to start doing the green routes after about twenty sessions…"

Then the instructor realised he was talking to himself. He smiled as he saw the two new arrivals walk to the overhang with a few, barely visible, holds identified by blobs of black paint.

"Nobody has ever climbed that," he called, "it is impossible."

Stephanie looked at Nork. "Nobody would build a wall that could not be climbed," she said, "it would make them look silly."

Nork nodded, then clipped himself into a rope, which Stephanie prepared to feed out.

"It's quite safe," said the instructor to Doris," he will never get off the ground, but regulations mean I will still have to put a mattress underneath."

This delayed them for a few minutes, long enough to attract a small crowd of guests, who gathered for a laugh. Then Doris watched the boy climb quickly and effortlessly to the roof. Their climbing instructor went white, while the rest of the audience gave nods of approval.

"Come down," shouted the instructor, "you're going to kill yourself!"

A few seconds later, Nork had reached the lip of the overhang, where he pushed three fingers into a crack, then locked them in place by spacing them apart. Using his powerful tummy muscles, he curled his body upwards, his feet searching for the tiny ledge above the roof that he had spied from the ground. Then the rubber toe of his specialist rock boots just caught something. This is what rock climbers call a 'delicate move', since he was upside down with his body stretching across a genuine section of blank wall.

"Two foot of slack," he called calmly.

Stephanie was in complete control of his safety. Give him too much rope, and any fall would result in a dangerous swing; too little slack, and it would pull him back, halfway through the lunge she knew was coming.

Nork understood this was the hardest move he had ever tried to make, not helped by the instructor screaming in terror. However, knowing the girl from the reception desk was watching him, somehow gave him the extra strength required. He slowly curled his body upwards, making the upside-down toe hold ever more precarious as he removed his fingers from the hold in the roof. Just as he felt his toe beginning to slip, a powerful lunge took him upwards to grab a three-finger pebble. He swung from this for a brief moment, then lunged higher for a pocket, into which he threw a fist. A few seconds later, he reached up to touch the white line at the top of the wall. After clipping his rope through the bolt, Stephanie lowered him back down.

The climbing instructor was already racing through the hotel, where he rushed into Peter's office without bothering to knock.

"A boy has just climbed the black route!" he shouted, before collapsing into a chair, fearing that he was about to pass out.

Peter smiled. He knew the climbing-wall company would never have built a truly impossible route, because it would make them look silly. A few minutes later, he was racing to the side of the building to discover a crowd standing in complete silence.

"Good heavens!" he exclaimed, as if he were seeing things, because now a girl was upside down, at the very edge of the overhang, a surreal image due to her long hair drifting down in a slight breeze…But he must remember he was over fifty, with a loving wife, unlike the men in the audience who, he suspected, were all gazing up, dreaming that one day she might become their rock climbing partner…and maybe a lot more.

Stephanie had watched Nork carefully, so knew the hard 'upside-down move' was mostly to do with gymnastic agility. Physical strength was less important, at least for somebody who weighed under ten stone, and had just rowed a wide-beam boat across quite a lot of ocean. In any event, she was eventually able to touch the white line that acted as the summit. As Nork lowered her back down, the now substantial crowd stepped back to gaze in awe and wonder, as if she was a magical goddess who had just landed from another planet!

Peter pushed his way to the front of the audience, then announced himself as the owner of the hotel.

"That was rather fun," responded Stephanie, pointing casually upwards.

In truth, she knew it to be the most desperate thing she had ever done, but she liked surprising people.

Peter understood that now the 'black route' had been climbed, all those who had previously failed, and pronounced it impossible, would have to come back. This lady had just earned him the profit from 1,000 cups of coffee, plus a substantial improvement in his reputation. Somehow, he would have to expand the bunkhouse to accommodate all the new customers who would come flocking to look at the wall. Then he studied the lady.

"You're the girl in the rowing boat," he exclaimed, "… all at sea!"

"It was fun," she said.

Peter's brain was alive with wild ideas. "Potholing?" he asked.

"I believe we were the first to do the route that comes up to your basement," she said, "five years ago. That was great fun too."

"So," said Peter, "I am looking at a lady who can row across an ocean, climb the hardest rock known to man, and puts through new potholing routes…and here's me, having started a hotchpotch of outdoor activities without any pre-meditated plans. Then a few minutes ago, I was sitting in my office, thinking about…whatever it was…but what I have just witnessed seems to have cleared my brain of anything that has gone before! I only know that I would be mad to let you go without…though I can't think straight at the moment, because my mind is too full of seeing you hanging upside down to organise my thoughts into anything sensible."

A murmur of approval came from the crowd. Peter understood the entire audience of male climbers were hopelessly infatuated with the girl. But that was their problem; thankfully his own concern was limited to…then the idea came…He had unexpectedly come across a manager for his new outdoor centre.

"I'll arrange a dinner party on my yacht," he said, "tonight at eight. You know the one, it's moored in the harbour now."

OK, free food, thought Stephanie, *we'll be there!*

*

Cautiously, Nork boarded the yacht, where a lady in a maid's uniform directed him to a flight of stairs that went below decks. He looked around to make sure Stephanie was still following. Thus reassured, he descended to the bottom step, where he stopped abruptly. Ahead was a large oval table, around which a dozen or so people were seated. He looked about the cabin to check the escape routes. Then Stephanie squeezed past him, before also stopping. She had frequently seen dinner parties like this at the hotel, but only when somebody important was attending. Now, all the diners had turned to look at her, and presumably Nork, as if they were the guests of honour. Knowing what Nork would be thinking, she took his hand, then located Peter, whom she tended to trust. She then did a quick count of the other guests, or would have done, had her gaze not spotted Jim. What on Earth was he doing here, reaching across the table to hold the hands of a lady sitting opposite? With some relief, Stephanie realised Jim's sole interest was gazing at the girl in a way that said 'nothing else in the world matters'. Then the lady broke free and walked towards them.

"Nork, I presume," she said. Then she lost control, and threw both arms around him. "I'm so sorry for the way I neglected you before," she cried.

"Huh?" said Helen, who was also seated. Hurriedly she stood up and, advancing from the side, also threw her arms about Nork, in a way that told the world 'he belongs to me'.

Stephanie knew that Nork would feel himself to be trapped, so might take flight. To prevent this, she came in from the other side, making it not so much a group hug, but a rugby scrum, in which a totally bewildered Nork was caught in the middle.

Peter blinked. Even in his student days, he had never attracted so much attention from the ladies. Nork was one great big magnet...or, as Helen had said, 'a double-dream sugar lump!'

Stephanie understood the situation completely; this was the start of Nork eventually drifting away from her. Not that 'her work here was done', because she would always be his aunty, but from now on, she just knew it would be different. This inevitable fact was emphasised by Helen, whose determined expression clearly communicated that her sole interest in life was to become Nork's partner. Then, a small boy came to stand close by.

"I'm Nork," he said. "Are you the man who found the pothole?"

"Certainly hope so," said Stephanie, "because if not, it would mean there are three Norks, and that's way too confusing to deal with!"

This made all the dinner guests laugh, which lightened the atmosphere into something far less formal. Stephanie sensed Nork senior had also become less nervous, and let go her embrace. Then the first lady backed away, which left Helen in sole control of the situation. She pulled Nork towards the two empty chairs, to make sure she sat beside him. Stephanie gave a sad little smile, then went to where Helen had previously been sitting, which happened to be next to Peter. Then she looked at the first lady who had made the presumption about Nork, and realised it was Jane. She decided the entire dinner party was going to be spent working out all the confusion, as to why everybody was where they were.

After a very friendly meal, Peter turned all his attention to Stephanie. He wanted to talk sensibly about his rapidly evolving plans for his outdoor centre.

"The management post," he mentioned as a throwaway remark, "is £12,000 a year, reviewed after three months."

Stephanie stared at him in astonishment. "Most weeks I've been lucky to take home £40," she gasped.

"I admire your honesty," Peter responded, "so will not offer to meet you in the middle. The £12,000 a year is non-negotiable, except upwards, in three months' time."

He offered her a hand. "Shake on it," he said, "and the deal is done."

After the handshake, Peter got up and left the room. Doris, whom she knew to be his wife, smiled at her.

"Welcome to the team," she said.

Then Peter returned. "I like the way you trusted me on a handshake," he said, "now it is my turn to show my trust in you."

"You just fed me," she interrupted. "What is there not to trust?"

This made everyone sitting around the table laugh again.

"Completely honest as well," said Peter. Then he handed her a wad of £10 notes. "An introductory bonus," he added, "so now the deal is properly done."

"Not quite," said Stephanie, "because I need to justify my wages. Let me think...yes, it might work. Your American tourists, after using the Bonnie Prince Charlie escape tunnel and the rowing boat, what happens after you have taken them across the loch, like Helen mentioned?"

"A power boat picks them up. Then they go home to tell their folks all about it, probably with some degree of exaggeration."

"And what if I owned a bit of land with a cottage on the other side of the loch? Fix it up for me, and it would sleep fifteen as a bunkhouse. Also, I believe it was the place where Bonnie Prince Charlie spent his first night on the run from whatever it was. Sadly, it has gas lights now, but you could easily take them out, and hang up some oil lanterns…if you like?"

Doris gave a respectful cough. "I think the Trades Description Act might have a problem with that," she said.

"No," said Peter, "if Stephanie says it is what she believes, then who can prove she believes otherwise? Like when somebody invented Robin Hood. This eventually became folklore, which strengthened to a legend. Try telling anybody from Nottingham now that Robin Hood never existed, and you would be driven out of town…presumably using a bow and arrow, purchased from one of their many tourist shops!"

Peter turned to Stephanie. "Sadly," he added, "our rich American friends like comfortable beds at night. Also, the other side of the loch goes nowhere, unless one happens to have a hovercraft, or machete to clear a jungle path around the loch. So, an overnight stay would still just mean them getting the power boat back the following morning."

Nork now felt more confident in his new surroundings, and quite liked the way Helen was holding his hand beneath the table. It made him want to take her rock climbing – or something else. Though why the tingles travelling up his arm made him feel sufficiently brave to talk to all these people, he had no idea.

"Stephanie knows a way through the bog," said Nork,

"something nobody else in the whole world has discovered how to do."

Stephanie smiled and, blushing slightly, nodded.

"I believe Bonnie Prince Charlie also knew the way," she said. "But there is a lot of zigzagging to do, so it's about five miles to reach the first hard ground on the far side. From there, I suppose, your American guests can be picked up in two Land Rovers, and taken to the ferry road. No, not Land Rovers, but a tractor, with a trailer, like they used for taking land girls out for haymaking during the war. It will sound better when they tell their folks back home. As for the comfortable beds…reckon the cottage would take eight, but the only heating comes from open log fires."

Peter thought for a moment. "Forget the probationary period," he said, "I'll get my lawyer to write up a contract tomorrow. £18,000 a year, but for the next five years, we get to use the cottage where Bonnie Prince Charlie once stayed. You, I am afraid, will have to live in the hotel, from where it will be easier for Nork to walk to school…until he's old enough to get insurance to become an instructor in whatever the Bonnie Prince Charlie Outdoor Centre becomes. Over to you, Stephanie."

*

Helen closed her eyes. How on Earth was she going to tell her parents that she was walking to school with a boy called Nork, who came from Nowhere, and that she would be staying in this Scottish town…hopefully forever?